I0780393

The Assassin Baltimore

Jim West

Copyright © Year 2024
All Rights Reserved

Copyright by Aurora Publications

The mounted cowboy over the state of Texas is the trademark of Aurora Publications.

This is a work of fiction. Names, characters, places, and incidents either are product of the author's imagination or are used fictitiously, and any resemblance to any actual persons, living or dead, events, or locales is entirely coincidental.

ISBN:
Hardcover: 978-1-964289-66-3
Paperback: 978-1-964289-65-6

Other books by Jim West

DNAlien
DNAlien II
DNAlien III
Living Within a Strange Mind Volume I
Living Within a Strange Mind Volume II
Genocide by GMO
The Making of an Assassin – Atlanta

Thanks to everybody who had a hand in writing this book. Especially those people who provided the inspiration for the original book, *The Making of an Assassin - - Atlanta.*

And thanks to some who graciously allowed me to use their names throughout the book. As is my habit, I use the names of friends and relatives in all of my books, but never so their true characters can be positively identified. Such is the curse of knowing me. However, this time, I strayed and must give special thanks to Jewell Heeger and Carrillo/Tibbels, P.L.L.C.

Jewell unwittingly became one of the main characters that actually portrays her in her position as a Flight Attendant for American Airlines. A long-time friend, she also helped in the continuous editing process.

The law firm of Carrillo/Tibbels risked its professional reputation by allowing me to portray it as one of the many firms whose ridiculous advertisements sicken all of us. As a matter of fact, they have been my personal lawyers for well over a decade, and I respect and admire them greatly. Needless to say, they have a terrific sense of humor outside of the courtroom.

And, as always, thanks to John Fleenor for providing a stinging commentary about my assault on the English language. Never failing to point out the many errors in my narrative, he's been a steadfast friend for more years than I'll admit to being alive.

And, to all those out there who keep telling me to keep writing, thank you. You are truly the reason that I'm doing this.

Prologue

"American 2361, contact departure 125.2," the Dallas/Ft. Worth International Airport (DFW) tower controller directed the MD 80 that had just taken off from runway 35L.

"Twenty-five-two," acknowledged First Officer Jim Lashley as he watched Captain Brett Heeger flying the departure route they had been assigned in their clearance to the Baltimore/Washington International Airport (BWI). Glancing at his radio, Jim changed the frequency on the secondary control to 125.2, keyed the microphone, and said, "Departure, American 2361 passing eight for ten."

"Roger American 2361, climb and maintain Flight Level (FL) 230," the controller replied.

"Climbing to 230," Jim acknowledged as he watched Brett set 23,000 in the altitude window on the autopilot display.

"230", Brett said, pointing to the display and engaging the autopilot. "Autopilot's on."

"Roger, 230, autopilot on," Jim replied as he glanced at the systems to ensure everything was set to keep the plane climbing to the assigned altitude, on the assigned heading, and holding the correct airspeed.

A couple of minutes later, as they passed 10,000 feet, Brett reached up and hit the button that made a chime within the cabin, advising the Flight Attendants (FAs) that the sterile period was over and they could resume their duties.

"Any plans for the night?" Brett asked as he slid his chair back a few inches, lowered the armrest, and removed his earpiece and microphone.

"I'm having dinner with an old Marine buddy," Jim answered as he slid his chair back. "What about you?"

"No plans," Brett answered as he turned the overhead speaker on.

"American 2361 cleared direct Little Rock, climb and maintain FL330, contact Ft Worth Center on 128.25," came the instructions from departure.

"2361, direct Little Rock, 330, 28.25," Jim replied, switching the radio as directed, and then said, "Ft Worth, American 2361, passing 190 for 330, direct Little Rock."

"Roger, 2361, now cleared direct Charleston, rest of route remains unchanged," came the voice over the speaker.

"Now direct Charleston," Jim responded. "Any ride reports ahead?"

"Light chop over Little Rock at 350 about 30 minutes ago, nothing else," came the reply.

"Roger, thanks," Jim said, nodding as Brett entered the fix for Charleston into the GPS and engaged it to navigate the plane.

"I'll be off for a minute," Brett said. "You've got the jet."

"I've got it," Jim answered as Brett reached down for the handset that connected the cockpit to the cabin speaker system.

Listening to the standard spiel about how happy they were to be flying everybody to Baltimore and that it was going to be a smooth ride and seatbelts and yada yada yada, Jim reclined his chair a little and watched Brett make obscene gestures as he was making his usual speech. Grinning and shaking his head, Jim knew this was going to be a fun three day trip with a Captain that had a sense of humor. He almost wished he could hang out with Brett at one of the local bars just a few blocks from the hotel where they were staying for the night.

But his assignment tonight with Muddy Water was to meet retired Marine General Gene Barker about an upcoming mission. Having known General Barker since serving two tours as a Reconnaissance (Recon) Marine during Vietnam, Jim had followed Gene's advice for several years. The first had been to complete a program that allowed Jim to become a Marine officer and pilot. After another tour in Vietnam flying the F-4 and the war was over, Gene recommended that he accept an assignment to a Marine Reserve Unit and join a clandestine organization known as Dark Water.

Dark Water was the enforcement arm of an international security company named Black Water. Any time Black Water needed to encourage or discourage actions involving their clients, Dark Water was sent to ensure the desired effects were accomplished. As a Marine reserve pilot, Jim was sent across the world for several years to make sure the desires of Dark Water were fulfilled.

Then, as Jim approached retirement from the Marines, Gene was instrumental in securing an interview for him to become a pilot with American Airlines. No longer able to travel overseas to perform the requirements of Dark Water, Gene ensured Jim became one of the unknown members of the enforcement arm of Black Water within the United States, Muddy Water.

Baltimore was going to be the second mission Jim had been assigned since joining American Airlines and Muddy Water, but it was far from the numerous missions he had accomplished for almost 15 years with Dark Water. His first assignment with Muddy Water was just a couple of months ago to eliminate a problem in Atlanta. Even though Jim knew that certain actions were necessary, it still bothered him to be the instrument that resulted in the death of the target.

True, some of the previous missions had been resolved with no violence. But Jim harbored no doubts that by the time he was called to resolve an issue, it was well past the discussion phase. Now, immediate and final actions were required. From growing up on a small farm in West Texas, Jim had changed from a naive young man to a hardened enforcer regardless of what the company required.

Two tours as a mud Marine and losing his entire squad on a small insignificant hill in Vietnam forever changed the farm boy. Now, the loss of life of another meant little after seeing what any enemy would inflict on the combatants. Whether on the battlefield or in the clandestine world of global politics, someone was going to die. Jim only knew that he didn't want to be that someone.

Page Left Blank Intentionally

Chapter 1

Jim was sitting at home Friday afternoon, waiting for his wife, Jennifer, to get off work. They had planned to go to dinner with some members of his old Marine Squadron, VMF 112, at Naval Air Station (NAS) Dallas. He had been assigned there until his retirement almost two years ago but maintained close contact with several of the other members and their wives.

Having mowed the yard of their new Mesquite home, Jim had already showered and was just relaxing when the phone rang. "Hello," he said, wondering if it was American Airlines calling about his upcoming trip tomorrow or something to do with dinner tonight.

"Good afternoon, Jim," came the very familiar voice of General Barker. "Any plans for this evening?"

"Good afternoon, General," Jim replied. "As a matter of fact, Jennifer and I are meeting Colonel Bull Winkle and his wife for dinner later. But you're certainly welcome to join us."

"I appreciate that," Gene told him. "I'd love to see Bull, but I've got to get back to Quantico in a couple of hours.

Would it be all right if I came by for a few minutes or so before Jennifer gets home?"

"That would be fine," Jim answered. "When will you be here?"

The doorbell rang as Gene told him, "How about answering the door? I think you'll find the answer standing on your porch."

Smiling, Jim hung up the phone and walked to the front door. Opening it, he said, "General, I'm not surprised that you'd already be here when you called. You seem to have some inside information as to where I am just about any time you want to know. Am I under surveillance?"

"Of course not," Gene said, shaking Jim's outstretched hand. "I just happen to know that a gentleman of leisure, such as yourself, would be taking advantage of the days you have off from flying and doing your wife's bidding. And probably would be glad for a little stimulating conversation this afternoon."

"I'm always glad to have you stop by, stimulating or otherwise," Jim replied as he shut the door and ushered Gene into the living room. "Would you like something to drink?"

"I don't suppose I could trouble you for a Jack and Coke, could I?" Gene asked as they continued on toward the kitchen. "By the way, how does Jennifer like her new house?"

"She's happy," Jim answered as they entered the kitchen. "I still think it's too much, but she insisted on having a second master bedroom and bath in case we need to bring my mother here to live with us in the future."

"How's your mother doing?" Gene asked.

"For now, she's capable of managing on her own. But you know how fast Alzheimer's can get and the house in Frisco just wouldn't accommodate the three of us," Jim said as he reached into the cabinet and removed an unopened 1.75 liter bottle of Jack Daniel's. "And you know what they say, you lose them a little each day until they are no longer there."

"I know. I lost a good friend that way," Gene said. "A terrible disease. For the individual and the family.

Whatever happened to just having a regular bottle, a fifth?" Gene asked as Jim sat the bottle on the counter and took two glasses from the adjoining cabinet.

"I'm doing my part to cut down on carbon emissions," Jim told him as he filled two glasses with ice and a healthy shot of whiskey. "I've single-handedly reduced the chances of global warming by at least 50 percent by making fewer trips to the liquor store just by buying the larger bottle."

"Ah, global warming," Gene said as he took the finished drink from Jim. "Don't get me started on the absurdity of that little issue. Semper Fi!"

"Semper Fi," Jim repeated as they touched glasses and toasted the Marine Corps and their common bond. "Now, what brings you my way today? Stimulating conversation or something else?"

"I'd say a little of both," Gene answered. "Shall we take a walk around the yard as we talk?"

"Of course," Jim answered as he opened the back door. "I guess this must be some issue with our common interest in national security."

"Very insightful," Gene told him as they walked toward the rear of the yard. "This is probably closer to your remark than you'd guess. And... extremely sensitive in nature."

"What makes this one different than any of the others," Jim asked as they stood looking at the far-off skyline of Dallas.

"I guess the biggest change is that we want you in on the planning stage of this one," Gene said. "And you'll have a partner as we try to reach a peaceful solution."

"What do you need me to do?" Jim asked, wondering why he was being asked to help with the planning. Never before had he done any more than just execute the final solution.

"We need you to be in Baltimore a few times next month," Gene answered. "The first night or day you're there, we need to get you to Quantico for the briefing and your input on how you'd like to proceed with the problem we're having."

"What's the problem?" Jim asked.

"A certain Chief Executive Officer (CEO) is proving to be a major obstacle in the acquisition of some minerals we need for NASA's ongoing satellite program," Gene explained. "He believes that this is his chance to become a very wealthy individual at the expense of our requirements. Basically, he's trying to charge tenfold the price of a critical component because he controls the majority of a certain mineral. That's unacceptable."

"What's his connection?" Jim asked, wondering why they just didn't offer money to sway the CEO to do what the company needed.

"Do you remember what we needed to do during the construction of the SR-71?" Gene asked.

"Some of it," Jim answered, nodding. "Something to do with the titanium for the body, I believe."

"Close," Gene said. "The problem came from a lack of rutile ore, the basic requirement to make titanium. Not really a lack of the ore, but a problem of getting the ore in sufficient quantities without arousing suspicions about the program."

"I remember," Jim said. "The Soviet Union had the ore, and we couldn't buy it without alerting them as to how critical it was."

"Exactly," Gene confirmed. "We used several dummy companies and some third-world countries to purchase the ore and provide it to Lockheed for the titanium. And that's just one example of how we have to work around shortages of material here in the US. So, national security is an issue even though it's a small matter of extortion that forces us to persuade this individual that his interests are secondary."

"What about this partner I'm getting?" Jim wanted to know. "How's he involved?"

"Actually, he's a she," Gene told him. "If the plan works out as we envision, she'll be posing as your wife for the operation."

Just as Jim was about to question the basic plan involving a fictitious wife, Jennifer opened the back door and called out, "General, I didn't know you were coming today."

"Spur of the moment," Gene said as he walked to meet her. "You're looking as lovely as ever, but I still don't understand what you see in this disreputable husband of yours."

"He's handy," Jennifer replied as she hugged Gene. "Mother always said that if you can't find one that's handsome, at least find one that's handy."

"I guess handy works for him," Gene said, laughing. "He certainly isn't too pretty."

"Sometimes he cleans up pretty good," Jennifer said, smiling at Jim. "Sometimes."

"I know I'm not just another pretty face," Jim said as Jennifer slipped her arms around his waist. "But I make up for that with charm and wit."

"That you do, dear," Jennifer said, kissing his cheek. "That you do. General, how about letting me refresh your drink and we can dissect my husband's obvious flaws."

"I'd love another drink," Gene said, following Jennifer toward the house. "But I don't have near enough time for all the obvious flaws, let alone those that aren't so obvious."

"Would it be okay with you, kind folks, if I joined you for a refill?" Jim asked as they entered the kitchen.

"As long as you mind your manners," Jennifer told him, refilling Gene's glass and making one for herself. "We'll be in the living room should you want to join us after you get your own drink."

"Now, can you stay for dinner with us?" Jennifer asked as she and Gene took seats on the couch. "We're meeting Bull Winkle and his wife at a great little restaurant called Tomato Joe's Pizza and Pasta."

"I'd love to," Gene answered as Jim came in. "But I've already told Jim I've got to get back to Virginia tonight. Maybe on my next visit."

Shortly after Gene left, Jennifer sat beside Jim on the couch and said, "We need to talk about something."

"Any something? Or something in particular?" Jim asked, smiling at her.

"I'm serious," Jennifer said, putting her hand on Jim's arm.

"I'm listening," Jim said, noting the change in her attitude.

"It's about someone at work," she started. "I don't know just what to do anymore."

"What about this someone?" Jim asked, wondering what was happening.

"It's one of the guys in accounting," she answered. "He's been bothering me."

"What do you mean, bothering?" Jim asked.

"He's been making inappropriate remarks, trying to get me to go to lunch. Or to go out for a drink when you're on a trip," she told him as tears filled her eyes.

"Do you want me to say something?" Jim asked as anger rose quickly.

"Not yet," Jennifer told him. "But, if he doesn't stop, I'm not sure if I can continue to work there." "Quit," Jim said. "We don't need the money. And you certainly don't have to take that sort of crap from anybody."

"But I love my job," Jennifer said, wiping a tear from her eye. "I need something to do when you're gone. I can't just sit around the house. An, I'm not about to join one of those old lady cliques that play cards all day."

"All right," Jim said, standing. "I'll let you handle this any way you want. But you know I'll take care of it if you need me to get involved."

Jennifer stood and put her arms around his waist and told him, "I know you would. But, for now, I'll try another time or two to get him to understand that there's no way. I worked too hard to get what I wanted, and he's not going to cause any problems that could affect that."

"I guess you mean me," Jim said as he pulled her against his chest. "And I'm sure you can resolve this little issue. Now, let's go clean up and get ready to go to dinner."

Chapter 2

The following morning, after Jennifer left for work, Jim checked his travel bag to make sure he had clean clothes for the three days he'd be gone. As much as he'd like to get some more information about the upcoming assignment, he had two more trips before he could possibly get any Baltimore layovers unless he could trip trade with another First Officer. Another issue was whether his relatively junior seniority would allow him to get a schedule that had BWI layovers.

His sign-in for today's trip wasn't until 12:30, but he wanted to get to the airport early in case there were any changes he needed to make to his manuals or navigation publications. Plus, the bid lists were going to be out, and he could spend some time looking at the layovers he'd need to perform the contract for Muddy Water.

Leaving his standard I Love You note on the kitchen counter, Jim took his suitcase and headed for the door. Tossing his suitcase into the rusting old pickup that was his airport car, he rechecked his pockets for his company keys and ID badge. As he was backing out of the driveway, a white pickup stopped, blocking his way.

Moving the gear shift into park, Jim got out and walked to where the pickup sat waiting. As he approached the passenger side, the driver stuck a large envelope out of the window, saying, "This is for you, Mr. Lashley."

Jim had barely taken the envelope when the pickup sped off down the road. Shaking his head at the company's methods, Jim carried the envelope back to his pickup and got in. Ensuring the almost invisible seal was intact on the envelope, he continued out of the driveway and headed for DFW. Once on loop 635 around the north side of Dallas, the traffic became increasingly heavy, and Jim realized that he'd have very little time before the required one hour ahead of departure to be signed into the computers at the airport; so much for doing all of his publication changes before takeoff. Guess he'd take care of it on the first leg to Denver if he didn't finish it.

Finding a parking place just yards from the employee train, Jim opened his suitcase and tossed his keys and the envelope inside. As he was locking the pickup doors, he saw the two-car electric train making the final turn before arriving at the small loading station. Hurrying inside before the train could discharge the passengers going home, Jim noticed his Captain for the month holding the door open, waiting for him.

"Running late, are you?" Brett Heeger said as Jim stepped into the small car.

"I guess," Jim admitted as he took a seat on one side of the car. "I thought I was going to be early, but the 635 traffic was a mess."

"It can be that way," Brett admitted. "I've got to come in on 114 from Rhome, and that little two-lane road can be a problem if there's an accident or anything. So far, I've only had to call the schedulers one time in over 15 years of living out there."

"I know a Flight Attendant that lived seven miles from the airport, normally a 15-minute drive to the employee parking lot," Jim recounted. "One morning, she got caught in traffic, and it took over an hour to get here. She wound up parking at the terminal to not be late and had to pay parking fees of almost 100 dollars by the time the trip was finished."

"Like you said, nothing's guaranteed in driving around here," Brett admitted. "Unless you sleep down in the crew room, the odds are that you'll have trouble one of these days making it by sign-in."

A few minutes later, they pulled into the employee loading area of the terminal and joined the people from the other car heading upstairs. The mix of Flight Attendants, pilots, mechanics, and other airport personnel represented a cross-section of the airline business. Just another day at the office for most of them.

Entering Flight Operations, Brett headed for one of the numerous computers to sign in while Jim used the one beside him. Once signed in, Jim typed in the code for the crew names and saw that it was same Flight Attendants as the last trip.

Next, he saw an envelope with navigation publications changes and the bid sheets for next month's flying in his box. Taking them, he grabbed his flight kit bag with all of his manuals and headed back into the computer room. Not seeing Brett, he headed out into the terminal and walked to the gate where their airplane had just arrived.

When the crew finally came out of the jet bridge, Jim was standing by the door with his bags. The departing Captain stopped for a moment and told Jim that the plane was good, but the cleaning crew was having to do a little extra due to one of the passengers not quite getting all of his upset stomach into the little 'puke pouch' at his seat.

Tossing his kit bag into the right seat, Jim ran through the memorized checks of all the aircraft systems and reviewed the log book. Out of the cockpit, he opened his suitcase and retrieved the envelope he'd gotten at his house. Shutting the suitcase, he put it into the coat closet beside the open door of the airplane and stuck the envelope in his kit bag before placing it into the rectangular holder beside his seat. Grabbing his flashlight, he headed outside to check the exterior of the plane.

Back inside, Jim opened the envelope and noticed a profile of what appeared to be the main target of his next assignment. Along with the photo, there was a description of his position as CEO and a summary of his life outside of the company. Ten pages of data showed that the company had done its usual thorough job of providing information about the upcoming mission.

Hearing Brett coming down the jet bridge talking to one of the Flight Attendants, Jim stuck the pages back into the envelope and placed it in his bag beside his seat.

Chapter 3

The flight to Denver was uneventful as Jim flew the plane and Brett ran the radios. Less than an hour after landing, they were heading back to DFW with Brett flying and Jim running the radios.

Approaching the Red River, they began the descent to land on the west side of the airport. Knowing that there would be a long taxi route over to the gates on the east side, Jim keyed the microphone and asked, "Any chance of 17 center?"

"Stand by," came the answer.

A couple of minutes later, the controller came back and told them, "Turn left heading 120 to intercept 17 center localizer, descend and maintain five thousand until established on final, contact tower 127.5."

"Left 120, five thousand, localizer 17 center, and 27.5," Jim replied, looking at Brett as he nodded his acknowledgment of the new clearance.

"Tower, American 2635 descending to five for 17 center," Jim said after switching to the new frequency.

"Roger American 2635, do you have 17 right in sight?"

Seeing Brett nod, Jim replied, "Affirmative tower, 17 right, is in sight."

"Now cleared visual to land 17 right, American 2635," the tower controller told them.

"Cleared to land 17 right, American 2635," Jim replied.

Clearing the runway about three-quarters of the way down, Jim switched to the ground controller and got clearance to taxi to the terminal. Once there, Brett parked and shut down the engines. As soon as the checklist was complete, Brett opened the cockpit door and began saying goodbye to all the passengers as they walked by.

Gathering their bags, the entire crew walked to their next gate for the flight to Tucson. "Mind pulling the paperwork?" Brett asked as they approached the gate agent's stand. "I'll do the cockpit stuff and walk around."

"Not a problem," Jim said, stepping around the stand to an open computer. "I'll bring them down for you to sign."

"Great," Brett said, heading for the door to the jet bridge. "I've got training next month and need to refresh myself on what the First Officer has to do."

"Excuse me, Captain Heeger?" the gate agent asked as he approached.

"Yes," Brett answered. "What can I do for you?"

"You and the crew have been reassigned, sir," the agent said, handing Brett a piece of computer paper. "You're now going to Baltimore instead of Tucson."

Brett took the notice and stepped up to the computer where Jim was about to pull up the flight plan. "I'll take care of this," Brett said, signing in.

Waiting for Brett to finish, Jim watched the agent change the flight number to 2361 and the destination from Tucson to Baltimore, leaving in 45 minutes.

"What happened?" Jim asked as the Flight Attendants walked up.

"Equipment change," the agent replied as passengers looked at the change on the board above the agent. "They put a 757 on the Tucson trip due to an earlier cancellation."

"Still want to do the walk around?" Jim asked as Brett continued to work on the computer.

"No," he answered. "I need to call the flight office to make sure we get credit for the extra hours this change will make. I'll see you down there in a few minutes."

Holding the jet bridge door open for the Flight Attendants, Jim wondered if this change was truly a scheduling issue or if, once again, either Dark Water or its subsidiary, Muddy Water, had managed to direct operations to its benefit.

As he got to the airplane, he saw a man with the blue pants and shirt that the mechanics and ramp personnel wore writing in the logbook. "Here ya go," the man said, handing the logbook to Jim. "Just signed off the draining of the aft lavatory (lav). Guess it wasn't flushing right, but it's good now."

Taking the book, Jim noticed the Baltimore Orioles baseball cap the man was wearing. "Thanks," Jim told him as he carried the logbook into the airplane.

Setting his suitcase in the coat closet and his kit bag in the right seat, he opened the logbook to see the sign-off. A plain white envelope was between the pages, simply marked 'BWI FO.' Looking back toward the cabin where the Flight Attendants were busy getting ready for the passengers, Jim slipped the envelope into his kit bag and put it in the space beside his seat. Looking out the window, Jim saw the same man with the ball cap looking up at him. As he watched, the man removed his ball cap and walked away. Now Jim was positive that Black Water had instigated the sudden change that would send him to Baltimore.

Finished with the cockpit checks and exterior inspection, Jim took the envelope from his bag and went into the forward lav. Noting the unbroken seal along the flap, he opened it and saw Call 410-328-7448 upon arrival at the hotel written on the single sheet he found inside. After writing the number on a piece of the paper he tore off, he tore the envelope and the remainder of the paper into small pieces and flushed them down the toilet.

Stepping back into the cockpit he asked Julie, the Flight Attendant who worked first class, for a Dr. Pepper and a slice of lemon. As she was handing him the can and a Styrofoam cup with ice and the lemon on top, Brett stepped onto the plane and asked, "Got another one of those, Julie?"

"Just for you, Brett," she said, smiling. "You Texas boys sure do like your Dr. Peppers."

"I suppose you're a Coke fan, growing up in Atlanta," Brett told her as he sat his bag on his seat. "Please get the rest of the ladies up here, and I'll explain what's going on."

Tossing the paperwork on the center console, he asked Jim, "Want to hear this or wait until I get back?"

"I'll wait," Jim replied as he picked up the flight plan. "I'll set up the cockpit for the departure and change my airport pages from TUS to BWI."

A couple of minutes later, Brett stepped into the cockpit, put his bag in the holder to the left of his seat, and sat down. "Well, the good news is that you'll get home a day earlier. We're done when we get back from BWI tomorrow night. And we still get paid for the third day! Hope you didn't have plans that just got shit-canned."

"Nothing that I can't live with," Jim said. "I'll just call home when we get to the hotel and tell my wife I'll be getting home tomorrow night."

"Looks like we'll have some tourist time tomorrow morning if you're interested in seeing what's left of a once-famous city," Brett said as he set his instruments up for the takeoff.

"What's left?" Jim asked.

"Yep," Brett told him. "There's not much left of the old Baltimore. Most of the beautiful old buildings downtown are falling apart. The area around the bay is still nice unless you get a couple of blocks away. Then, the rest of the city is checkerboarded with ghettos and a few nice residential areas. Have you ever been there?"

"Nope," Jim answered. "This will be my first time. Maybe I'll take a little stroll around tomorrow morning and see what it's like."

"Just be careful," Brett recommended. "I'm not sure exactly where the layover hotel is, but don't wander off too far. I've never seen a city that goes from ghetto to good every other block. Must be because of their Democratic raisings."

"I'll watch out," Jim said, smiling at Brett's obvious political leanings. "What are you going to do?"

"Believe it or not, I've got an old Air Force buddy that lives there," Brett answered. "I'll give him a call when we get in and see if I can't have either breakfast or lunch with him. Want to join us?"

"Thanks, but I'll find something to do," Jim said. "What time do we leave tomorrow?"

"Not until 6:30 that evening. We won't get home until almost 9 o'clock tomorrow night," Brett answered. "At least the traffic won't be bad that late."

A few minutes later, the gate agent stuck his head in the cockpit and told them all the passengers were on board and that he was closing the door.

"Well, I guess we better start the engines," Brett said, smiling. "It would be a tough flight unless we get at least one running."

Chapter 4

The routine flight to BWI arrived on schedule, and the hotel van was waiting just outside the terminal as they exited. Thirty minutes later, the entire crew had been assigned rooms and were heading for the elevators.

As soon as Jim tossed his suitcase on the bed, he called home to tell Jennifer that his trip had changed and it would be close to 10 o'clock when he got home tomorrow night. Next, he called 410-328-7448 as instructed.

"Light Industrial Waste," came the answer after the first ring.

"Good evening," Jim replied. "I was given this number to call when I reached Baltimore."

"Yes sir," the voice said. "Please stand by for General Barker."

"Jim," the familiar voice of Gene came on the line. "How was the trip?"

"Rather unexpected, I'd say," Jim answered. "Just how far do the company's arms reach?"

"Now, what makes you think the company had anything to do with your reassignment?" Gene chuckled.

"Oh, I don't know," Jim said, shaking his head. " Pickups that block me from leaving my house and scurry off after giving me an envelope that just happens to coincide with your assignment talk the other day. Something about mid-sequence flight changes and strange hats on maintenance personnel. Need any more 'coincidences'?"

"I'm pretty sure that's exactly what it was. Just another coincidence," Gene told him. "But I hope you're able to bring your suitcase downstairs to the lobby after you change out of your uniform. Say in about 15 minutes?"

"Do I really need my suitcase?" Jim asked.

"Only if you don't want to wear the same clothes you come downstairs in until noon tomorrow," Gene told him. "I've made arrangements for you to spend the night at Quantico and help us with the planning early tomorrow morning."

"I guess I better get changed and head downstairs if I'm going to make it in 15 minutes," Jim said, resigned to the fact that he actually had little choice.

"More like 11 minutes since you wasted time debating the necessity of my suggestion," Gene retorted. "I'll be in the car parked outside the hotel."

Hearing the line go dead, Jim pulled his uniform off, hung everything in the closet, slipped on a pair of jeans and a T-shirt, pulled his black 'airline' boots on, grabbed the suitcase with the original envelope now inside, and headed out the door. Making sure it locked and the Do Not Disturb sign was displayed, he took the stairs that were at the end of the hall to avoid possibly running into any of the crew in the elevator and checked the lobby before leaving the hotel.

A black Suburban with dark tinted windows was parked beside the door as Jim walked out. The rear passenger door opened, and Gene said, "You're late. I thought I taught you better than that. Timeliness is a virtue. Tardiness is a sin. Where do you think the world would be now if the Big Bang had been delayed even a second?"

"Probably we'd be right here-----now!" Jim said, grinning and taking the Jack and Coke Gene was offering him.

"That's what I like about you. Always have a ready answer," Gene said, raising his glass.

"I'm even right...occasionally," Jim said, raising his glass. "Semper Fi."

"Semper Fi," Gene replied. "We have about 30 minutes before we get to Quantico. Did you bring the information we gave you?"

"Of course," Jim said, tapping the suitcase on the seat between them. "Boy Scouts and Marines. Always prepared."

"Never doubted you for a second, but I've got mine out already," Gene told him. "Let's not waste any time digging through your dirty underwear. Jerry, please raise the window."

As the dark window separating the rear seats from the driver rose, Gene held up the photo of the target and said, "This man, Harry Wellington, is the CEO of Wellington Mineral Acquisitions. He has one of the few contracts for Lithium mined in Australia, Argentina, and Chile. Those three countries account for almost 90 percent of the known Lithium production in the world. We've offered to buy his contracts at what would be an astronomical profit for his company, but he is holding us hostage because he knows we need his product."

"What about buying his company's stock through the people who manage our retirement fund?" Jim asked, knowing that Black Water had offshore accounts that handled the funding for all the Dark Water and Muddy Water operations, as well as personnel salaries and retirements.

"We've tried that," Gene answered. "But his family owns over 90 percent of the stock and controls the board of directors where any major contract decisions are made. Every attempt at negotiating has been met with the same demand, four hundred million dollars for his Lithium contracts."

"Is that really excessive?" Jim asked. "What about the other sources? Could we get what we need elsewhere?" "We estimate that our need for Lithium would exceed the other producers, especially if you exclude Bolivia, and Wellington is negotiating with them for exclusive rights in that country," Gene answered. "Not to mention that four hundred million dollars is probably the value of all of the Lithium in South America at the current price. And then it would take years and billions of dollars to extract it. We've offered forty million.

Now, there is one other source, but so far, it's unattainable," Gene continued. "Afghanistan has probably close to a billion dollars' worth of Lithium. But as long as the war continues over there, nobody will invest the assets to try to get it. That's one of the main reasons Russia fought for years to get in, and we're involved there, too."

"What are the plans we're working on at present?" Jim asked.

"How much did you get to read about Harry so far?" Gene asked.

"Not much. Just glanced at the pages," Jim answered. "I'd planned on looking at them tonight in Tucson."

"Understand," Gene said, holding the pages out for Jim to see. "Harry is rather fond of good food, expensive liquor, and exotic ladies. Oh yes, toss in some illegal gambling. But as much as he likes gambling, he sucks at it. I mean, he truly sucks."

"Are we planning on blackmailing him?" Jim asked, reading the top page. "I don't see how that would resolve the board of director's issues."

"Not blackmailing, but you're here to discuss the options we're exploring," Gene answered. "We're also working on the other members of the board. There are four of them, and we think we can get three to support our offer."

"How do you plan on doing that?" Jim asked, looking at the page describing the members of the board of directors.

"By trying to convince them that the time element for the offer makes it to their advantage instead of waiting several years to see this sort of profit," Gene admitted. "That and running a little...let's call it a hustle, for lack of a better word, on Mr. Wellington. That's where you and your exotic new wife come into the picture."

"And when do I get to meet her," Jim asked as he saw the signs announcing the outskirts of Quantico.

"You've already met her," Gene said, smiling. "But you'll see her again in the morning."

Chapter 5

The next morning, Jim was woken by the sound of someone knocking on the door of his room. Initially not knowing where he was, he quickly remembered the dorm-like apartment from his first visit and briefing with Dark Water.

"Just a minute," Jim said as he threw the sheets and blanket off. "Let me get some clothes on."

Pulling on his jeans and T-shirt, Jim opened the door and saw an unknown man wearing khaki pants and a knit shirt with a logo and the words Muddy Water written underneath. "Good morning," the man said. "I'm Rob, and I'll be your escort this morning. How soon can you be ready to meet the rest of the group for breakfast?"

"Give me 15 minutes to take a quick shower and brush my teeth," Jim said, recognizing the uniform from previous visits, but instead of Dark Water, the name had changed.

"I'll be back in 15 minutes," Rob told Jim as he shut the door.

Pulling his jeans, T-shirt, and underwear off, Jim started the water running in the tiny shower and waited for it to get warm enough. Grabbing the washrag from the towel bar and the small wrapped bar of soap, Jim stepped into the shower and quickly washed. The shampoo bottle was vintage hotel, as was the soap, and Jim simply left them on the small shelf as he finished rinsing and toweling dry.

Putting on fresh underwear and socks with yesterday's jeans and shirt, he was just finishing brushing his teeth when he heard the knock. Rinsing his mouth, Jim laid his toothbrush and paste back on top of his shave kit and opened the door.

"Ready?" Rob asked.

"I guess as ready as I'll get today," Jim said, smiling as he thought about how many *Robs* he had met since starting work for the Black Water group so many years ago. Now he just thought of them as Rob number 100 plus. The exception is one encounter with a female that he dubbed Robin even though he didn't really meet her. Only saw her profile from a distance.

"If you'll just follow me," Rob said as he led the way down a long hall with several numbered doors on either side. "We're meeting for breakfast in one of the conference rooms. It's been set up for the members of your group and General Barker."

Exiting the hall, they crossed a large circular lobby, and Rob entered the required code in one of the several doors that exited the lobby. Once inside the room, Jim saw three round tables with five chairs arranged around each. A buffet of breakfast foods was arranged along the wall opposite the door, and carafes of juice and coffee sat on each table, along with a tablet, pen, and name for each seat.

"The others should be here shortly," Rob told Jim. "Please find your seat and get whatever you want for breakfast. I'll be back after everyone finishes here today unless you need anything else."

"No, I think I'll be fine for now," Jim said as he saw the small cardboard name place that read M. Lashley.

Just as Rob turned to leave, the door opened, and Gene came in wearing the same khaki pants and shirt with the logo but Black Water written on it. "Good morning, Jim," Gene said as he crossed to the table where he and Jim were supposed to sit. "How was your night?"

"As good as a tiny room, uncomfortable bed, lukewarm shower, and minimal sleep can be, I guess," Jim said, shaking Gene's hand. "How about you?"

Smiling, Gene answered, "My accommodations are slightly better than yours, but then I spend much more time here than you do. But it still beats living in the field, doesn't it?"

"Maybe a little," Jim said as he followed Gene to the buffet table. "I sure don't miss the mud, mosquitoes, and lousy food if you got any at all. And the mess tent wasn't too much better when you weren't out on patrol."

"You should have joined the Air Force if you wanted luxurious living," Gene said as he loaded his plate with scrambled eggs, crisp bacon, hash browns, white gravy, and an English muffin.

Filling his plate with the same, Jim followed Gene to the table, saying, "The only thing I don't see to make this a great breakfast is Tabasco sauce."

Smiling, Gene took a small bottle from his pants pocket before sitting down and asked, "Like this?"

As they were taking their seats, Jim glanced at the other name places and didn't recognize any of them. Half expecting to see Rob, Rob, and Rob at the other seats, he just saw M. Somebody, M. Somebody else, and another M.

Somebody. It was like Smith, or Green, or Johnson. All common names.

Within minutes, the room was filling up with several men dressed in what Jim thought of as the company uniform. As they filled their trays and carried them to different tables and seats, two of them arrived at Jim's table and took seats.

"Good morning," each of them said, addressing Jim and Gene.

"Good morning," Jim and Gene replied almost in unison.

Thinking it somewhat strange that neither of the men introduced themselves, Jim thought it best to just follow suit and let his name place provide any information if they wanted to know. They apparently knew each other, and almost everyone else nodded at each other as they either found their seats or returned with trays of food.

With his back to the door, Jim didn't see the entrance of the only female that had arrived. Making small talk stopped abruptly when Gene interrupted his discussion on airline food, hotels, and Flight Attendants.

"Excuse me, Jim," he said, looking at the person arriving at their table. "I believe you somewhat know this lady. But since some of the others here may not, gentlemen, please let me introduce Miss Jewell."

Jim turned in amazement as he saw Jewell standing behind the open seat to his left. "Jewell," he said when he finally regained the ability to speak. "It's been a while."

Placing her tray on the table, she replied, "Not really, Jim. You just haven't paid attention lately. I seem to remember a gas station in Mesquite on Main Street just west of Preston. And a restaurant in Atlanta more recently."

Jim sat back in his chair, his fork left on the half-eaten plate and asked, "So that was you. How long have you been with this company?"

"That's a subject we never discuss," Jewell said as she took her seat. "Just as we never ask who Rob is. Or Robin in some cases."

"Well, now that we're all here," Gene announced to break up the conversation. "Let's get this little planning session underway. Rob, would you please start the briefing and handle the questions that will definitely arise?"

Chapter 6

A middle-aged man stood at one of the other tables and raised a remote that lowered a flat-screen TV covering most of the wall behind him. Almost immediately, the picture of Harry Wellington appeared. "This man, Harry Wellington, owns the controlling interest in Wellington Mineral Acquisitions. The company was started by his grandfather during the great coal mining days. Since then, they have expanded into numerous other minerals," Rob continued. "That's not to say they actually mine any minerals. The company just acquires contracts for the minerals and then makes contracts with the actual producers."

The picture changed to four other people dressed in suits, most of them appeared to be in their 60's or 70's. "These men comprise the members of the board of directors," Rob explained. "Two, the men on your left are both uncles of Harry. They've been on the board almost since birth and own almost 20 percent of the stock between them. Since they are brothers of Harry's father, they will continue to hold those positions until they die."

"The other two are also members of the Wellington family, but by marriage and serve more or less at the discretion of their wives. They are also in control of almost 20 percent of the stock," Rob explained. "Fifty-one percent of the stock is in the hands of.... you guessed it. Mr. Harry Wellington."

"The remaining nine percent is actively traded on the open market, as is some of their stock occasionally when they temporarily need extra funds," Rob continued. "But, to remain on the board, they must start each calendar year with the original number of shares. Any of them can trade up to 10 percent of their shares at any one time or combination of trades, but never more than 10 percent in total. And they must have the original number of shares for the majority of the days of any calendar year as well as have it at the end of any calendar year."

"Is that why you couldn't buy enough stock to force a sale of the Lithium contracts?" Jim asked, doing the mental math.

"Exactly," Rob concurred. "Even if we could buy each available share when everyone had their 10 percent on the market, plus the other nine percent, we'd have less than 20 percent. We'd have to have all four of them vote with us to override Harry's vote if he had his 10 percent on the open market. Which, by the way, he's never had any of his shares being traded. We think it's because he doesn't trust his uncles or uncles-in-law."

"Now, anyone can see the futility of pursuing that approach. So, let's move on to the most feasible plans," Rob stated. "Blue team, what have you got?"

As another man walked from his table to take the remote, he said, "We believe we've developed a scenario that has an excellent chance of working."

As he was changing the picture on the screen, Jim looked around the room and noticed that the words beneath the logos were either red, as the two men at his table, blue, as at the table where the man now talking had been, green, the other table, or black. The only ones with black were the initial speaker and General Barker. Thinking back to his other visits here, he was sure he'd seen white lettering also, but couldn't be positive.

"We think we must make Harry believe that the price of his Lithium contracts will soon lose over 90 percent of their value," the blue team speaker explained. "To do that, we've envisioned a scenario where our two out-of-town guests provide him with some inside information that will practically guarantee that he will drop his price tag of four hundred million dollars."

Jim leaned over to Jewell and whispered, "I think they are referring to us."

"Probably so," she whispered back. "But any of these guys could be from out of town. Especially the other two at this table, for example."

"What makes you suspect them?" Jim asked, looking at the two men.

"Red letters," Jewell said, nodding at their shirts.

Before Jim could ask what the different colors meant, Gene cleared his throat and glanced at both of them.

Looking back up at the screen after being mildly chastised, Jim heard the speaker continue, "We know that Harry frequents an underground gaming room affectionately known as Dunnahoe's Crapshoot. It's located in the Locust Point area in what was the master suite of the house. Larry, the current Boniface, has been running this little enterprise for over 15 years. It's not especially widely known, but it's no secret either. Current and past Mayors, Chiefs of Police, and other well-known political figures have been known to visit Larry at one time or another."

"It's because of the reputation of the place, as well as the status of its frequent visitors, that we are restricted in our use of the establishment," he explained. "However, we do have one possibility that we're pursuing."

"What's that?" Gene asked, knowing the repercussions of any action involving the politically placed individuals that he knew went there.

"We have secured the assistance of one of the blackjack dealers," the speaker answered. "He's Harry's favorite dealer, and we know that Harry has managed to persuade him to bend the rules ever so slightly to give Harry a minor advantage."

"How did you determine that?" Gene asked. "I can't imagine Larry allowing any infraction of the rules. He has too much reputation at stake to show any favoritism."

"We learned that the dealer was suddenly driving a leased Porsche 911," the blue speaker explained. "We traced the lease back to...."

"Let me guess," Jim said. "Mr. Harry Wellington."

"Close," the speaker answered. "One of Harry's uncles, a member of the board of directors. Blood appears to be thicker than ethics."

"Okay, how do you expect to use this information," Gene asked. "I don't see blackmailing a dealer as a way to encourage Mr. Wellington to lose millions of dollars. Even he would have a hard time losing that much at blackjack."

"Oh, we don't plan on doing anything more than having that dealer be missing when Harry comes to play," the speaker explained. "We know that the dealer sticks the little finger of his right hand out when looking at his cards if they total 13 to 16 so that Harry knows not to hit anything over

11. We've spent countless hours taping and watching him to learn the signs. Trust me, we know how this is working. And the dealer knows that we know."

"How does his being missing help us?" Jim asked. "All that means is that he'll lose any advantage in the odds."

"That's the point," the speaker explained. "Harry is a terrible gambler. Without his advantage, he loses close to ten thousand dollars on any given night. Oh, sometimes he'll win a little. But over the last eight months we've been watching him, he's lost close to one hundred thousand."

"All right. But you just admitted that we can't get him to lose enough to really make any difference, "Jim said. "What good does it do to change dealers? And how do you know what day he'll go there anyway?"

"First answer, we're changing dealers to ensure that a couple of out-of-town guests end up as winners at the same table where Harry is probably losing," came the explanation. "Second answer, Harry always goes there when a certain lady from the Wellington corporation goes there. And we definitely know when she'll be there."

"How do you ensure I'll win? And how do you know when that certain lady will be there?" Jim asked.

"You'll win more often because the dealer will signal when to stand by holding his left thumb up when he looks at his cards. The lady will be there when we tell her to," Gene said, knowing exactly which lady they were talking about.

"If anybody wants anything from the buffet, please do so now," the speaker suddenly told them. "I need to have a word with my team before we resume the briefing."

Chapter 7

As the blue team was meeting, Jim asked Gene, "What do the different colors of the lettering on your shirts signify?"

"Blue is for operational planning, green is support, and red denotes those assigned to execution of the plans," Gene answered. "Black is for headquarters, and you may have noticed some with white; they're administration."

"I guess I thought all of the people that you had in the field were guys like me," Jim replied. "Sort of outside the mechanics of the operation. More like contract personnel."

"Most of our field people are just that, contracted to do certain jobs, like you or Jewell," Gene told him. "But we do have a very small contingency of field operators that are here for their expertise. And occasionally, we need them on a moment's notice to replace one of our contract people who are unable to complete the mission if it becomes time-critical."

"Why are these two gentlemen here with us today?" Jim asked, nodding toward the two red-lettered men at their table.

"Backup plan," Gene told him.

"Oh yes," Jim said, nodding. "I remember, always have a plan, a backup plan, and a way out."

"Exactly," Gene said as the speaker returned to the front of the room.

"Sorry for the delay," the speaker said as he resumed the briefing. "A slight adjustment to our plan, but we'll take care of it after we conclude here since I know one of us must be back in Baltimore in a few hours, and I don't want to waste everyone's time with minor details that were overlooked by my team."

"You mentioned some out-of-town people that were to be at Larry's place," Jim said. "I'm assuming that you're referring to the lady sitting here and myself."

"You are correct," the speaker answered. "You two are the crucial part of this plan."

"What's our role in the gambling aspect?" Jim asked. "Are we there just to distract Harry? And, how do you know he'll take any notice of us?"

"First answer, the gambling issue is merely a way to get you introduced to Mr. Wellington without arousing suspicion," the blue leader answered. "Second, not just distract, more to provide a forum for you to disclose some inside information about one of your company's products that will have a major impact on his Lithium holdings. And lastly, if you remember the briefing material you were provided, Mr. Harry Wellington has an eye for exotic ladies."

"What is my company, and what's the product?" Jim asked.

"Rob, would you please give him the company data now?" the speaker asked the original speaker.

As the small folder with some papers was delivered to Jim, the speaker continued, "You can study the data for the next couple of weeks to ensure you know your role, but I don't want to waste time today with the nuts and bolts of that portion."

Jim took the papers and glanced through what appeared to be a standard company organizational chart with product information, locations of field offices, heads of divisions, and an overall summary of the entire operation from conception to future financial projections.

"The basics of this plan are that you and the lady beside you will meet Harry at Dunnahoe's Crapshoot early next month," the blue speaker told him. "The exact date will depend on your schedule. There is some flexibility in the time frame, but we need to complete this no later than two months from today."

"The two gentlemen sitting at your table will be the backup for you should the situation require," he continued. "But it presents problems that we'd like to avoid. Additionally, we're pursuing two other possibilities. We want to use them as a last resort, but again, we want this concluded as soon as possible."

"What is their role?" Gene asked, referring to Jim and Jewell.

"She's there to pique his interest," the speaker answered. "He's there to make Harry believe that his financial interests are in jeopardy if his company gets the patent they are working on."

"How many times will we meet Mr. Wellington?" Jim asked. "And how do you plan to prevent him from discovering our identities? And where did this company I own come from?"

"We anticipate it will take at least two, maybe four meetings between the three of you," the speaker said. "If it goes longer than that, we may need to take a more dramatic approach. As to your identities, I'll let the green team take over that aspect."

"Thanks," a man from the green table said, taking the remote. "These are pictures of both of you taken within the last month."

Jim saw himself walking through the DFW terminal in uniform and another picture wearing civilian clothes in what appeared to be a Walmart.

"Now, this is what you'll look like when you assume the identity of Mr. Billy Pratka. CEO of Pratka's Pharms," he continued.

The screen showed what was unrecognizable as Jim. His almost solid gray hair was shoulder length, a retro 70's mustache adorned his upper lip, a rather pronounced paunch slightly stretched the fabric of his shirt beneath the unbuttoned suit jacket, and the wireframe glasses magnified the mass of wrinkles that surrounded his eyes.

The next pictures were of Jewell in the same order. She was in some terminal wearing her uniform, others in jogging shorts, and in jeans with a tank top. Next came several pictures of her with long dark hair reaching halfway down her back, a clinging black silk dress that was cut almost to her hip on one side, four-inch heels, and an obviously enhanced chest. Contacts changed her eyes from green to golden brown, and the makeup made her completely unrecognizable.

"How do we change from photo number one to the not-me photo number two," Jim asked. "And why did you give me a lazy man's pot belly? You make me look like a damned Air Force desk jockey."

Smiling at the remark, the speaker answered, "We'll have a room in the hotel where you'll be staying on your trips to BWI. As soon as you arrive, you'll come to our room, and we'll start the makeover. There will also be an adjoining room for your lovely wife. When you return from the meetings, you'll come back to those rooms for your conversion back to the real you."

"What about getting to Larry's place?" Jewell asked. "Will I be staying in the same hotel?"

"Yes, you're staying in the same hotel. We're working on making sure you get assigned trips to BWI that match his," came the answer. "If we can't get the trips, we'll make sure you have days off and travel on your own. From your hotel, both of you'll be driven to a five-star Four Seasons hotel, where a limo will take you to Larry's. The limo driver knows nothing of this operation and is completely unaware of the fact that you aren't actually guests of the Four Seasons. If questioned, he'll place you at that hotel where we'll actually book and occupy rooms under the name of Pratka. Those two people will be identified by the hotel as the Pratkas if ever needed. He only knows he was paid by Pratka's Pharms to be available on demand for your requirements."

"Not to bring up another issue," Jim interrupted. "But how did you get my flight schedule changed yesterday?"

"That's not that difficult," the speaker told him. "Just a matter of having one of our contract personnel ground an aircraft that resulted in needing the equipment change for the following flight due to the number of passengers. We don't like to use that option; it could be problematic if it occurs often enough. Plus, we don't want to interfere with any company more than absolutely necessary. This was sort of a last-minute decision to make sure we have the plan firmly in place for your flying schedule next month."

"Can you give him a quick overview of his company?" Gene asked.

Changing the screen to mirror the same data on the pages that Jim held, he said, "Pratka's Pharms is reflective of the combination of farming origins and pharmaceutical aspects. Billy Pratka grew up in the Midland and Odessa area of Texas. That explains his horrendous accent."

"Now that's unnecessary," Jim said, smiling. "As long as I don't have to adopt a New England snob accent and pretend to be a graduate of Harvard or Yale, I can get along just about anywhere in the US."

"I'm sure you can," came the reply as he smiled. "Now, since Billy comes from the oil-rich area of Texas, it also explains how his company was initially funded and why he has an interest in both food products and the pharmaceutical aspects of engineering various methods of improving everything from beef to broccoli."

"The major thing this plan does is to provide Mr. Wellington with some potential problems with his Lithium contracts," the blue team leader said, standing at his table. "Your company just happened to stumble upon a replacement for the declining Lithium production during an attempt to combine a genetically engineered bacteria to react with kelp or seaweed. Since kelp is abundantly available all over the world, it would be an extremely cheap food product."

"How does that replace Lithium?" Jim asked.

"I'm getting there," the blue leader said. "The other mineral you were experimenting with is diatomaceous earth or DE. Being another readily available mineral, the combination of bacteria, kelp, and DE was thought to be a way to provide cheap nutrition to cattle operations, mainly feedlots. And it could be an alternative for human consumption without the DE additive."

"The idea was that the kelp and bacteria produced an increased weight gain at an extremely low cost compared to conventional feeds. And it produced less waste because it was more completely digested. Combine that with the properties of DE that reduce the insect issues around animal waste; you have a viable product," he finished.

"The thing that brings this into focus for the Lithium, or battery part of the problem, is that during some research activity, one of your scientists inadvertently left a nickel-plated instrument in the modified bacteria/kelp/DE mix overnight. The instrument he was using became electrically charged and became the basis for the research into a replacement for the Lithium-ion battery. This new battery will be a variation of the Nickel Cadmium, NiCad, and will hold a charge longer, recharge in one-tenth the time, and avoid the overheating issues of both the NiCad and Lithium-ion batteries."

"And you expect me to pull this off?" Jim asked. "You're talking to a dumb-assed country boy. Maybe you should go to Harvard or Yale for someone who can explain what you just tried to explain to me. I've got a hard enough time figuring out if I need AAA or D batteries."

Jewell raised her hand and said, "Excuse me, but on that note, I need to go to the lady's room. I can't be expected to swallow some of the yarn that's being spun at this table."

"Now's as good a time as ever to take a break," the original speaker said, standing from the table where he'd been waiting. "We'll resume in 10 minutes so everyone can stretch their legs."

Chapter 8

Jim was sitting at the table with Gene when Jewell returned from the restroom. "So, what do you think?" he asked as she sat down.

"Interesting," she answered. "My part is rather easy. Just sit around and look pretty."

"The way you look in the makeover photos?" Jim asked. "That makes your job a cinch. I think even the Pope would take a second look."

"Are you saying I look like an altar boy?" Jewell joked.

"Not one I've ever seen," Jim replied, smiling. "But then again, I'm not Catholic."

"Okay, if we're ready," the blue speaker announced, seeing that everyone was back. "The issue about your intimate knowledge of the scientific or production aspects of the fictitious battery or how electrical production takes place is unnecessary. You merely own the process and the pending patent."

"Won't he be suspicious if I tell him how we discovered the process?" Jim asked.

"If he asks about it, just tell him the real secret is the genetically modified bacteria," the speaker explained. "That's what causes the kelp to produce an enzyme or acid that reacted with the nickel. The key to the bacteria is which gene was inserted or exchanged."

"That sounds scientific enough for someone like Billy Pratka," Jim said. "What about if he does any in-depth looking at the company or if he has access to patent records?"

"The company, Pratka's Pharms, has been an incorporated organization since 1976. The subsidiary that is doing the research on kelp was incorporated into the Pharms corporation last year," he said. "Before that, it was a small research lab originally located in Palo Alto, California. Black Water acquired the company sometime during the 1960s and has used it for several different operations. The only information available since we've controlled it is whatever we decide to provide, and that varies according to our operations."

"We'll have every aspect of this issue covered," the speaker continued. "We've actually applied for the patent, even though it's completely unworkable. We've also got certificates of incorporation on file in California and Texas, showing all of the organizations as actual taxpaying companies. The information in your packet will familiarize you with all you need to know. Should you want to embellish it in any way, that is entirely up to you. Just know that we may not be able to fix a problem you introduce in a timely manner. So, unless necessary, we prefer you not modify our plan. That's why we're here today, to iron out any issues that either of you uncover or notice based on your own experiences."

"I'm assuming my role is to just be the distraction," Jewell said.

"You're the reason Mr. Wellington will even want to talk to you guys," Gene told her.

"That's right," the blue speaker agreed. "Having Billy Pratka sit at a table with a strange dealer won't gain us an audience with Harry. Our story wouldn't stand a chance if it was pitched out of nowhere. It has to be drawn out of you; otherwise, Harry wouldn't give it any credence. I'm sure he's had wild schemes presented every day since he's been CEO. The real work here is to get him interested and convinced that his Lithium contract is worth little more than the forty million we've offered. The bait is the shiny lady. The hook is the bookish semi-reluctant multimillionaire named Billy Pratka. How you play him is what will make this a successful operation. Or not."

"Do we have all the documents we need?" Gene asked.

"Of course," the original speaker told him. "We've got passports, driver's licenses, marriage certificates, and photos of them together at various locations, everything a married couple would be expected to have."

"What about problems between me and Harry?" Jewell asked. "How do I handle that?"

"You're happily married," the speaker told her. "I'm sure he's going to make a pass, probably several, when Billy isn't watching. But your constant refusal will serve our purpose far better than any romantic entanglement. If we were trying to blackmail him, we'd use another approach. Just be a fun-loving, husband-loving, family woman who enjoys a day playing cards."

"What about the cash for the game?" Jim asked.

"You'll be given fifty thousand dollars for each night we need to work, Mr. Wellington. The money will be provided when you leave the hotel," the speaker answered. "Any money left after you come back to the hotel will be given back and used again on the next trip to Larry's."

"What about getting from the Four Seasons back to our hotel?" Jim asked.

"The car and driver that took you to the Four Seasons will be waiting to bring you back to your hotel," the blue speaker answered. "Just make sure you enter the Four Seasons so the limo driver thinks you went inside. Our driver will be where he dropped you off at a side exit after the limo leaves."

"Why don't we break for lunch and then do a quick wrap-up?" Gene suggested. "I know Jim's got a little time issue, and I don't want to cause any problems with getting back before he needs to head back to the airport."

"That works," the original speaker said as everybody started getting out of their chairs. "The staff will remove anything left from breakfast and bring in the lunch buffet."

"I'm afraid you're restricted to this room or the lobby just outside," Gene told Jim and Jewell. "I need to go make a few phone calls, so where would you like to wait?"

"How about the lobby?" Jim asked Jewell.

"Sounds good to me," she answered. "These chairs aren't the most comfortable anyway. I hope the lobby has something better. Is there a restroom in the lobby?"

"Yes, there is," Gene answered, walking toward where everybody was exiting the room. "And there are couches and a couple of phones if you need to make any calls. Just dial '9' for an outside line or '0' for the company operator if you need to make anything other than a local call."

Jim and Jewell followed Gene out and walked to one of the vacant couches before saying anything. "What's happening in your life?" Jewell asked, taking a seat.

"Same old thing," Jim answered, sitting down on the opposite end of the couch. "Fly my trips, mow the yard, take out the garbage, and change the oil in the cars, just standard husband stuff."

"How's Jennifer?" Jewell asked, looking at Jim.

"She's fine," Jim told her. "She loves her job and has plenty of friends from my days in the Marines and from her office. She seems happy."

"And are you happy?" Jewell asked.

"I suppose so," Jim answered. "I miss flying the F-4, don't really enjoy the airline flying, and can't get into yard work. But in general, yes, I'm happy."

"No kids?" Jewell asked.

"Nope," Jim told her.

"Ever thought about what might have been?" she asked, watching for his reaction.

"Of course," Jim admitted. "I've also thought about what would have happened if I hadn't been on that hill in Vietnam. Or what would have happened if I hadn't become a pilot. I've made choices in my life, as have you, but I can't truly say I'd do anything different if I could start over."

"You're the one person I've really wondered about," Jewell said, looking down at her hands in her lap. "I've had several opportunities, but never really considered them to be long term."

"Well, I guess there are some very unlucky gentlemen out there," Jim said, reaching over to touch her hand. "I can't imagine any man not wishing he could be with you."

"That's one of the things I've admired about you, Jim," Jewell said, looking up. "You've always been open and honest."

"You could have said handsome and suave," Jim said, smiling.

"Oh, now I remember why it never worked out with us," Jewell said, laughing. "Your modesty was always in the way."

"Not to change the subject, but what do you think of the plan?" Jim asked.

"Seems pretty straightforward," she replied. "I'm sure it's going to take several visits with Mr. Wellington to get him to believe that his financial issues are in jeopardy."

"I wonder how many times we'll have to meet him. And, what is the backup plan?" Jim said as he watched the lunch buffet being wheeled across the lobby into the room they had been using.

Chapter 9

A few minutes later, when everyone was back in their seats, the original speaker announced, "As soon as everyone has selected their lunch and returns to their seats, we'll resume the briefing,"

After Jim and Jewell had filled their plates and returned to the table, Jewell saw a folder on her chair. Setting the plate on the table, she picked it up and opened it. Seeing the same information she had been listening to, she sat it on the table and sat down.

Jim looked at her questioningly as he put his plate on the table. "Looks like a copy of what we've been listening to," she said, seeing his look. "Guess they think I may need to step in if something happens to you."

"That sounds good to me," Jim said, taking his seat. "If nothing else, you can correct me if I drift off course when we're talking to Harry."

"I see you got your briefing material," Gene said, arriving at the table. "Good. I asked them to give you the same information Jim has. Do either of you have any questions about what the plan is or have any suggestions as to improve it?"

"It seems that you're placing a lot of getting this going on my being able to attract Mr. Wellington," Jewell noted. "Do you have another plan if something happens to me?"

"Of course," Gene said. "We have another asset who can step in, but since there's a connection between you and Jim that is apparent, we thought it best to use you. It will appear much more believable than someone Jim meets for the first time just minutes before you go to Larry's."

"What about subsequent meetings at Larry's," Jim asked. "Won't it appear strange when your replacement dealer continues to be there?"

"He'll only be there for the first meeting and maybe one more," Gene explained. "The original dealer will be on two weeks' vacation. Even if we only get one shot with our dealer, it will establish your credentials as an astute player. It may even help if you gave Harry a little subtle advice during the later part of the evening if you think he'd be receptive."

"What are your chances of getting the BWI layovers that get in early enough to pull this off?" Jewell asked Jim.

"Probably pretty good," he answered. "I took a look at the MD 80 schedule, and the BWI lines are pretty crappy. That makes it easier for a junior pilot like me to get the one I want. The senior guys will take the lines with more hours or better layovers. The one that looks the best gets in about 5:30 in the evening and leaves after 10 o'clock the next morning. That'll give me seven or eight hours of sleep after we get back to the hotel."

"What about you?" Gene asked Jewell.

"Not really a problem," she answered. "BWI trips usually suck. If I don't get assigned, trip trades are pretty easy since there are three of us on each trip and sometimes an extra. I don't envision a problem."

"Well, both of you, let me know if there's a problem with the scheduling," Gene said as he started to eat. "We try our best to let nature take its course in these matters, but direct intervention can be used as a last resort. Especially if we believe our interests are in jeopardy."

"Shall we begin?" the original speaker asked as everyone was now back in their seats. "Unless anyone has questions or suggestions, I think we can wrap this up within the hour."

One man from the green table raised his hand and asked, "Do we have time this afternoon to take some measurements of both people for the wardrobes?"

"What do you guys think?" the speaker asked, directing his question at Jim and Jewell.

"How long do you think it will take?" Jewell asked.

"Not long for you," the green speaker answered. "We'll just take the standard measurement as any tailor would do and then make adjustments for the breast augmentation we'll be doing. Our wig maker will be there also, so I'm guessing 30 minutes or so."

"That works for me," she replied.

"What about me?" Jim asked.

"We're guessing probably 30 to 45 minutes," the green speaker told him. "We'll start with the wig so that he can be done with you before she's ready. Then, the standard measurements, plus we need to fabricate the paunch and add that into the calculations for pants, shirts, belts, and jackets. We need to ensure you don't look like you buy suits off the rack. Everything must look custom-made."

Seeing Gene nod, Jim answered, "I've got plenty of time. What about the other issue of the wrinkles and glasses?"

"Not a problem," the speaker told him. "We'll use some high-definition photos to make the measurements for a plaster replica. Then, we'll manufacture some silicon patches to add to the area around your eyes. Everything, including makeup at the hotel before the meeting, shouldn't take more than 20 to 30 minutes."

"Sounds like you guys have done this before," Jim quipped.

"The head of our make-up department spent 30 years in Hollywood," the speaker told him. "This isn't his first rodeo."

"Anybody have anything else?" the speaker asked. "If not, you're free to leave when you've finished your meals and the wardrobe people have taken care of whatever they need. General Barker, if you've got time, I'd like to meet with you when you finish."

"We can get together in your office while I wait to take Jim back to Baltimore," Gene answered.

"Great," the speaker said. "I'll be there in 15 minutes. What I need to discuss won't take long, so any time you want to stop by will be fine."

Chapter 10

Less than an hour later, Jim and Gene were heading back to Baltimore. "What do you think?" Gene asked as they sped north along US 95.

"This could take some time," Jim told him. "I can't believe he'd rely on someone he met over a blackjack table to influence him to make a major financial decision. Especially to drop his price by three hundred and sixty million dollars."

"I think you're right," Gene said, shaking his head. "The man doesn't run a multinational organization and let some unknown individual influence his financial interests without doing a major investigation into the information he's given."

"I sure wouldn't," Jim agreed. "And using Jewell. She's a cute lady, but does the company seriously think a man would give up that much for any woman?"

"That's not the idea," Gene answered. "Her whole purpose is to get you close to him. I thought that was made clear in the briefing."

"It was, but it still comes back to her being the bait," Jim replied. "Remember the 'shiny lady' comment? I think the company is placing too much emphasis on Harry making decisions based on hormones."

"I understand your point," Gene said. "We know this is sort of a long shot. That was mainly what we discussed while you and Jewell were working with the wardrobe folks. There is considerable concern that we're wasting time."

"What's your opinion?" Jim asked.

"I don't think it will work," Gene admitted. "I'd give it about a five percent chance of success. At most."

"I'd give it less than that," Jim told him. "There are so many ways to disprove the idea of a bacteria, kelp, DE, battery. All he has to do is some basic research and see that none of the major producers have anything better than Lithium-ion. True, it has its limitations. But the NiCad battery was inferior to it in most instances. And acid-based batteries, you've got to be shitting me."

"I know it's sort of out there in concept," Gene said. "But you'd be surprised at how good this company is at providing background for their operations. I'd be willing to bet that within days, there will be articles in the Scientific American about this revolutionary new breakthrough in energy generation. And other literature will appear about the science behind our patented process. Don't discount their abilities to construct elaborate covers. Just remember all those cardboard tanks and planes we had in England before the Normandy landing. Sometimes the fake is easier to believe than reality."

Pausing, he continued, "This is a part of the operations that you've never seen. But it's a great example of how the company works. They try every avenue they think has even a slight chance before we pull the trigger on the final solution."

"I appreciate that," Jim said, nodding in agreement. "I'd hate to think that we're ready to eliminate someone just for financial reasons. Hell, I'd rather give the bastard his four hundred million!"

"The problem isn't just the money," Gene reminded him. "It's more about doing what's right. And setting an example. If he can extort the government like that, some other man, group, or company will think they can hold out for an exorbitant amount also. That's really the big issue here."

"You know I'll do whatever I'm asked," Jim told him. "But I really hate to waste my time on futile efforts. I'm a good soldier, and I'll do my best to follow orders. If the company wants me to try to charm this man, I'll be as charming as possible. But charm isn't one of my strong suites."

"Oh really?" Gene asked, smiling. "I've heard you say charm was one of your major attractions. As a matter of fact, I think you told me that charm and wit were what made up for your unattractive appearance. And that was just a day or so ago."

"So, what's the answer," Jim asked, changing the mood back to serious.

"Just follow the plan," Gene recommended. "Maybe a miracle will happen. Maybe someone at the top of the food chain will see the frivolity of this and look for other avenues."

"So, I'm to just close my eyes, shut my brain down, and do something I totally disagree with?" Jim asked.

"The answer is yes," Gene said. "You'll never know how many times I've had to do the same over the years. At least this dumb-assed decision won't cost lives. Over my career, I've had to keep silent while decisions were made that I thought lost lives unnecessarily. That's a hard pill to swallow."

"Why?" Jim asked. "How can you stand by and let something like that happen?"

"Because sometimes you're not seeing the bigger picture," Gene told him. "Do you think everybody beneath General Eisenhower thought the invasion at Normandy was a good idea? What if those down the chain of command had just refused to follow their orders? Sometimes, you have to trust the men making the final decision to know something you may not understand."

"I understand that," Jim replied. "I know that the poor grunt laying in the mud can't see why a particular hill is important. All he can see is what's left of his best friend bleeding in the mud beside him."

"Let's look at it this way," Gene finally said. "What happens if we're wrong? Mr. Wellington isn't going to shoot you or Jewell. The worst thing that can happen is that he berates you as a fool who got caught in a scheme to defraud him. Is that worth moving the ultimate goal to the next level. Possibly resulting in having to terminate him? What good does that do if we have a chance, even if it's ever so slight, to get what we need with no loss of life?"

"I know, " Jim told him. "I really do. But if we need to win this issue, if the goal of getting the Lithium is so important, if our national security is indeed at risk, why are we wasting time?"

"Because we have time," Gene answered. "We still have sufficient supplies to allow the company a month or two to find what I term a peaceful solution. None of us want the final solution. Up until now, you've only been asked to do what we've tried to do for months, if not years, in a more benign way. You've been the final solution whether you knew it or not. Now, you're moving up to the things that may ultimately result in that decision. We've got many people that can do what you did in Syria or the other places with Dark Water. Or in Atlanta. What we really need…what we truly need, are people who can make the miracle happen so that we don't need that last resort.

"So, you're asking me to take the leap of faith. To accept an assignment that I believe to be unworkable," Jim asked.

"Did you know what the real goal of every mission was that you were sent on when you were a Recon Marine?" Gene asked. "Or what you'd be asked to do every time you took off during your tour as an F-4 pilot? I doubt it."

The car slowed to exit US 95 as Jim reluctantly agreed, "I'll do my best to convince Mr. Wellington that he has a real problem. But I hope you folks have another approach."

As the car pulled under the overhang of the hotel, Gene reminded him, "A plan, a backup plan, or a way out."

Jim returned to his room and sat in the overstuffed armchair, reading the material while the TV provided some background noise. Hoping to find something that he could latch onto that would make sense about the grand battery scheme.

Maybe it was simply a matter of demonstrating that the solution was on the supply side of the equation instead of the demand side. Thinking back to the Cold War and the plans the US had enacted to reduce the Soviet Union's available cash, he wondered if the major Lithium producers could be persuaded to make major reductions in the price of the ore. Or, if rumors of new mineral deposits were announced, maybe doubling the current known quantities, then there could be a possible 50 percent reduction in price. Therefore, the value of any contract would be reduced since the same quantity of ore was used but at a much cheaper price.

Picking up the phone, he dialed the same number he had been given, 410-328-7448. As soon as he heard "Light Industrial Waste," he asked for General Barker.

"Please hold," the voice answered.

A moment later, the voice directed, "Please call 410-382-5968."

"Good afternoon, Mr. Lashley," the female voice announced. "Please hold for General Barker."

A moment later, Gene came on the phone and asked, "What can I do for you, Jim?"

"I'm sure you remember what happened to oil prices during Reagan's P

residency," Jim started explaining. "By persuading the Saudi oil companies to increase production, we enacted a threefold drop in oil prices. Since oil sales were the Soviet's major source of revenue, we essentially ran them out of business."

"With only one-third of the revenue to spend on their military and our increased production of military arms, they had no choice but to come to the negotiating table," Gene answered. "I remember it well. Are you trying to tell me we need to do the same with the Wellington company?" "Pretty much," Jim said, getting excited about how the plan may now have a better chance of achieving the desired result.

"Interesting concept," Gene admitted. "Let me get with the company and see what the higher powers think."

"If they were willing to bet on a kelp battery, I think they'll see the more optimistic option of combining a supply side issue with the technological advancement portion. If you were faced with a dramatic drop in the price of a commodity and a potential obsolesce issue, the prudent choice would be to recalculate the value of your assets. Mainly, sell before the market value drops and wipes out your portfolio."

"I think you have something there," Gene said, agreeing with him. "I'll run this up the flag pole and see what we get."

"I'm sure you know that this startling discovery of new deposits and a market drop in Lithium prices needs to be enacted as soon as possible," Jim reminded him. "Since we're planning on presenting our nickel kelp battery to him in about two weeks, he needs to be convinced that the price drop isn't temporary and that your forty million dollar offer is looking more attractive."

"I'll get back to you tomorrow," Gene said. "I really do think this may give us a fighting chance. Thanks. I knew we hired you for more than just a pretty face."

"I know," Jim said, laughing. "My charm and wit."

Chapter 11

Jim met the rest of the crew in the hotel lobby for the trip back to the airport. Waiting for the van driver, Brett asked him, "Do anything interesting here in Baltimore?"

"Nope," Jim answered. "Watched a little TV. Read some. I pretty much just laid around. What about you?"

"I just hung out in my room last night," Brett told him. "Then my buddy picked me up this morning, and I spent most of the day with him and his wife. Pretty domesticated, I guess. Whatever happened to running the bars and trying to get enough sleep to fly the next day?"

"I think it's called maturity," Jim said, laughing. "Or maybe that's just another word for growing old."

"I guess," Brett agreed as they started loading their bags into the van. "I don't know if I miss those days or not. Been too long to remember."

"You're right about that," Jim agreed as the FAs all came out, and the van driver put their bags in the rear of the van. "I've been married over 20 years, and running the bars is a long-distant memory."

"You've been married 20 years?" Julie asked.

"At least," Jim grinned as the van pulled out, heading for BWI.

"How long have you been with American?" she asked.

"Only a couple of years," Jim replied.

"You're the rare one," she said, smiling. "Most of our pilots have had at least two wives. I'm starting to believe that it's a requirement to make Captain."

"I guess I'll stay a First Officer forever, then," Jim told her. "I'd rather not have to start all over again trying to understand another woman. I've finally figured out what makes this one mad."

"Yet you still piss her off!" Brett laughed.

"Can't help it," Jim acknowledged as they pulled into the airport. "But it's generally something new. Maybe I should know better, but at least I've avoided the biggies." "What are the biggies?" Julie asked.

"You know, having her find strange panties in your suitcase when you come home from a trip. Lots of hang-up phone calls. Those little biggies," Jim said.

"I'd say that avoiding those little biggies would be important," she said, nodding. "Anything else in your book of No No's?

"Anything to do with how she's spending your money. The increasing size of her wardrobe. And really stay away from the increasing size of the clothes in her wardrobe," Brett recommended as they started getting their bags from the rear of the van.

After tipping the driver, they headed into the terminal, dragging their luggage behind them. Seeing their assigned gate, they made their way through the departing passengers like salmon swimming upstream.

Finally, at the gate, Brett told Jim to pull the paperwork and bring it down to the plane. As the rest of the crew walked down the jet bridge, Jim started getting the flight plan, crew list, and all the necessary papers. The agent was standing at the next computer helping passengers who had just arrived for the flight when an elderly man came up to Jim.

"Are you the pilot for this flight?" the man asked.

"I'm the First Officer," Jim told him. "How can I help you?"

"My granddaughter is on it going home to Dallas, where her mother lives," he answered. "She's just a little nervous."

"How old is she?" Jim asked, tearing the sheets apart that they would need in the cockpit.

"She's only seven," came the reply.

"Let's go say hello," Jim suggested, ready to go down to the airplane. "Maybe that will make her a little less nervous.

Jim followed him over to where a cute little girl sat with a small suitcase covered with unicorns. "Hi, Miss," Jim said as he knelt down. "What's your name?"

She glanced at her grandfather and said tenuously, "I'm Vicki Mischelle."

"Hello, Vicki Mischelle," Jim said, holding out his hand. "I'm Jim. Captain Heeger and I will be taking you to Dallas to see your mother."

"My daddy calls me Sticky," the little girl said. "What does your daddy call you?"

"He used to call me Butch," Jim answered. "Unless I was naughty. Then he'd call me James."

"Do you have any kids?" she asked.

"No," Jim answered. "My house has white carpet. You can't have kids if you have white carpet. But right now, I have to go get the airplane ready to fly to Dallas. Or your mother will be calling me James because I was late getting you there. I'll tell the ladies that will be with you on the airplane that you are a special friend of mine and to take real good care of you. All right?"

As she watched Jim stand up, the grandfather said, "Thanks, sir. I really appreciate that."

"No problem," Jim said, turning for the jet bridge. "I think I was young once myself. The world can be a big scary place when you're that small and think you're all alone."

"Anyway, thank you," he said, shaking Jim's hand. "Too many people forget what being alone and scared is like when they grow up."

"Trust me," Jim said, turning to leave. "There are still scary things out there after you grow up. Have a nice day."

"Miss Julie," Jim said as he tossed his suitcase in the closet. "There's a little girl traveling all alone on this trip. Would you mind letting her step into the cockpit when she gets here? And, could I get a Dr. Pepper with a slice of lemon?"

"Yes, and yes," Julie said, smiling. "Don't tell me another woman has stolen your heart. After 20 years, you've fallen for a younger woman."

"At that age, they're happy with a plastic ring from a box of cornflakes," Jim quipped as he set his kit bag in the seat. "Once they're over 20, it's got to be a two-carat princess cut set in white gold. And don't even start about the formal gowns that get worn once. And matching shoes....and purse....and hair and nails and on and on."

"Who's getting rings and gowns?" Brett asked as he came in.

"Just discussing what happens when little girls became grown women," Jim said, handing Brett the flight plan for his signature.

"They found men," Brett said, signing the paper and setting it on the Flight Attendant's seat by the open door. "Men then found women. Women then found they could get anything they wanted from men. Men then found beer. Now that that's settled and world order has been restored let's load up and get the hell back to Texas. I know a woman that will be happy just to see her man."

"You?" Julie asked incredulously.

"Of course it's me," Brett said, smiling and getting into his seat. "Because I'm bringing home my paycheck.....before starting checklist, please, Jim."

Chapter 12

The flight back to DFW was uneventful, and Jim found the parents of the little girl waiting for them when he and Brett got to the terminal. After listening to Vicki excitedly telling her parents about the flight and seeing where the pilots worked, Jim and Brett told them how nice Vicki had been and hoped to see her again on another flight.

"We're such good PR agents," Brett said once out of hearing. "There should be a special pay section for that. You know, a bonus if passengers like us."

"What about putting a tip jar beside the door," Jim joked. "Like in a bar. That way, we don't have to pay income tax on it."

"Who gets the tips?" Brett asked as they entered the flight operations area to put away their kit bags. "I should get the most since I'm the most important one on the plane."

"Maybe so," Jim countered. "But I'll bet the Flight Attendants think they do most of the work. At least with the passengers. They'll want the biggest share."

"What percent do you think you should get?" Brett asked as they headed for the employee train station.

"Probably 75 or 80 percent," Jim answered.

"Why should you get that much?" Brett asked.

"Wasn't I the one that made the little girl happy?" Jim stated. "Since I'm the one that did that, I should get most of it."

"How about you get all the tips from the kids, the Flight Attendants get all the tips from the coach passengers, and I get it from the first class," Brett replied as they boarded the first car and waited for both cars to fill up.

"I don't see any of us getting rich from tips either way," Jim told him. "I've never had a job where I got tips anyway. Marines don't get tips; they get shot."

"You got shot?" Brett asked as they headed for the employee parking lot.

"A couple of times," Jim answered.

"That sucks," Brett told him, nodding.

"Could have been worse," Jim said as they prepared to get off the train. "Plenty of guys lost arms and legs. Plenty of guys never came back. I'm one of the lucky ones."

"Any plans before next week?" Brett asked as they headed for their cars.

"Nothing special," Jim told him as he got to his pickup. "I'll see you in four days."

"See you then," Brett said, walking away. "Maybe I'll put that tip idea in the suggestion box when we come back."

"Good luck with that," Jim said, getting into his pickup. "I just don't want to be involved with the argument over a couple of dollars. I'll take my paycheck and go home happy."

On the way back to Mesquite, Jim pulled into Tomato Joe's to get a pizza to take home. After ordering one called 'The Most,' he got a Shiner Bock and asked if he could use the phone.

Calling home, he told Jennifer that he was bringing dinner home and would be there in about 30 minutes. Just as he hung up and returned to his beer, a man wearing a Baltimore Orioles ball cap walked in, took a seat just down the bar,

and asked if his to-go order was ready. Hearing that it would be another 10 minutes, he ordered a beer and sat back.

Jim watched him out of the corner of his eye, wondering if there was any significance to the ball cap. Leaning back so he could see if the man was paying any attention to him, Jim wished there was a mirror behind the bar so he could see the man's face without appearing to be watching him.

Finally, the man turned to Jim and asked, "You from around here?"

"Mesquite," Jim answered. "How about you?"

"Seagoville," he told him. "Just moved here a couple of months ago."

"Let me guess," Jim said. "You came from Baltimore."

"No," he answered. "I lived in Pensacola, Florida."

"Just that the ball cap made me think you were from Baltimore," Jim said, sipping his beer.

"That's my dad's team," he replied. "He grew up in Baltimore and always followed the Orioles even after we moved to Florida."

"I understand," Jim told him. "I always liked the Brooklyn Dodgers when I was a kid. Then they moved to LA, and I gave up on them."

"I'm Bob," the man said, reaching over to shake hands.

"Jim," Jim said, shaking his hand. "Pleased to meet you. Come here often?"

"Only when I want a good pizza," Bob said. "And I make sure it won't be ready when I get here, so I have an excuse for a beer or two."

"Good plan," Jim said, laughing. "I found that you get an extra beer if you wait to order until you get here."

"That's true," Bob said. "But they seem to plan on serving at least one more beer, telling you it will be another couple of minutes before your food is ready."

"Yep," Jim said, nodding. "And as soon as they give you the beer, your food is suddenly ready, and they put it on top of the oven to keep it warm."

"I have noticed that, too," Bob agreed. "Pretty sneaky."

"Of course, but the food is great, the beer is cold, and the owners are friendly," Jim said. "I'll take that over the pizza chain restaurants any day. Even if they do sneak in that extra beer every now and then."

"Speaking of guessing, I'll bet you're with American Airlines," Bob said.

"Yeah, the uniform sort of gives it away," Jim agreed. "Just got back from a trip and stopped for pizza on the way home. Doesn't make much sense to change clothes just to drive home."

"I guessed that," Bob said. "I didn't figure you were heading to the airport since you're here drinking beer."

"I never thought about that," Jim acknowledged. "Maybe I better either take off the epaulets and wings or just take off the shirt and wear a T-shirt. Don't want people to think pilots drink before going to work."

"I'm sure it happens," Bob said. "But I'd bet they don't do it in public where they would be seen. I'm sure most people would figure out that you're heading home."

"Probably," Jim agreed. "But, there's always one ass that wants to make a scene or be recognized for his public service for exposing the horrible truth about pilots and alcohol."

Just then, Jim's pizza came out of the oven, and he said, "Nice to meet you, Bob. I've got to get home to the little lady before she starts wondering why it's taking so long."

"Good to meet you," Bob said. "Maybe I'll run into you here again sometime."

"Could be," Jim replied as he paid for the beer and pizza. "It's one of my favorite restaurants around here."

"Damn, I'm getting way too suspicious," Jim thought as he headed home. "Seeing company people everywhere I go. I'd be having a heart attack right now if he'd told me his name was Rob instead of Bob."

Pulling into the driveway, Jim reached over and picked up the pizza box from the passenger seat. He was almost out of the pickup when he noticed an envelope that had been hidden when he put the pizza on the seat. Opening it, he saw a single page that read, 'Lithium prices to drop dramatically due to new deposits uncovered in Australia.'

"Damn," Jim thought as he folded the envelope and stuck it in his back pocket. "Now I know at least three people that aren't named either Rob or Robin. Now there's a Bob. How the hell did they know I'd be there? They had to have followed me from the airport. That's got to be it. They know my schedule and where I park; there's no other rational answer."

Chapter 13

The following week and final flight for the month passed uneventfully. Jim had received his bids for the next month's flying and had four Baltimore layovers. All of them arrived just after five o'clock and left the following day at noon. That would be perfect for what he needed to do. The only thing he didn't know was if Jewell would manage to be there. Gene had told them that he would make sure she was at the hotel each night, but he'd feel better knowing everything was in place.

Four days before he was scheduled to leave for the first day of the three-day trip, Jim had just finished washing and waxing the Corvette and walked back into the house. Getting a can of Dr. Pepper out of the refrigerator, the phone rang as he was pouring it into a glass full of ice. "Hello," he answered.

"Good afternoon, Jim," came the familiar voice. "I noticed you've got a good schedule for next month."

"Not bad for someone as junior as I am," Jim responded. "What are you up to today?"

"Thought I'd come over this evening and take you and Jennifer out to dinner," Gene told him. "That is if it's all right with you."

"Sounds great," Jim said. "What time?"

"How about if I get there about five?" Gene answered. "Then we can have a drink while Jennifer refreshes. I need about 30 minutes or so of your time to go over some last-minute details before you go to Baltimore."

"That works for me," Jim replied. "I'll call Jennifer and let her know. She'll be excited to see you and go out tonight."

"Do I need to bring a bottle of Jack over?" Gene asked. "I assume you still imbibe occasionally."

"No need, sir," Jim told him. "I've got a fresh bottle and plenty of Coke. And you can come over anytime, but I need to take a quick shower before you get here."

"Don't tell me you've been doing manual labor," Gene laughed.

"Just washing and waxing the old 'Vette," Jim answered.

"How's it running?" Gene asked.

"Good," Jim said. "I just don't get to drive it much. Jennifer doesn't like it. Too noisy, too rough riding, too hot in the summer, too cold in the winter, too windy with the top down. I usually only drive it when I go meet her for lunch or other times when I'm by myself."

"Amazing how things change," Gene told him. "I seem to remember you guys driving that little buggy across half of the United States. Did she mind it much back then?"

"No," Jim answered. "At least she didn't say anything."

"Tell you what," Gene said. "I'll swing by a little early, say in an hour, and we can take it for a spin before she gets home."

"Sounds good," Jim agreed. "I'll hit the shower, and we can go to a little place I know and have a quick beer."

"Excellent!" Gene said. "I'll see you in an hour."

After calling Jennifer and taking a shower, Jim checked the oil in the 'Vette and pulled it back out of the garage. Letting it idle to warm up, he was sitting behind the wheel when Gene pulled in at the curb.

"Sounds good," Gene said, walking up to the car. "Ready for a little drive?"

"Just let me shut the house," Jim said, getting out of the driver's seat. "Why don't you drive?"

"Thought you'd never ask," Gene said, getting behind the wheel.

"I'll be right back," Jim said, heading for the open garage door. Going inside and pressing the button to bring it down, he went through the house and came out the front door, locking it behind him.

"Anywhere in particular?" Gene asked.

"Just head north and then take 80 west," Jim said, shutting his door. "There's a little bar just off Gross Road."

"I think I know the place," Gene said, backing out of the driveway. "Tomato Joe's?"

"That's the place," Jim said, laughing as Gene accelerated down the street. "Just try to get us there alive."

About 15 minutes later, Gene pulled into the parking lot and shut down the engine. "Still a great car," he said. "But I'll take my sedan if I need to go more than a couple of blocks."

"It's not a good riding car," Jim told him, shutting his door. "I'll admit that I wouldn't want to travel across the country in it again. Guess I'm getting used to comfort, too."

"Comfort ain't bad," Gene said as they went up to the bar. "Not bad at all. Even more so the older I get."

"Two Shiners," Jim said as they took seats at the empty bar.

As soon as the bartender delivered them, Gene said, "Semper Fi."

"Semper Fi," Jim repeated, tapping his beer against Gene's.

Ensuring the bartender was away, Gene said, "We're sticking with the original plan. Since the impending price drop will cause some consternation, we're hoping even the slightest push will convince him, or his board, if necessary, to negotiate."

"Are you planning anything else with the board members?" Jim asked, taking a sip of his beer.

"Definitely," Gene told him. "In case Harry doesn't see reason, we need another approach."

"Do you really think he'll go for the kelp crap?" Jim asked. "I still believe the new discovery is a better solution."

"We're looking at that and every other way of convincing him that Lithium is the last of that generation for electrical storage," Gene said, nodding. "I know it's sort of out there, but we're going to do a little background that will support your claim. And, we'll portray that it's still in its infancy."

"What do you plan to do on that?" Jim asked.

"We'll have an article placed in the American Scientific Journal," Gene answered. "It will describe a small research facility in southern California that's on the cutting edge of bio-engineered cells that retain electrical charges."

"When are you going to do it?" Jim asked.

"It'll be out the first of the month," Gene told him. "That way, he can see it after your first meeting, and it'll back up your story."

"Too bad we couldn't get it in last month's issue," Jim said. "That would make it even more creditable. "

"I know," Gene acknowledged. "We even thought about pushing this entire operation a month or so later because of that. But the final decision was that if he saw the article, he'd have too much time to do his own research, and we might not have time to get a complete cover in place for every contingency."

"I suppose you have all the 'fronts' in place," Jim responded, nodding.

"We've got most of it in place right now," Gene confirmed. "We'll have the final touches completed by the time you and Jewell make your first contact with Harry."

"I've got the cover story pretty much down," Jim told him. "What about the people on the company roster? Any name changes or phone number issues?'

"Nope," Gene answered. "All of the phone numbers actually connect through our offices in Quantico. All of the 'employees' are members of the staff of Muddy Water."

"Even the California area codes?" Jim asked.

"Every number will be redirected to our facility," Gene assured him. "We even have a molecular biologist on call who will fully explain the science behind the kelp thing."

"Where did you get a scientist that's willing to explain a fictitious procedure?" Jim asked.

"Young man out of Texas A&M," Gene replied. "Actually, we came across him when he was working on his doctorate. Believe it or not, he discovered a genocide involving a GMO produced by a major agrichemical company right here in the United States."

"Genocide by GMO?" Jim asked. "I guess there's a downside to every technological advancement if the wrong people get it. How'd you manage to convince him to support this program?"

"The company, whose management of one division was behind the genocide, hired Mr. Jackson after he brought it to the attention of the company President and that of a retired Texas Governor," Gene explained. "That company happens to be in debt to our organization for some assistance we provided in patent infringement involving a certain African country. Mr. Jackson fully understands the issues at stake and wants to be part of the program."

"Is he 'part' of the program?" Jim asked. "Is he another 'Rob'?"

"Not yet," Gene replied. "But we're keeping an eye on him. He has potential, sort of like you. Maybe someday we can arrange a meeting between you two. You'd like him."

"What about Jewell?" Jim wanted to know. "Is her schedule going to fit mine?"

"Most certainly," Gene answered. "She traded all of her schedule to get Baltimore on the same days you'll be there."

Taking a sip of beer, Gene asked, "Are you comfortable with this arrangement between you and Jewell? I know there's some history between you two, and I sure don't want to cause any problems."

"There won't be any problems," Jim told him. "Jewell and I go way back, but it was also a long time ago. She knows I'm happily married and not interested in some long-distance romance. Or any romance regardless of the distance."

"Well, you two need to be convincing around Harry," Gene advised. "He's no dummy, and your act must be perfect. That's what worries me. You act like a loving couple, and it starts to get out of hand."

"We'll cross that bridge when we get to it," Jim said. "There've always been temptations along the way. I plan on treating this as two old friends playing a role that stops the minute the assignment is over. Nothing more."

"Good," Gene said, finishing his beer. "Now, let's get back to your house and take your lovely wife out for a nice dinner. I'll meet you in Baltimore on the first night to bring you up to date on any changes or problems."

Chapter 14

Each trip of the month was to leave DFW at eight o'clock in the morning, going to Mexico City and back, and then to Tucson, Arizona, to spend the night. The next day was from Tucson to DFW, sit for almost three hours, and on to Baltimore. And then, the third day was returning from BWI to DFW.

The first morning, Jim was in flight operations at 6:30, checking to make sure there were no changes to his flight publications. Having brought a cup of coffee from one of the kiosks in the airport, he was looking at the list of crewmembers when a short rather round man with four stripes on his shoulders stepped up to a computer just two down from Jim.

"Good morning," the man said as he tapped on the keys with barely a glance at Jim.

"Good morning," Jim replied. "Where are you headed this morning?"

"Mexico City," the man said, continuing on the keyboard. "And you?"

"Mexico City," Jim said, closing the space between them. "I'm Jim Lashley."

"Robert Bandy," he said, extending his hand. "Guess I'll be your Captain for this month."

"Yes, sir," Jim acknowledged, shaking his hand. "Nice to meet you."

"You, too," Robert told him, turning back to the computer. "I'll be done here in a couple of minutes, and I'll brief you on the trip."

"Wow," Jim thought. "I'm going to get briefed on the trip. I can hardly wait to see how this is going to work out."

A few minutes later, Robert pulled the flight plan and accompanying paperwork from the printer and said, "First, I'm sure you're previous military because of your age and the fact that you're still a First Officer. I've found that most former military pilots think they're just a step above those of us that came up through the civilian channel."

"Now, I think that those of us who don't have a military background know more about the airline business because we've spent our lives here," Robert continued as he looked up into Jim's eyes. "I expect you to show me the same respect that you'd show higher-ranking officers in whatever branch of the military you came from."

"Not a problem," Jim replied. "I'm the co-pilot, and you're the Captain. That's the way it is, and I don't have any issues with civilian pilots."

"Good," Robert said. "Now, when it's your leg to fly, I expect you to follow the flight plan to the letter unless you ask me for any deviations you might think are necessary. If I'm going to make any changes, I'll tell you if I think it's necessary. But you'll generally know because I'll be clearing it with the controllers before I do it."

"Understand," Jim said as he thought about how long this month was going to be with such an arrogant ass as this Captain. "If there's nothing else, I'll go do the preflight and make sure the plane's ready."

"That's fine," Robert said. "I'll be down in a few minutes to brief the Flight Attendants. If you see them, please tell them I need them to come up to first class when I get there."

"I'll do that," Jim said, walking to where he had left his suitcase and kit bag. "I'll see you there."

When he got to the gate, Jim noticed that the airplane hadn't arrived and that two Flight Attendants were sitting in the passenger area. "Good morning," Jim said as he walked over to where they were sitting. "Any chance you're going to Mexico?"

"Afraid so," one of them answered. "You too?"

"Yep, I'm Jim," he told them.

"I'm Amber," she said. "I'm your number one. This is Carolyn."

"Hi, ladies," Jim acknowledged. "I'm supposed to tell you to meet the Captain in first class when he gets here."

Amber looked at Carolyn and said, "I told you, it's the same Captain I was talking about."

"Do you know him?" Jim asked.

"Oh, yes," Carolyn said, shaking her head. "He's rather well known among the Flight Attendants. I've never flown with him, but the stories are out there."

"I've flown with him a few times over the years," Amber told him. "And the stories are true. But I'll let you decide for yourself what you think."

"I've already gotten a hint," Jim said as he watched the airplane pull into the gate. "Maybe it won't be as bad as I think it'll be."

"You'll see," Amber told him as the gate agent opened the jet bridge door. "By the time we get to Tucson tonight, I'm sure you'll know what we're talking about."

"Maybe it's just my turn in the barrel," Jim said, smiling and heading for the gate. "I'll see you down there. And don't forget, gotta get that briefing!"

After completing the exterior check of the airplane, Jim came up the stairs and saw Robert talking to the three Flight Attendants. Shaking his head at Amber as he passed, he quickly set his instruments up for the departure.

Just as he finished and put the pages from his navigation books in the order he'd need them on the holder, Robert stepped into the cockpit and said, "I'll fly this leg to Mexico and brief you on the departure in a minute."

"You gotta be shitting me," Jim thought as he watched Robert set up his instruments. "Every pilot here has flown the standard departures from DFW a thousand times. And this ass is going to explain it to me?"

Amber stuck her head in the cockpit and asked, "Jim, coffee or anything?"

"Coffee, black," Jim said, smiling at her.

"Anything for you, Captain?" she asked, rolling her eyes at Jim.

"I'm fine," Robert told her. "I'll call you when we're ready for our meals."

"Yes, sir," she answered, shaking her head as she left the cockpit.

"Okay," Robert said as he turned to look at Jim.

"We'll be flying the......," he continued as Jim tuned him out but kept a slight smile on his face.

That evening, when they had gotten to the hotel in Tucson, Amber looked at Jim and made a drinking motion as they were waiting for the keys to their rooms. Nodding,

Jim waited until she showed him her room key with the number where he could read it.

In the elevator, Jim said, "Well, guess I'll see everybody in the morning. Good night, Captain."

Hearing the responses, Jim got off and headed to his room. Changing into jeans and a T-shirt, he headed for Amber's room, not knowing exactly what to expect.

Before knocking on her door, he looked both ways down the hall to make sure he wasn't being watched. When the door opened, he stepped in, and Amber shut the door behind him. "So, what do you think now?" she asked as they took seats.

"I'll live," Jim said, shaking his head. "I may not like it, but I'll make it through the month."

"Told you," she said, nodding in agreement. "But that's not the reason I asked you to stop by."

Surprised, Jim asked, "What's the reason?"

Amber handed Jim an envelope from the nightstand and answered, "Baltimore. There's been a change of plans."

Jim watched her eyes as he took the envelope and opened it. The typed note explained that Jewell would be unable to make it to Baltimore, but the operation would still continue. Now, Amber would be posing as his wife.

"When did you get this?" Jim asked, handing it back to her.

"Yesterday," she told him. "It was delivered to my house along with a description of what we're supposed to do in Baltimore. There was also a brief description of what your role is and the background of your character and mine."

"What is your background in this?" Jim asked, wondering what had happened to Jewell.

"I met you in college, we dated for a few years, married now for ten years with no children, live in Midland, my father owns several hundred acres with mineral rights and oil wells, we vacation in the Caribbean a couple of times every year, we're in Baltimore looking at some housing areas with the expectation of buying a block of townhouses that are mostly burned out or abandoned, and I love you dearly," she answered with a smile.

"Oh, before I forget," she continued. "Robert will be removed from the trip when we get back to DFW tomorrow. He's being replaced by a new Captain who needs the trip with an experienced First Officer before he can complete his upgrade program. How lucky is that?"

Chapter 15

The following morning, Jim was already in the hotel lobby when Robert came down to turn in his room key. "How was your night?" he asked as he got a cup of complimentary coffee.

"Fine," Jim said. "Watched part of a boring movie and got eight hours of uninterrupted sleep. You?"

"Good," Robert said, taking a seat while they waited for the Flight Attendants to arrive. "But I got a phone call from crew tracking this morning."

"Really? What did they want?" Jim asked, knowing the answer.

"There's some new Captain that needs this trip to finish his checkout," Robert answered. "There's going to be a Check Airman in your seat, but you'll be in first class for the trip to Baltimore, and the Check Airman will sit in the jump seat for the trip back to DFW to observe the flight."

"That's fine," Jim said. "I get paid regardless of which seat I'm in. You've got the best deal, though, going home and getting paid as if you'd flown the entire trip."

"That's true," Robert agreed as the three FAs came into the lobby. "I guess you military types didn't have that in your contract."

"Nope," Jim replied as he stood to go out to the van that would take them back to the airport. "We were paid to get shot at 24 hours a day and for about half of what I'm getting now. I can hardly wait until I'm a Captain and double my pay again---and nobody shooting at me."

The flight back to DFW went as smoothly as possible with Jim wondering if he could make the rest of the month with a Captain that needed to feel as if he was in charge of every aspect of the flight. Barely keeping his mouth shut, they finally got off the airplane in DFW, and Jim said, "Sorry to lose you, Captain. But I'll see you next week for the same trip."

"You too," Robert said, carrying his bags up the jet bridge. "Next trip maybe I'll let you brief me on the legs you're going to fly. I think that would be good practice for when you finally do make Captain. Matter of fact, I think it should be required of every Captain to let the First Officer brief their flights. What do you think?"

"That's an excellent suggestion, sir," Jim said with the words almost sticking in his throat. "I'm sure all of the First Officers would appreciate the opportunity. Especially us military types that never got to watch a Captain brief his flight, I mean crew."

Wondering if Robert caught the sarcasm, Jim headed to the gate for the flight to Baltimore. "You are sooooo lucky," Amber said smiling as she caught up with Jim at the new gate. "I'd call in sick if I had to sit in the cockpit with that tubby little prick for hours at a time. I don't know how you guys sit that close for that long anyway."

"Ninety-nine percent of the guys, or gals, are great," Jim said as he waited for the new Captain and Check Airman to finish the paperwork. "Matter of fact, it's almost fun. Getting to hear all sorts of stories, different backgrounds, ex-wife stories, occasionally a good joke, and it sure beats working for a living."

"Okay," she said as she headed for the airplane. "I'll have you a Dr. Pepper on ice when you come down. And I suppose you want a slice of lemon with it?"

"Of course," Jim said before turning to greet the new Captain. "Us first-class passengers need to be spoiled."

"Jim Lashley?" the Captain asked.

"Yes, sir," Jim answered as the gate agent handed him his first-class ticket.

"Hi. I'm Mike Wheeler," he said, extending his hand. "Just call me Mike. I assume you know you're in first class going to Baltimore and will be back flying the trip home."

"Yes, sir," Jim told him. "And I know this is a check ride for you, so if you want to do the flying tomorrow, that's fine with me."

"No, I want you to fly the leg back home. I think they want to watch me watch you. I just wonder who's watching them?" Mike said, laughing.

"I'll just sit in back and watch the Flight Attendants," Jim joked as they started down the jet bridge. "Maybe I'll learn something back there."

As soon as all of the passengers were on and briefed about how to fasten a seatbelt, Amber took Jim's empty glass and promised to give him his choice of meals for the flight to BWI before she got in her jump seat.

The flight went as advertised and landed a few minutes early. As everyone gathered outside of the terminal, the hotel van pulled in and let another crew off before the driver started loading their bags. The trip to the hotel was short, and Jim nodded at Amber as they got their room keys. As they got off the elevator a few minutes later, Jim said, "See you guys in the morning."

Hearing the same thing echoed by everyone, he went into his room and changed into his jeans and t-shirt. Barely dressed, he grabbed the phone before the second ring, saying, "Hello?"

"Come to room 302," the voice said. "Your co-worker will be in the adjoining room, 304."

Jim hung up and grabbed his room key and a bottle of water before hanging the 'Do Not Disturb' sign on his door. Taking the stairs down to the next lower level, he opened the stairwell door and saw 302 on his left. Knocking, the door opened, and a fiftyish man with a bushy beard met him. "Come on in," he told Jim. "We've got 20 minutes to transform you. It probably won't take that long, but the lady next door might. Want something to drink?"

"I brought some water," Jim said. "What do you want me to do first?"

"Strip down to your shorts and socks," the man said as he picked up what looked like a lady's corset, except it extended the belly instead of holding it in.

Over the next 15 minutes, the man used rubber cement to add a mustache to Jim's face, put deep wrinkles around his eyes, and fit a wig of long grey hair. Next came what was obviously a tailor-made suit, silk shirt with French cuffs, and monogrammed gold cuff links with P/P in black onyx. The shoes were well polished and probably cost a week of Jim's salary. Finally, the glasses were added, and Jim looked at himself in the full-length mirror.

"Wow, I'm still good-looking!" he announced just as the connecting door opened. Turning, he looked at what used to be Amber and just said, "Damn."

"You likey your little wifey?" she said as she slowly turned around.

Shaking his head, Jim could only repeat, "Damn."

Just then, the door opened, and Gene came in looking at both of them. "I wouldn't recognize either of you," he said as he walked around each of them. "Good job, folks. Ya'll can take a break in 304. I need a minute with these two before they head down to the lobby."

As soon as the connecting door closed, he asked, "Think you're ready?"

"As ready as I can be," Jim answered. "I've spent more time memorizing my new life as I did learning the F-4. And it had many more systems than my Pratka's Pharms company."

"I'm sure you'll do fine," Gene said, nodding. "How about you, Amber?"

"No problem," she told him. "I just smile a lot, let Harry stare at the new and improved cleavage, and pretend I think my dear husband, Billy Pratka, is the love of my life."

"Guess that about does it then, "Gene said. "Why don't you go into your makeup room and let me talk to Jim for a minute? We'll knock when we're ready to go down to the limo."

As the connecting door shut, Gene looked at Jim and asked, "Curious as to why we pulled Jewell and replaced her with Amber?"

"Yes," Jim answered. "I was surprised when you made the change after we had planned everything earlier."

Gene paused for a minute and then explained, "I made the decision after I had dinner with you and Jennifer. I certainly didn't want to be the reason anything could happen between you and Jewell and affect your marriage. I've grown very fond of Jennifer, and I didn't want to take the chance that something might develop with Jewell. I know you think you can handle it, but if there's even a slight chance of something, I'm not comfortable being the reason it happened."

Jim nodded and said, "I'm sure you want to make sure nothing happens. I don't either. But I can promise you, nothing ever would."

"I'm sure you feel that way," Gene said, agreeing. "But I've seen too many good marriages go under because of a close relationship between two of our people. Especially when they're pretending to be loving, and alcohol is involved. I can't take that chance with you and Jennifer. And, since it's my decision, that's what I decided. Is it going to be a problem with you and Amber?"

"No, sir," Jim said. "I'll treat her like a loving wife at Larry's and a colleague when we get back here to become our former selves."

"Good, now let's get your wife and go meet Mr. Harry Wellington," Gene said, knocking on the connecting door.

Chapter 16

Gene's car took Jim and Amber to the Four Seasons, where they were given fifty thousand dollars in cash and entered the hotel through a side door. Exiting mere moments later through the lobby, they were greeted by the driver of a new black stretched limo.

As soon as they were seated in the luxuriously appointed rear, the driver whisked them to the circular drive that brought them to Dunnahoe's Crapshoot. Dropping them at the front door, the driver pulled away to await their departure whenever they were ready to return to the hotel.

As soon as Jim and Amber approached the massive double doors, a well-dressed gentleman opened the doors and greeted them. "Good evening," he said as he held the doors open. "I'm Larry. Welcome to my home."

"Thank you," Jim said, taking the outstretched hand. "I'm Billy Pratka, and this is my wife, Maria."

"So very nice to meet you, Maria," Larry said, taking her hand and giving her a slight bow. "May I escort you and your husband to our little gaming room?"

"Of course," Amber said as she took Larry's arm. "I can hardly wait. I've heard so much about this place."

"I hope it lives up to your expectations," Larry said as he slid two doors open, revealing a large room with several tables set up for dice, roulette, blackjack, and different poker games. "Would you like to have a drink or select a table?"

"Blackjack table would be perfect," Jim answered. "Then probably a few drinks would be in order."

"This way," Larry said as he led them to where three blackjack games were in progress. "There's two open seats right here just waiting for you to take all of my hard-earned money."

"I doubt you lose too much money here," Jim laughed. "How do I purchase chips?"

"You can either play cash, and the dealer will make the conversion, or I'll send my manager over if you'd prefer to change all of your dollars for chips right now," Larry answered.

"We'll just play cash then," Jim said as he held out a chair for Amber.

"That's fine," Larry said as Jim took the seat beside Amber. "I'll send a waitress for your drink orders, which, of course, are complimentary."

As Larry walked away, Jim pulled ten thousand dollars from his jacket pocket and placed it on the table, saying, "I'd like hundred-dollar chips, please."

"Certainly, sir," the dealer said as he removed a stack of chips from the racks beside him. "If there's anything else you need, just let me know. And good luck!"

For the next 30 minutes, Jim and Amber played hand after hand, winning more often than the other players. Jim had noticed the left thumb raised every few hands and took a hit accordingly. Amber sat to his left and followed suit.

Looking around, Jim wondered if Harry would actually show up when a beautiful lady in a black evening gown took one of the vacated seats and placed ten thousand dollars on the table.

"Good evening, Miss," the dealer said as he counted the money and slid a stack of chips over to her.

"Good evening," she said, pulling the chips toward her. "Where's Jimmy tonight?"

"Not sure," the dealer said. "They just called me to step in for the evening. Is there anything I can do for you?"

"I'd like a martini, extra dry," she said as she put ten-hundred-dollar chips on the betting line.

Nodding at the waitress who was passing by, he gave her the martini order and kept dealing the cards.

Jim leaned around Amber and said, "Good evening, Miss. I'm Billy, and this is my wife, Maria."

"Nice to meet you," she said. "I'm Valerie Rose. Please, just call me Val."

A few minutes later, another player left the table as Jim continued to play and joke with Amber and Val.

"This seat open?" a man said as he walked up to the table.

"Hello, Harry," Val said as she accepted his kiss on her cheek. "Of course, it's open....for you!"

As he took the seat between her and Maria, Val said, "Harry, this is Billy and Maria. They've been kind enough to keep me company while I waited for you."

"Nice to meet you," Harry said to Amber, going from her eyes down to her cleavage and back up.

"Very nice to meet you, too," she said. "And this is my husband, Billy."

Barely glancing at Billy, Harry said, "Nice to meet you, Billy. Haven't seen you folks around here before."

"First time," Jim said as he watched Harry put three ten thousand dollar stacks on the table. "First time in Baltimore, too."

"What brings you up our way?" Harry asked as he took his chips.

"Investment," Jim answered as the cards were dealt.

"What are you interested in?" Harry asked, looking at his cards.

"Housing," Jim told him as he split the two cards and placed another stack of five hundred dollar chips on the line.

Moments later, the dealer revealed a total of 19 on his cards and took everybody's money except one of the split hands Jim held.

For the next few minutes, the conversation was light and covered mostly mundane subjects. After several losing hands, Harry pulled another stack of bills from his jacket and said, "If it wasn't for the pure joy of sitting between two beautiful ladies, I'd give up for the night."

Leaning over to let him see down the front of her dress, Amber said, "Oh, please don't give up yet. I'm sure you'll get lucky later on tonight."

Staring at her cleavage, Harry smirked and said, "I always get lucky, sooner or later."

"I'm sure you do," Amber smiled and asked. "What do you do besides play blackjack....and get lucky."

"I own Wellington Mineral Acquisitions," he told her, focusing all of his attention on her.

"What do you acquire?" Jim asked, watching Amber play him with her banter.

"Minerals," Harry answered with a slight glance at him. "What do you do?"

"Mainly trying to produce increasing viable food and greater nutrition," Jim answered as he watched the dealer raise his thumb.

"How do you do that?" Harry said as he tried to keep his eyes off Amber and on his cards.

"We try to change the basic cellular structure of the grain," Jim said, tapping his cards to signify an additional card.

"Sounds way too exciting," Harry said as the dealer revealed that he had lost again and Jim had won.

"Not really exciting," Amber told him as she put her hand on Harry's arm. "But, rather financially rewarding."

"That's always good," Harry remarked. "But, isn't that pretty much part of the whole genetically modified organism, or GMO, thing that's causing an uproar in the population?"

"Yes, it is," Jim answered, leaning over to look at Harry. "But I think most of the opposition will fade as we prove the success of our products and testing proves no problems."

"What about the housing investment?" Harry asked as another hand of cards was dealt.

"We're looking into buying sections of abandoned or dilapidated townhouses here in Baltimore," Jim answered, tapping his cards for another card.

"That's got to cost millions," Harry said as he watched Jim win another hand while he lost. "Your seeds must really be profitable to afford an investment like that."

"Not that profitable," Jim laughed. "Fortunately, my dad was lucky enough to buy some worthless farmland out in west Texas."

"And how is worthless land fortunate?" Harry asked, looking directly at Amber.

"Worthless for farming," Amber told him. "But very lucrative for oil."

"Oh, really?" Harry responded suddenly, paying more attention to Jim.

"I'm happy to admit, yes," Jim said, smiling. "And, of course, Maria's father just happens to own a few hundred acres in the same area."

"Now that's what I call fortunate," Harry laughed as he pulled additional cash from his jacket and looked at Amber. "Beautiful and rich. Simply irresistible."

"Robert Palmer," Jim said, watching Harry's unabashed flirting and interest in Amber.

"Who?" Harry asked, never taking his eyes off Amber.

"Robert Palmer," Jim said, admiring Amber's expertise in keeping Harry hoping for something more. "He sang the song 'Simply Irresistible'."

Tossing his cards down a few hands later, Harry announced, "Well, this is about enough losing for one night. How'd you folks like to have dinner with me tonight? I know a great seafood place that I'm sure you'll like. And, since you're planning on spending some time in Baltimore, it would be my pleasure to show you some of the good parts of this town."

Jim looked at Amber and asked, "What do you think, dear?"

"I'd love it," she said, smiling at Harry. "I think Harry may be just what we need here in Baltimore. An expert on fun places to go. Isn't that right, Harry?"

"It'll be my pleasure," Harry said, turning slightly to address Val. "Will you go with us, my dear?"

"Can't, darling," Val answered, standing and kissing him on the cheek. "I've got some early morning shopping to do. "But you guys have fun, and I hope to see you next time you're in Baltimore."

"Shall we go?" Harry asked, standing while Val got up. "I'll be glad to drive and show you some of the interesting areas around here on the way."

"What if we take my car," Jim suggested. "We can stop back by here or drop you anywhere you need to go."

"Sounds good, " Harry told him, thinking it would give him more time to flirt with 'Maria.' "I'll meet you outside after I make sure Val is okay."

Chapter 17

Jim and Amber were standing by the limo when Harry came walking back from telling Val goodnight. "Nice," he said as they got into the back. "I figured you'd have rented a car."

"This is much better," Amber said as she put her hand on Jim's leg. "We can enjoy our evening and not worry about having too much to drink or getting lost trying to find where we want to go."

"That's the biggest thing to me," Jim said. "I don't have a clue where I should go or how to get there. And there are more than a few scary areas in this city after dark."

"They're scary even in the broad daylight," Harry agreed. "Makes me wonder why you want to spend your money trying to remodel the blight in some of these areas."

"Good Samaritan, I guess," Jim answered. "Maria and her sisters wanted to do something for those less fortunate, so here we are."

'Just a moment," Harry said and looked at the driver, asking, "Do you know where Lumbini restaurant is?"

Hearing that he did, Harry then said, "That's where we need to go."

"Is Lumbini good?" Amber asked as the driver rolled the dividing dark glass up.

"Excellent," Harry told her. "It's more Indian cuisine than pure seafood, but it's some of the best in Baltimore. A little pricey, but that shouldn't matter since you're my guests."

"I don't think I've ever had Indian food," Jim told him. "I've heard it's rather spicy."

"It's a little spicy, but I think you'll enjoy it," Harry replied.

"Nothing wrong with trying something new," Amber said, looking Harry in the eyes. "We're here for some adventure, as well as try to help build a community."

Smiling back at her, Harry asked, "Why Baltimore? I'm sure you have communities in Texas that could stand some renovation."

"Baltimore is such an old historic city," she explained. "One of my sisters was up here a year or so ago and told the family how deplorable some of the areas were. Billy and I agreed to try to rebuild one side of one block. Two of my sisters agreed to do the same. Sort of a family project."

"I wish you luck," Harry said. "There's a reason those areas are abandoned. Until that reason is removed, I'm afraid you'll end up with the same problems."

A few minutes later, they arrived at the restaurant, and the driver opened the door for them. Jim told him they'd be back in an hour or so and if he wanted to go get something to eat, just be back within the hour.

After being escorted to a table near the rear of the restaurant, Jim asked, "Is it always this easy to get a table? I thought I saw several couples standing at the front."

Harry just smiled and answered, "I have a standing reservation here. I recommend the Shrimp Tikka Masala. It's one of my favorites."

"I'll let you order for us," Amber said, smiling at him. "I'm sure you know what's best."

Harry glanced at the maître d' and waited for him to arrive. "We'll have three orders of Shrimp Tikka Masala and a bottle of Egon Muller Scharzhofberger Spatlese Riesling, please."

"So, tell me about your food business," Harry said, glancing at Jim before returning his attention to Amber."

"Nothing special," Jim answered. "We've been doing GMO work for several years and are proud of some of the enhanced protein content of our grains. We're also doing some work with cattle to improve the growth rate and muscle percentages. It's especially worthwhile in the lean breeds, such as longhorn. "

"Tell him about the California place," Amber remarked. "It's going to be one of our best new products."

"I'm sure Harry doesn't want to hear about seaweed," Jim told her.

"It's more than seaweed, and you know it," she rebuffed him. "It's got more potential than that corn thing you're so proud of."

"What's happening with seaweed?" Harry asked, trying to show support for 'Maria'.

"He's making a new type of feed for cattle," Amber answered. "It's also got great potential for people, too."

Harry looked at Jim and said, "Tell me about this revolutionary new product that Maria thinks is so important."

Jim glanced at Amber with a look of mock chastisement and said, "It's not that revolutionary, just a twist on what the Japanese have been doing for centuries."

"It's more than that," Amber argued. "Most people only know about it if they eat sushi. And this is much better than a wrap for rice and fish."

"You're going to feed sushi to cattle?" Harry asked incredulously.

"No," Jim answered. "We're developing a high protein slurry that uses kelp as the basis. Our facility in Palo Alto is leading the research into developing a sustainable food supply from an almost infinite amount of available and cheaply harvestable plants."

"Seaweed soup?" Harry smirked. "I can't imagine many people in any culture, other than the Japanese, that would enjoy that."

"The slurry is just the base," Jim said, shaking his head. "We bake it into pellets after we harvest the kelp and combine it with various minerals, genetically modified bacteria, and other ingredients that we can flavor to meet the taste of any culture."

"Who'd want to eat pellets?" Harry asked as their food arrived. "Can you imagine what our meal would look like if it was a pile of pellets? Might taste like shrimp, but most people would rather have the real thing."

"What Billy's talking about are just the ingredients," Amber said, taking a taste of her shrimp. "But I'll agree that this is delicious, and I'd certainly prefer it to any pseudo shrimp tikka or whatever it's called."

"This is delicious," Jim agreed as he took a sip of the wine. "Nobody will ever develop a replacement for good food. Sort of like thinking tofu is a substitute for real meat.

Or bean curd. Man's meant to eat meat. Real meat for real men. That's nature's way."

"Now I can agree with you on that," Harry said, raising his wine glass.

"That's why the kelp program was originally designed as cattle feed," Amber explained. "The people part was an offshoot and meant mainly for countries that can't grow enough food for their population. Either vegetable or meat."

"So, what's the difference in food for cattle or people?" Harry asked as they continued to enjoy their meals.

"Mainly the taste," Jim said, wiping his mouth with his napkin. "Animals, other than man, don't need different flavors. Since grass is their main diet or other varieties of plant, it's simple to reproduce that taste."

"But the biggest thing we add to animal feed is diatomaceous earth, known as DE," Jim continued.

"What's DE," Harry asked. "Is it a mineral?"

"Sort of," Jim told him. "It's actually fossilized algae. Very porous and abrasive. The porosity allows it to suspend the kelp slurry, and the abrasive characteristic is useful in insect control."

"Let's not get into the insect stuff," Amber said, making a face. "That part is gross and not suitable for dinner conversation."

"You probably know about it since you're into minerals," Jim told Harry.

"I'm more into rare mineral deposits," Harry said. "Like praseodymium, or neodymium, or promethium."

"Lots of 'iums'." Amber joked. "What are they used for?"

"All sorts of things," Harry said, smiling at her. "From batteries to magnets and lasers."

"Oh, tell him about your electrical thing," Amber told Jim. "That's sort of like a battery, the way that guy in California explained it."

"What's this about a battery?" Harry asked suddenly interested in Jim's operation.

"Probably nothing," Jim answered, looking at Amber in mock disapproval. "Our researcher just advised me that there was some unexpected electrical activity in one of the tests involving a sample of DE-enhanced kelp slurry."

"What happened?" Harry asked.

"I'm certainly not a scientist," Jim explained. "But it seems that a nickel-plated instrument was inadvertently left in contact with a dish of the slurry overnight, and it imparted an electrical charge to the slurry."

"And how does that translate into a battery?" Harry wondered.

"Well, Jim Jackson, the research scientist in charge of the facility, thinks he can dry the charged slurry into thin sheets and combine them into a new type of battery," Jim explained. "He says it's a variation of the old NiCad battery combined with the Lithium-ion battery. Because of the DE, it's very lightweight. And something, maybe an acid or alkali produced by the modified bacteria reacting with the kelp or another ingredient, produced a charge much like a lead acid battery."

"That's enough talk about weeds and dirt and batteries," Amber said, knowing the seeds of interest had been planted. "I'd like to know if Harry will be available to accompany us to dinner next week when we come back to look at one of the areas we're considering."

"I agree," Jim said. "And this time, it's on me. But we'll let Harry pick the place since he was certainly right about this restaurant. Fantastic meal. I can't wait to see where there's more fabulous food."

"It would be my pleasure," Harry said, directing his attention to Amber. "This has been an absolutely wonderful evening. Even after losing so much at Larry's, it's still one of the best evenings I've had all year."

"That does it then," Jim said as they finished eating. "We'll plan on meeting at Larry's next week. If you'll give me your card while we take you back to your car, I'll call you next week and coordinate the date."

"Most definitely," Harry said as he put ten hundred dollar bills on the silver tray the maître d' had delivered. "I'm already excited to take you to another of my favorite restaurants."

Chapter 18

After dropping Harry off back at Dunnahoe's Crapshoot, Jim told the driver to take them back to the Four Seasons. As they were making the short drive, Amber looked at Jim and asked, "Well, what do you think?"

"Harry seems nice," Jim said, motioning for her not to talk.

Jim knocked on the dividing glass, and when it was down, he asked, "Did you get a chance to go eat?"

"No, sir," the driver replied. "But I always bring something and some drinks. I keep a small cooler here in the front seat with me."

"Good thinking," Jim told him. "We appreciate your assistance tonight. We'll be back in a few days, and I'll ask for you when we reserve the limo for our next trip."

"Thank you, sir," he responded as they pulled into the hotel.

"Good evening, sir. Madam," the driver told them after opening their door.

"You too," Jim said, handing him two hundred dollar bills. "We'll see you next trip."

Amber held Jim's arm as they entered the lobby and walked toward the elevators. Looking back to ensure the limo was gone, Jim changed directions and went to the door leading to the first-floor rooms and out to where the car from their hotel had dropped them.

As they exited the building, the car they had arrived in came from the parking lot and stopped beside them. Speeding back to their hotel, Amber asked, "Why did you 'shush' me back there?"

"I don't know just how secure the rear of the limo is," Jim answered. "And, I saw Harry hand the driver one of his cards as he got out. Not sure why, but it could be so he can ask him if we said anything."

"Or, it could be he just wanted to hire him someday," Amber argued.

"I'm sure Harry has plenty of information about local limo services," Jim told her. "You could be right, but I'll bet he wanted to talk to the driver about where he took us and if he heard anything interesting."

Arriving at the hotel, they went to room 302 and knocked. Gene opened the door and said, "Welcome home, folks. Give me a quick 'how did it go' before you change back into your real clothes."

"Pretty good," Jim said as he pulled at the mustache that was beginning to bother him. "I think Amber did an excellent job of getting Mr. Wellington's attention."

"You think I overplayed it?" she asked.

"No," Jim said, shaking his head. "I'm referring to leading him into wanting to know about the fictitious battery. You finally got him interested in something besides your chest area."

"How'd that go?" Gene asked.

"Amber sort of eased the subject into the discussion about kelp and cattle," Jim said, proud of how she had played Harry.

"You certainly pretended it was nothing," Amber remarked. "I was afraid we'd never broach the subject if I didn't say something."

"And you did a great job," Jim repeated. "I was wondering how to turn the conversation without seeming too interested in talking about my business, but I thought he was going to get whiplash when he snapped his head from looking down your dress to me. I didn't think anything would break his attempt at trying to seduce you."

"Sounds pretty good for a first contact," Gene said, nodding. "Let's get you out of those clothes, and you can head back to your rooms. We'll contact you later this week for a more intensive debrief."

When Amber went through the connecting door to 304, Jim handed Gene the cash he had brought back and started taking off his suit. "Looks like you did okay at the table," Gene told him as the makeup man started removing the fake wrinkles and wig.

"Not bad," Jim said, taking off his trousers. "Certainly better than Harry."

"What do you really think?" Gene asked after putting the money in a briefcase on the bed.

"Too early to really know," Jim said as the fake belly bulge was unfastened and placed in a large suitcase. "We got his attention, and I'm sure he'll do some investigating before we see him again. But I think the seeds of doubt have been sown and may reinforce the price of Lithium issue."
"That's the best we can hope for at this stage of the operation," Gene said. "But I was referring more to you and Amber. How did that play?"

"She did good," Jim admitted. "She was a little more forward than I expected. But that really got Harry's interest. And, looking back, she played it perfectly. Just enough distraction and just enough encouragement without seeming to be an easy make."

"Amber is one of our best agents," Gene agreed. "She's had lots of experience working with us. Not to mention, she's got to play you airline pilots and most likely numerous male passengers."

"She plays her part well," Jim laughed. "I'm sure Jewell would have done as well, too."

"Oh, I'm positive she would have," Gene agreed. "But how comfortable would you have been with her obvious flirting with Harry?"

Thinking about it for a couple of seconds, Jim answered, "Probably not very."

"That's another reason I decided to make the change," Gene said. "I know you, and I know Jewell. The chemistry between you two could have caused a problem then or later if you're too close for the rest of this operation."

"How are we on the seaweed battery stuff?" Jim asked as the makeup man tried to remove the last of the adhesive from his face.

"Good," Gene replied. "Phones are all set up; Jim Jackson is fully briefed and ready to provide the scientific explanations. Two additional references to the kelp procedure are being released within the 'scientific community' as we speak. All in all, we're ready to press on with this approach."

"And the other, the backup plan with the other shareholders?" Jim asked.

"Showing some progress," Gene said, shaking his head. "But I really don't think it's our best option. If this works, and I think it stands a good chance, we'll approach Harry after your next meeting and make an offer. That is if you think the timing is right. Otherwise, we'll wait another week."

"Not to ask the question, but here it is....what happens to Harry's stock if something should happen to him?" Jim asked.

"Equally divided among his uncles," Gene replied.

"So, still no way to get a majority of the votes without at least two people," Jim said, nodding.

"No," Gene agreed. "But, if we're forced to implement the final solution, the uncles will most assuredly vote together. And, given their age, I'd bet that current cash beats long-term risk. The thought of giving up forty million at this point in their lives outweighs the benefits of maybe getting more later. Especially since everything will point to a most probable decline in their Lithium contract value, I think we'll get our objective. But, as always, that's not how we want to resolve this. I'm hoping that you and Amber will convince Harry to take a more reasonable option. Now, get back to your room, and I'll give you a call in a couple of days."

Chapter 19

Jim came downstairs the next morning and was having a cup of coffee while he waited for the rest of the crew to arrive. Mike arrived a few minutes later with his suitcase and kit bag. "Good morning, Jim," he said as he got a cup of coffee.

"Good morning," Jim replied. "Everything go okay yesterday?"

"No problems," Mike answered. "Little crap like nonstandard radio calls. Didn't tell him I was changing something on the panel, just normal things that everybody does or doesn't do at one time or another."

"Sounds about right," Jim said, nodding. "They've got to find something to rag about to show you they're doing their job. Anything we need to do on the way home?"

"Not that I know of," Mike said. "If he wants to see something, let him ask. Otherwise, you fly, and I'll supervise. And I don't expect to need to say a word to you other than what the book says I have to say."

"I understand," Jim said, smiling at his relaxed attitude. "What's your background?"

"Air Force," Mike told him. "C-141's. You?"

"Marines," Jim answered. "F-4's."

"Given your age, I'd guess Vietnam," Mike guessed.

"Three tours, two on the ground and one in the F-4," Jim said. "Retired in the Reserves a couple of years ago. Now, just waiting for that huge retirement check when I'm almost too old to spend it."

"Congratulations," Mike said, smiling. "I made it through seven years total. Airlines were hiring, and I figured I'd make more flying people instead of rubber dog shit out of Taiwan."

"Good choice," Jim said, laughing. "I didn't have that option. Too old when my commitment was up after flight training and my scenic tour in the land of Ho Chi Minh."

"Good morning," Amber greeted as she walked from the elevator. "How's my favorite couple of pilots today? Ready to get me home with an empty airplane and an hour early?"

"Probably neither," Mike laughed as he saw the rest of the crew getting off the elevator. "But I'll try to at least be on time. You'll have to talk to the gate agent about putting the passengers on another flight."

After landing at DFW and telling everybody goodbye, Jim got his pickup from the employee parking and headed home. Knowing Jennifer was still at work, he decided to stop by her office and surprise her. He parked beside her car and walked into the reception area, waving at the girl talking on the phone. Just down the hall, he was about to walk into Jennifer's office when he heard her talking to someone. Pausing to listen, he heard her say she needed to get back to work.

A second or two later, a 40-ish man walked out of her office smiling. Almost bumping into Jim, he said, "Excuse

me.   Aren't   you   Jennifer's   husband?"
"Yes," Jim said, extending his hand. "I'm Jim."

"Hi, Jim," the man said, shaking his hand. "I'm Charlie. Good to finally meet you."

"Good to meet you, too, " Jim said as he started into Jennifer's office.

"Hey, Jim," Jennifer said as he walked in. "This is kind of a surprise."

"Thought I'd stop by and see if you wanted to do anything for dinner tonight," Jim said, looking at her slightly red face. "Anything wrong?"

"What do you mean?" she asked, blushing even more.

"You just look like you've got a little fever or something," he told her. "Your face looks sort of flushed."

"No, I'm fine," she told him, averting her eyes. "What do you want for dinner?"

"I thought I'd get a couple of steaks and grill them with some asparagus and brussel sprouts."

"Sounds good," Jennifer replied, giving him a slight smile.

"Okay. I'll have a bottle of Merlot open when you get home, too," Jim said. "By the way, who was that guy you were talking to before I got here?"

"That's Charlie Weitzel. His uncle owns the company," she whispered. "He's the guy I was telling you about."

"Ah", Jim responded. "Any luck on resolving that little issue?"

"Not yet," Jennifer said busying herself with some papers on her desk. "I'll see you in a couple of hours."

"You bet," Jim said, turning to go. "Anything else you'd like?"

"No," she said, still fussing with her papers. "But you can get anything you want for dessert if you're interested."

"I'll think about it," Jim said, leaving. "Love you."

"You, too," she said quietly as he left.

Jim stopped at the Piggly Wiggly on his way home and picked out two thick-cut rib eye steaks and vegetables. Passing the frozen food section, he grabbed a half gallon of Blue Bell Pistachio Almond ice cream.

At home, he put the steaks on a platter, dusted them with a liberal amount of Montreal Steak Seasoning, and set them aside. As he was washing the vegetables, the phone rang.

After drying his hands, he walked into the living room and answered, "Hello?"

"How was the flight home?" Gene asked.

"Standard....uneventful," Jim answered. "How are things back east?"

"Pretty normal for a mad house," Gene said, chuckling. "But, I'm not back east. I'm about 15 minutes from your house if you've got time for a quick visit."

"Plenty of time," Jim said. "I was just getting some steaks ready for dinner tonight. I'll run out and get one for you if you'd like to eat with us."

"I appreciate that, but I'm sort of pressed for time this evening," Gene answered. "I've got to meet someone else after I talk to you. And then I'll head back to Quantico."

"Time for a drink when you get here?" Jim asked.

"Not today," Gene answered. "But, thanks. I'll see you in a few minutes."

Jim had just put some charcoal briquettes and a couple of pieces of Mesquite in the bottom of the grill when he heard a car pull into his driveway. Going back through the house, he opened the door just as the bell chimed.

"Come in, General," Jim said, greeting Gene.

"Thanks," he replied. "Sorry to make this so quick, but we've got some activity with our little operation that I wanted to discuss."

"No problem," Jim said, leading him into the living room. "Please, have a seat."

Sitting on the couch and facing Jim as he sat in the well-worn recliner, Gene said, "Harry has had his staff busy since your evening with him."

"What's he looking for?" Jim asked, knowing it was most likely about Pratka's Pharms or the kelp battery issue.

"You, to start with," Gene told him. "And Amber. They did a search for Billy Pratka and his wife Maria early this morning. Fortunately, we had a complete history in a place that would be found regardless of the search method."

"Then they did a search of the company records, which were impeccable, and inquiries into the Palo Alto facility," he continued. "It's pretty much as we anticipated, and all of the background information we supplied should hold."

"That sounds good," Jim said, nodding. "Are you anticipating any problems, or do we continue the approach we've started?"

"For now, we'll keep Billy and Maria involved," Gene answered. "We still think it stands the best chance of working. Plus, it gives the uncles more reasons to push for a corporate sale based on financial uncertainty. And, even if we resort to a final solution, we need them to vote in our favor. Either way, it's important to follow the path we're on."

"Anything else I need to know?" Jim asked, wondering why Gene needed to come to Texas to tell him what he already assumed.

"Just wanted to tell you that we're looking into how to implement the removal of Mr. Wellington, should it come to that," Gene answered.

"How do you plan to do that?" Jim asked. "Are you going to use the two guys with red logos I saw at the briefing with Jewell?"

"No," Gene told him, pausing for a second. "Have you ever heard of a tree named Cerbera odollam?"

"Can't say as I have," Jim answered. "Is this a botany quiz?"

"No, just a little education," Gene smiled. "You went to a restaurant that specializes in Indian cuisine, and the Cerbera odollam is native to India. Over there, it's commonly known as 'Othalanga'. That's another word for suicide tree."

"You plan on poisoning Harry?" Jim asked.

"Of course not," Gene answered. "But you and Amber may have to."

Chapter 20

During the next four days off, Jim spent several hours watching where Charlie went for lunch or after work. Noticing that he seemed to favor one of the small out of the way restaurants, Jim started formulating a plan in case he continued to harass Jennifer. All he needed to do was gather the few materials he would need to discourage Charlie from bothering her again. Or any other woman.

Now, Jim was ready to get back to work; the small yard and a few chores around the house were taken care of. He hoped Jennifer could take care of the problem of Charlie without him and he was looking forward to seeing what would happen regarding Mr. Harry Wellington.

The only thing that made going back to work unpleasant was the thought of having to fly with Robert. Mike had been enjoyable. . . good pilot and good attitude. But there were those few pilots that nobody wanted to fly with, and generally, for a good reason.

As he signed in for the flight, Jim noticed that Robert wasn't listed as the Captain. Not recognizing the name, he looked around to see if there was anyone with four stripes nearby. Not seeing anyone, he looked back at the Flight Attendant's names. At least Amber was listed, and he knew they would be able to see Harry and try to give him the impression that his Lithium contracts were even more in jeopardy than he originally may have thought. Jim didn't really want to be the one to cause his demise. And he didn't know how Amber felt about the final solution.

Grabbing his bags, he walked to the gate where they were scheduled to leave for the trip to MEX. When he got there, he saw a Captain talking to the gate agent. "Jim Lashley?" the Captain asked as Jim walked up.

"Yes, sir," Jim replied.

"I'm John Clark," he told Jim. "I guess your regular Captain called in sick this morning. I was sitting reserve and got the call about two hours ago."

"Good to meet you, John," Jim said, shaking his hand. "Anything special happening on the flight?"

"Not that I know of," John told him. "I just pulled up the paperwork, and everything looks good to Mexico and back."

"Great," Jim said. "I'll go down and get everything checked out."

"I'll be down in a couple of minutes," John told him as he turned back to the computer.

As Jim was opening the door to the jet bridge, Amber yelled at him, "Hold the door, please!"

"Thanks," she said as she followed him to the airplane. "I guess you saw that fat boy Robert isn't with us."

"Happily," Jim answered. "I just met the new Captain. Don't know anything about him. Can't be any worse, though."

"Dr. Pepper?" Amber asked as she put her bags away.

"When I get back," Jim answered as he put his suitcase in the closet and tossed his kit bag onto his seat. "John, our Captain, should be here before I get back. Tell him what a nice guy I am and how much you like flying with me."

"Sure," Amber said, laughing. "Let's not start lying to him before he gets to know us. I'll just tell him you haven't crashed one yet."

"That's good enough," Jim said as he headed down the stairs to make sure everything looked all right on the exterior of the airplane.

When he got back, John and Amber were standing in the first-class area talking. Jim slid into his seat, took the paperwork from the console, and started setting his instruments.

"How'd it look?" John asked, getting into his seat.

"Fine," Jim said, handing the paperwork to him. "Do you want the first leg to Mexico?"

"Which leg did you fly last trip?" John asked as he set his instruments for the takeoff.

"The return," Jim answered, getting his charts out of his bag.

"Why don't you fly down, and I'll fly back," John said, putting the paperwork back on the console.

"Sure," Jim said as Amber stepped into the cockpit, handing Jim his drink.

"Just to let you know," John said as Amber left, "I just finished my checkout, and this is my first unsupervised trip to Mexico City."

"Not a problem," Jim said, grinning. "I've been down there so many times I almost speak Spanish."

"Just let me know if I'm about to do something stupid," John told him, nodding. "I'd rather not screw up on my first trip without the guiding hand of our supervisors."

"I'm sure you won't have any problems," Jim said as the passengers started filling the airplane. "And, I don't care if you fly each leg. Or, just take the ones you want."

"We'll just rotate the legs, like normal," John said as the gate agent told them all the passengers were on. "Normal is always good."

The first two days of flying went as scheduled. Landing at BWI, Amber sat beside Jim in the hotel van and asked, "Doing anything exciting tonight?"

"Not really," Jim answered. "I may go look around some tomorrow if the weather's good. How about you?"

"Nope," Amber said, smiling. "Just relaxing and enjoying a good book. Maybe go out for something to eat this evening if I don't like anything on the hotel restaurant's menu."

"Food here's not too bad," John said as the van pulled into the hotel. "I've spent several nights here and can recommend the clam chowder. And, the blue crabs are excellent."

"That sounds good," Amber said. "I'll probably just get room service so I don't have to dress up. Just lounge around in my flannels."

"Then I guess I'll see everybody tomorrow," John said as they got their bags.

"You bet," Jim said as they walked into the hotel and got their room keys. "Good night, everybody."

As he was changing into his jeans and T-shirt, the phone rang. "Hello," Jim answered.

"Room 302." the voice told him before hanging up.

A few minutes later, as he was changing into a different suit and getting his makeup applied, the connecting door to 304 opened, and Gene came in with a magazine.

"Your company just got some good recognition," he said as he showed Jim the cover of the Scientific American.

"What's it say?" Jim asked as the mustache and wrinkles around his eyes were being applied.

"Just that a promising development in the field of electrical micro-storage is being researched by a small company attached to Pratka's Pharms," Gene told him as the makeup artist was adjusting the gray wig.

"Do we know if Harry has seen the article?" Jim asked, checking his appearance in the mirror.

"He's seen it," Gene told him. "We had a couple of our local people discussing the article at a restaurant where they would be overheard by two of Harry's uncles. And we know one of the uncles stopped by the newsstand across the street from the restaurant and bought a copy. I'm sure it was brought to Harry's attention because one of his assistants was busy on his computer the next day looking for any other information on the process."

"I'll look at it on the way to the Four Seasons," Jim said, taking the magazine. "I need to at least know what the article says in case he brings it up."

"That's why I brought you a copy," Gene said as Amber came in, ready to play her role as Maria.

"You look just marvelous, Billy Pratka," she said, smiling at him. "Are you ready to take your wife out for a fun night of gambling and dining?"

"Of course, my dear," Jim answered again, admiring the striking change in her appearance.

"By the way," Gene told them as they prepared to go down to the car that would take them to meet the limo. "Harry's favorite dealer is back. Remember, he raises his little finger on his right hand when you shouldn't take a hit. We've got to let Harry win a little tonight."

Chapter 21

After being dropped off at the Four Seasons, Jim and Amber exited the lobby to the waiting limo. Noting the same driver as before, Jim nodded and told him they were going to Larry's again.

Harry was already at the blackjack table when they walked in. Walking to the table where only one chair was open, Jim said, "Good evening, Mr. Wellington. Would you mind if Maria sat here beside you?"

Harry turned and smiled, saying, "I'd love to have your beautiful wife sit beside me. Maybe she'll bring me better luck than she did last time I sat beside her."

Jim handed Amber a stack of hundred dollar bills as she took the open seat on Harry's right, saying, "Oh, Harry. You know you don't need luck. A smart, good-looking guy like you makes his own luck."

Jim stood behind Amber as several hands were played. Finally, a seat opened on Harry's left, and Jim set several stacks of bills on the table as he took the seat. "Never been much of a spectator," he said as he placed his first bet of five hundred dollars. "Watching others play is like watching plants grow."

"And growing plants is your business," Harry remarked as another set of cards were placed in front of the players. "How do you explain that little boring detail?"

"Growing plants makes me money," Jim said as he won the hand. "Just like this game is going to do."

Amber leaned over in front of Harry, giving him an almost unobstructed view down the top of her extremely low-cut dress, and said, "Oh, Billy. Let's not discuss plants tonight. But my luck doesn't seem to be as good as Harry's."

Handing her two more stacks of bills, Jim said, "That's okay. Last time, Harry was losing, and he bought us dinner. Tonight, you're losing, so you can buy him dinner."

"Now, that seems fair," Harry said, laughing. "Seems dyslexic, but still fair."

A few hands later, Harry turned to Jim and asked, "How's the housing project going? Find any good prospects?"

"Still in the research stage," Jim said, asking for another card. "There are so many areas of Baltimore that need to be bulldozed and just start over. I'm starting to agree with what you said last week."

"What's that?" Harry asked as he looked at his cards.

"We could revitalize the entire city, but the underlying problem is the residents, not the buildings," Jim said, noticing the dealer raise his little finger.

"And I don't think you can ever change that little problem," Harry said, shaking his head at the dealer. "Until the culture of the residents changes, you'll be right back where you are today in less than a decade. And you've wasted millions of dollars."

"You're probably right," Jim answered, refusing another card. "I sure don't have the answer to the overall problem."

Pulling his winnings to him, Harry asked, "Speaking of answers, I saw an article about your research out in California. How's that going?"

"Pretty good, I guess," Jim told him. "Mr. Jackson, the project manager, seems to think he may have an experimental unit later this month."

"How does he plan to test it?" Harry asked.

"He's talking with Boeing to get permission to use one of their older satellites as the test system," Jim answered as the next hand was dealt.

"Think they'll let you experiment with one of their satellites?" Harry asked, looking at the dealer's hand. "That would be one hell of a gamble on their part, sending an unproven electrical source into space."

"Not an actual launched satellite," Jim explained, asking for another card. "One that was built but never sent into space. We just want to substitute our battery for the one designed to initially power it."

"Tell him about the solar thing," Amber said as she leaned over and looked around Harry so he would look at her again.

"That's just one of Jackson's unproven theses," Jim told Harry. "He comes up with some pretty wild ideas."

"Does it have anything to do with the battery research?" Harry asked, glancing down at Amber's dress before looking at Jim.

"Sort of," Jim said, smiling at Amber. "He thinks that the kelp will enhance the solar collection of energy for the batteries. Something about chlorophyll being a natural means of converting sunlight into energy. Don't get me to lie about it. All I know is that you need sunlight to grow plants."

"Still an interesting concept," Harry acknowledged as he looked at his growing pile of chips. "It all seems like wishful thinking, though. I'll still trust in tried and tested methods."

"Really?" Amber asked. "Don't you think that science can improve almost everything that nature has given us? Look at computers. Before them, people were using an abacus. How long do you think it would take to do all of the calculations to send a man to the moon using a bunch of beans on sticks?"

"That's a little oversimplification, don't you think?" Harry asked, turning his attention to her. "I'm talking about proven science as an investment, not a research project."

"What do you think Bill Gates did when he started Microsoft?" she asked. "He invested in an idea, not a proven science."

"But the computer was proven; he just expanded on it," Harry pointed out. "That's a far cry from trying to make a battery from seaweed."

"Well, you invested in stuff to make batteries," Amber argued. "What about those minerals, all those 'iums' you said made batteries and magnets and stuff?"

"Yes, I invest in minerals," Harry acknowledged. "But they are all proven to make a current product. There's not much risk there."

"Except running out of the mineral," Jim told him. "What do you do when there's no more of one or the other? There needs to be an alternative."

"Running out isn't really my problem," Harry said as they continued to play. "Scarcity is how I make my money. I find a mineral that's in demand and has a limited supply;

then, I try to get control over the mining or production. If it becomes even more scarce, then I'll make even more."

"Until it runs completely out," Amber said, putting her hand on his arm. "What then?"

"There'll always be another," Harry assured her, placing his hand over hers. "My bigger problem is when I'm invested in what I consider a rare mineral, and it becomes less rare."

"How does it become less rare?" Amber asked, turning to give Harry a full frontal view.

Harry glanced down briefly and told her, "Take Lithium, for example. There is supposedly a new discovery in Australia. If true, it could cause the price to drop well below the threshold for my profit requirements."

"What will you do then?" Jim asked as he watched Amber squeeze Harry's arm.

"Try to get out from under my contracts," Harry answered as he smiled at Amber.

"Who would buy a contract for Lithium if they knew the price was about to drop?" Amber asked, leaning back. "That would be like paying a dollar today for something that would only be worth fifty cents tomorrow."

"I said there is supposedly a new discovery of Lithium," Harry explained. "There's always a rumor about new discoveries or fantastic deposits of minerals that turns out to be a fabrication or misinformation."

"Who would do that?" Jim asked as he nodded at Amber to signal they needed to get to dinner.

Amber pulled her chips to the edge of the table and announced, "Well, I don't know who wants to buy cheap dirt, chlorophyll, or ancient computers. I just want to go buy Mr. Harry Wellington the dinner we promised."

"A brilliant idea, pretty lady," Harry said, collecting his chips. "There's an excellent blue crab served at Phillips. I think you'll enjoy it."

"That sounds good to me," Jim said as he stood and gathered his chips. "Maybe we should start investing in restaurants; we seem to use them more than we do batteries or dilapidated townhouses."

"Oh, I forgot," Jim suddenly said, smiling as they walked from the table.

"What did you forget?" Amber asked, wondering what he was talking about.

"I forgot about all of those battery-powered appliances you keep in the nightstand drawer," Jim said, laughing. "Restaurants are a distant second!"

Chapter 22

After arriving at Phillips and entering the restaurant, Jim said, "Not quite as fancy as last week."

"No," Harry agreed as they waited to be shown to their table. "But I think you'll find that their food is as good as any five-star restaurant anywhere in the world."

"I know you selected this place," Amber said as she took Harry's arm, "but I want to be fair about the reciprocal dinners. I'm sure this isn't near as expensive as last week."

"She's right," Jim agreed as they headed for a table near the back of the restaurant. "I think we'll have to treat you next time we get to town. This may be good, but I can't take advantage of your good nature."

"Don't worry about my good nature," Harry said as they sat. "Good food and good company aren't measured in dollars. I'm going to recommend the blue crab dinner and calamari for an appetizer."

"We'll trust your judgment," Amber replied as she put her hand on his arm. "You were right last time, and I'm sure you know what's best here."

"We'll have three blue crabs, an order of calamari, and two bottles of De Loach Russian River Chardonnay," Harry told the waiter who had led them to the table.

"Excellent," the waiter answered, taking the unopened menus from the table. "I'll be right back with the wine. The calamari will be out in about ten minutes if that's all right."

"That's fine," Harry said dismissively. Turning to 'Maria,' he continued, "So, you were remarking about the inadvisability of buying something today that may be worth less tomorrow."

"Yes," Amber answered as the first bottle of wine arrived. "And then you said something about doubting the veracity of the discovery of Lithium. Why would you doubt that?"

"I think he's probably just being thorough," Jim answered for Harry. "There's always some unfounded rumor about something that could have a dramatic impact on your business."

"That's exactly right," Harry said as he raised his wine glass. "Sort of like your seaweed battery. If I was the energizer bunny, I wouldn't be looking for another job just yet."

"The bunny doesn't care where he gets his juice," Jim said, toasting both Amber and Harry. "But your point is well taken."

"How will you confirm or deny the rumors?" Amber asked as she tapped Harry's glass with hers.

"I'll have my geologists look into it first," Harry said, sitting back. "If they confirm that the location fits the type of formation where Lithium is normally found, then we'll have a little greater confidence in the discovery."

"Are you saying that you'll only use a geologist's report of the probability of potential mineral deposits?" Jim asked, setting his wine glass down.

"As a starting point," Harry answered, looking at him. "If the conditions meet their expert opinion of probability, then I'll send a team to look at the location and get samples of the core borings. Plus, there should be some magnetic resonation data that will reveal the size of the field."

"What will you do if it's true?" Amber asked as the calamari arrived.

"I've got a couple of options," he told her. "But, until I confirm this find, I'll keep my options open."

"What sort of options are you talking about?" Jim asked, putting some of the calamari on his plate.

"I've had offers to purchase all of my Lithium contracts," Harry answered cautiously.

"Do you have to get approval to sell your contracts?" Amber asked, noting Harry's seeming reluctance to discuss the issue.

"Not necessarily," he answered, looking at her quickly before returning his attention to Jim. "The board will have to approve anything of this magnitude, but since I'm the major shareholder, I don't foresee any problems."

"I know what you mean," Jim said, nodding. "Pratka's Pharms requires a majority vote of the board members for any expenditure over a certain threshold and the same for the sale of company assets. Fortunately, I hold well over fifty percent of the voting stock."

"It's the same with Wellington Mineral," Harry replied. "I control any decision regarding the financial dealings of the company."

"Billy is actually the sole shareholder of Pratka's," Amber remarked. "But I'm sure it isn't near as big as Wellington."

"It's a lot easier to control assets when you don't have to answer to shareholders," Harry said, nodding. "But, when your company is publicly traded, you have to answer for every decision. Especially when it could dramatically affect the stock price."

"I'm sure that's right," Jim said as their dinners arrived. "I'm used to making the decisions and living with what happens. I'd hate to have to explain everything to anybody else."

"What about you?" Harry asked, looking at Amber. "Don't you have some of the shares of the company?"

"I can have all of the shares if I want them," Amber answered, smiling at him. "Billy will give me anything I ask for."

"Let's not get too carried away with what you ask for," Jim said, grinning at her. "Maybe I'd sell you some of my shares. That's if you can get your dad to give you the money."

"You were talking about using one of Boeing's satellites," Harry said as they finished the first bottle of wine. "How long will you need before you know if the battery will power it? And how long do you believe it will supply the required electrical needs before recharging?"

"I don't have a clue," Jim admitted. "Jackson has full authority to pursue any avenue he believes necessary to either develop the battery or recommend dropping the program."

"Doesn't that give him carte blanch for ripping you off?" Harry asked incredulously.

"What do you mean?" Amber asked, wishing she could steer the conversation away from the battery issue and back to the Australia find.

"I mean, if he has the authority to continue the research, thereby ensuring his continued employment and salary, why would he halt the program? Any prudent man would want to do everything possible to safeguard his position," Harry told her.

Turning to Jim, he continued, "You said you alone had financial control over your company's assets. I think you're mistaken. It seems to me that this Mr. Jackson has a lot of control."

"He does," Jim agreed. "But, it's a minor percent of the company. Not to mention, I trust him explicitly."

"Trust is a valuable commodity," Harry stated. "I'll never give complete control over any aspect of my company to anyone, regardless of how much I trust them. Money, or the fear of losing it, will do strange things to a man."

"Maybe I'm a little naive," Jim told him as they were finishing their meal. "But, since I don't have to answer to shareholders, as you do, then I'll take the chance to give a valued employee the benefit of the doubt."

"Not to change the subject," Amber said as she saw the animosity growing between Harry and Jim, "who do you have to appease in your company?"

"Myself," Harry answered. "Even if I drive the stock price to the bottom of the barrel, which I'd never do, I still own the majority share."

"What if every other shareholder decided to dump their stock?" Jim asked.

"They're mostly family members," Harry told him. "Sure, they'd express concern if it looked like I was making a foolish decision. But they are really helpless to oppose any decision I make regarding financial issues."

"So, you're saying that because they're family, they'd support you even if it wasn't in their best interest," Jim countered.

"I didn't say they'd support it," Harry said, shaking his head. "I just said they lack the power to stop me. Big difference."

"Of course," Jim said, agreeing. "And, I'm sure you'd never make a decision that wasn't in your own financial interest. And that would prevent you from acting contrary to their interests."

"Exactly right," Harry said as Jim signaled for the check. "Just as you trust Jackson, my family trusts me."

"When do you think you'll know about the new Lithium stuff?" Amber asked as Jim put five hundred dollars on the tray with the bill.

"I'll know within a week if I need to send a team to Australia," Harry answered as they prepared to leave. "Why do you ask?"

"Just wondering," she told him, putting her hand on his arm and walking toward the door. "I was just sort of comparing it to how long it's taking for Billy's battery thing to be proven or not. I wish we could know within a week or two."

"We'll see," Harry said as they got into the limo. "When do you folks think you'll be coming back to Baltimore?"

"Not exactly sure," Jim said as they headed back to Larry's. "We've engaged a new company to look into the housing issue. They're supposed to present us with a concept and cost proposal sometime this week. I'll know more when they finish the investigation into financing and tax benefits from the city."

"Well, I hope you make it back soon," Harry said, looking pointedly at Amber. "Maybe you'll know more about your little seaweed project by then."

Amber smiled and replied, "And maybe you'll know if there's some expensive dirt in Australia."

"Or really cheap but overpriced dirt," Harry told them as they pulled into the parking lot. "But either way, I'm looking forward to seeing you again."

Chapter 23

As soon as they were back at their hotel and changing from their disguises, Gene asked how it had gone. "He's going to do some research on the Australia discovery," Jim told him as he sat waiting for the makeup man to finish removing all the additions.

"What did he say?" Gene asked.

"He plans on having his geologist look into the area of the discovery to see if it matches the general topography of other deposits," Jim answered. "Then, if it looks reasonable, he'll send a team to Australia to look at core samples and other data."

"I think we can make it through the first part," Gene said, thinking about what the company had done to fabricate the discovery.

"What about actual geologists going to the site in Australia?" Jim asked, rubbing where the rubber adhesive had held the fake wrinkles and mustache to his face.

"That's a little more difficult," Gene acknowledged, nodding. "We can provide much of the data they will be looking for, but it could be difficult to fool a trained geologist. Especially since his people know exactly what geological formations and the rock or soil compositions should be to indicate a Lithium deposit."

"What's our next step?" Jim asked, putting his jeans back on.

"I'll need to talk to our geologists," Gene told him. "We may be able to get some core samples from other regions, as well as the normal data that a geologist would need to evaluate the possibility of a deposit."

"I'd guess you have a week, maybe ten days," Jim said as Amber came into the room. "I believe he'll send his team over as soon as they recommend further study based on the data you can provide that looks like the correct topography. Which, by the way, will probably happen because you did such a good job of making it seem feasible."

"What do you think, Amber?" Gene asked, turning to look at her.

"I agree with Jim," she answered. "And it wouldn't surprise me if he started digging a little deeper into the kelp battery issue."

"What makes you think that?" Gene asked.

"He started asking about the Boeing satellites we were using, battery life, and a few other things that showed a keener interest than last time," she answered. "And I'm getting a feeling that he suspects something."

"What do you think he suspects?" Gene asked, frowning.

"I don't know," Amber answered, shaking her head. "I just got the feeling that he thinks something's wrong. His questions, somewhat the way he asks them, I can't put my finger on any specific thing, but I'm a little concerned that he knows more than we suspect."

"What do you think about that, Jim?" Gene asked.

"I'm not sure. But I do know that he's no fool. He'll dig into the Lithium story until he gets his answers," Jim replied. "And, as Amber said, I think he's digging around looking into our battery research. We need to make sure there's no loose ends that could unravel that part of our plan."

"I'll have the company do another trial investigation," Gene said, nodding. "They can access anything Mr. Wellington's people can get to. We'll double-check every channel, including the background data we put in the Scientific American."

"What about the uncles? Do we know if we can count on any of them to approve a sale of the Lithium contracts if we need to remove Harry?" Jim asked.

"I'm pretty sure," Gene conceded. "But we still need to keep pushing the plan until we need to resort to the final solution. Just remember, they are seeing the same information we're providing to Harry. But I doubt he's sharing all of the information he's gathering or will gather on either the Lithium deposits or the battery issue."

"I think you're right about that," Amber said, nodding. "He seems to be very controlling and extremely certain that he knows what's best for both himself and the company."

"I agree," Jim responded. "He's a little of a megalomaniac, and regardless of what his uncles think, or anyone else for that matter, he'll do what he decides is the best answer, even if it's wrong."

"I believe you're right," Amber agreed. "I've been around plenty of narcissistic personalities, and he'll top the list."

"Do you think you can exploit that?" Gene asked, looking at Amber.

"I'm not sure," she answered. "I know he's very interested in something more than a platonic relationship."

"That's for sure," Jim agreed. "I was surprised when he paid almost as much attention to me this evening as he did you."

"That's part of the reason I think he's suspicious," Amber revealed. "I practically had my hands on him every second I felt it wouldn't be too obvious. And he didn't pay the same attention as he did the first time."

"If he's ignoring you, even the slightest amount, it's not something that's normal behavior for him," Gene acknowledged, shaking his head. "That man can't stand rejection by any woman. And he relishes the chase. What do you folks think? Should we play the sex issue more?"

"I don't think so," Amber answered. "Maybe if I'd been a little more aggressive last week. Maybe. But if he truly suspects something's amiss, that would more likely confirm those suspicions."

"You're probably right," Gene told her. "Any dramatic change in either of your behaviors at this point wouldn't help our situation."

"Have you considered bringing in another lady?" Jim asked, thinking about the initial briefings with Jewell.

"What do you mean?" Gene asked.

"What if Maria's sister came with us next trip," he answered. "She's a fresh face, and there's no reason for him not to try his luck with her. If you intend on pushing the sex angle, I think that's a better way to go."

"I disagree," Amber told them. "I don't see Harry being swayed by any woman. Sex or no sex. He's too self-involved to let any sexual encounter mean anything other than an evening of pleasure. And by pleasure, I don't mean the woman's. I think men like him use sex to show dominance."

"She's probably right," Jim said, nodding at Gene. "I'm sure she can read a man better than either of us could ever hope to be able to do."

"Okay, let's scrap the sex angle," Gene decided. "Did you discuss the next meeting?"

"Sort of," Jim answered, "he just said he hoped it would be soon."

"I almost forgot," Amber said suddenly. "Jim told him that we had hired a company to do research on costs and tax issues on the housing idea. Do you have that covered?"

"That's an easy one," Gene told her. "There's a real estate investment company called the Time Group here in Baltimore that we've used to help in our acquisitions over the years. We'll just notify them that there may be some interest expressed in their work with Mr. Billy Pratka or his lovely wife, Maria."

"Do I need to drop their name next week?" Jim asked.

"No, he'll find them," Gene answered. "I think it would be better if he found them on his own. You know, showing you that he can dig into anything you're doing."

"That's a good idea," Jim said. "I'm sure he'll be sure to tell us what he's discovered when we come back next week. Letting him think he's too smart for us to hide anything works to our advantage. Maybe if his geologists think a trip to Australia would be in order, we can get at least another week or two."

"That's true," Gene said. "But, unless we can convince him the Australian deposit is real, it's all for naught. We've got to convince him that he may lose even the forty million we offered for the contracts."

"And the battery," Jim told them. "We need to make sure there isn't any way he can disprove the kelp concept until we decide whether or not to eliminate the man."

"Agreed," Gene said, turning toward the door. "You two, get back to your rooms and get some rest. I'll head back down to Quantico and see if I can't get the geologists out of bed. We can't afford to let Harry's men find any reason to express any doubt just yet."

Chapter 24

Two days after arriving back home, Jim was washing his Corvette when a black limo pulled up to the curb. Putting the soapy sponge into the plastic bucket sitting by the front fender, Jim wiped his hands on the towel that was lying in the seat of the car.

"Good morning, Jim," Gene said as he got out of the car and walked up the driveway. "Little 'Vette needs a good washing and waxing?"

"Not really," Jim answered as he greeted Gene and shook hands. "More from my boredom than needing to be washed. What brings you by so early in the morning?"

"Just thought you needed something more productive to do than washing cars," Gene replied as he admired the vintage Corvette. "But this is still one hell of a beauty. Hope you never give it up."

"Only when I get too old to drive it," Jim said, laughing. "Just what do you have in mind that's more productive than my training program for a future position as the head waxer at Hertz Car Rentals just outside Love Field?"

"Maybe just a little conference with a few colleagues," Gene told him. "We need to put our heads together and see if we're still on the right track with Mr. Wellington."

"All right, what do you need me to do?" Jim asked, wondering what the company had in mind.

"We need to fly to Quantico for a couple of hours," Gene answered. "There's going to be a gathering of minds, so to speak, this afternoon. We want you, Amber, and Jewell in on the planning."

"When do we need to leave?" Jim asked as he dumped the soapy water from the bucket. "And, more importantly, when do we get back?"

"As soon as you can put on some dry jeans," Gene said, looking at Jim's soaked pants and tennis shoes. "And, some boots. We'll be back by five or six tonight at the latest. Maybe earlier if we get moving."

"I'll be ready in ten minutes," Jim replied as he slid into the driver's seat. "Why don't you go in the house while I put the car in the garage and change? And, of course, call Jennifer and lie about what I'm doing today."

A few minutes later, as they were heading toward DAL, Gene told Jim, "We've made arrangements for Jewell to meet us at Quantico, and Amber is already at the airport waiting."

"Why's Jewell being brought in?" Jim asked as they pulled off Mockingbird Lane onto Lemmon Avenue. "I thought you had decided not to use her for this operation due to concerns about our previous relationship."

"Plans change," Gene said as they pulled into the parking lot for general aviation on the northeast side of Love Field. "We are running out of time and need to convince Wellington Minerals that it's in their best interest to take our offer of forty million."

Walking through the small terminal area, Jim saw Amber sitting in one of the leather armchairs that surrounded a round glass tabletop. "Hey," she said as he walked up. "Did we wake you up this morning?"

"Not a chance," Jim replied as she rose to join them. "Still a little of the farm boy in me, I guess. Can't stand to lay around in bed after the sun is up."

"Plane's ready, folks," the pilot told them as he walked in from the aircraft ramp side of the terminal. "We can leave as soon as everybody's here."

"We're all here," Gene answered him as he turned to Jim and Amber, "and if you're done with your morning greetings, we need to leave."

Slightly over three hours later, they were in a black company, Suburban, heading into the headquarters of Black Water and its subsidiaries. After passing through the double-fenced security gates, the driver dropped them off in front of the only entry to the massive building.

After tapping in the code that gained entrance to the cubicle, Gene held the door open while the three of them entered. Standing before the glass, Gene showed his ID and waited for the door to be unlocked.

Once inside, they were met by a lady wearing khaki pants and a tan knit shirt with the Muddy Water logo embroidered on the left chest area. "If you'll follow me," she directed as she headed across the lobby. "I believe everyone else is in the conference room, and a buffet table has been provided if you haven't had lunch."

As soon as they were escorted into the room, Jim saw Jewell at one of the tables talking to one of the men who was part of the makeup team. "Hey," Jim said as he noticed the name tags at the table included him, Jewell, Amber, and Gene.

"Hey, Gyrene," she said, hugging him. "How's it going with your new 'wife'?"

"Do you mean the real wife or the play wife?" Jim asked as Amber smiled at Jewell.

"I think she means me," Amber said, extending her hand. "Hi, I'm Amber or Maria, depending on where I am and what day it is."

"Good to meet you," Jewell answered. "I'm Jewell, as I guess you've figured out. I was the original Maria but fell out of grace with Jim because of his propensity to look for strange and new ladies to escort around the country."

"Wasn't my decision," Jim said, shaking his head. "I just follow orders."

"If you three are done posturing, we need to get this started," Gene said, returning to the table with a sandwich and some chips on a plate. "Grab something to eat and get back as soon as you can if you want to be home by evening."

As soon as they were all sitting, the original gentleman from their first meeting stood and addressed the group, "Good morning or afternoon, depending on where you came from. We'll try to keep this short so everyone can get back home today. Except for those of us who will probably be here all day and night trying to implement any of the changes or ideas that arise from this meeting."

Pausing to let everyone face his direction, he continued, "We've got some interesting information to give everyone, some good, some not so. First, the not so- - -Mr. Harry Wellington is proving to be somewhat reluctant to be persuaded that his best interests lie in accepting our offer for his contracts. The government negotiators ran several calculations showing him the results of even a ten percent drop in the price of Lithium, and that would affect his rate of return on his investment. The ROI, return on investment, would take twenty years to recoup what we are offering today."

"What about the other members of the board?" Gene asked.

"That's where the good news comes in," the speaker answered. "We've managed to gain possession of some internal memos that suggest that there's definitely some dissension within the board. Mainly, the uncles are pushing for the acceptance of our previous offer. We believe this is due to the difference in their age and that of Harry. They correctly see the bird in the hand as the only way to maximize their wealth. Not waiting another twenty years that they might not have."

"What about the battery program?" Jim asked as he finished his sandwich. "Have we made sure there's plenty of depth to our claims so it will stand the extra scrutiny we know he'll undertake?"

"We've put several more individuals on the issue," the speaker said, nodding. "We've placed numerous articles in various scientific magazines that allude to the feasibility of the process. "We've also put a Trojan horse into the Wellington company's main computer program that will direct most inquiries to our people. They've already gotten numerous fabricated studies showing the glowing results of current testing."

"And the Australian discovery?" Amber asked. "He's going to be looking into that aspect more than the battery thing, I think."

"Covered," the speaker answered. "We've got fake surveys and field data ready to provide using the same Trojan horse that will direct any inquiry to our website. I might add his geologists were busy looking into that the day after your last meeting with Harry. We were lucky you guys told us about his plans when you did. We might have been caught with our shorts down and a day behind getting the false data into their hands."

"Additionally," the speaker told them as he motioned to Gene to wait a minute, "we got several core samples from previous sites as well as the imaging that will prove the validity of our Australian site. These will be provided if his geologists actually come to the site of the discovery."

"What we're leading to," Gene said when the speaker finished, "is that we have provided Mr. Wellington with every piece of data necessary to convince him of the impending drop in Lithium prices, the feasibility of an alternate source of electrical power, and financial data to prove the prudent fiscal decision would be to sell the contracts. But he is still reluctant."

Pausing for a second, Gene continued, "So, here are the facts and what we see as the probable end of our negotiations. Everything we have given Harry has had little effect. Everything we've provided to the other board members suggests they will vote in our favor, but they don't have the shares to make the final decision. That leads us to what our company believes will be the only resolution: Mr. Harry Wellington must not be allowed to remain in control of his shares of the stock. We must take whatever measures are necessary to force the board to vote in our favor."

"You're talking about the final solution," Jim said, looking from Gene to Jewell to the speaker. "We still have another meeting with him later this week. What's the plan for that meeting?"

Chapter 25

Gene nodded to the speaker and asked him, "Would you please brief us on what the company's plan is from this point forward?"

"Certainly," the speaker answered. "As I've mentioned, we have everything in place in an attempt to get Harry and company to come to the bargaining table. And, we still have hope that either the uncles or the misinformation will convince Mr. Wellington to accept our original offer."

"Not to interrupt," Jim said, raising his hand. "Have you considered sending him a reduced offer that would correspond to the predicted drop in Lithium prices? If nothing else, it would serve to reinforce the whole new deposit scenario."

"No, I have to admit we haven't," the speaker answered. "That's a good suggestion. We'll send a revised offer over after this briefing. Reducing our offer by at least ten percent just might demonstrate that the government believes that a future decline is imminent. Thanks."

"Now, as to what we do if he doesn't accept our new offer. That depends on what you folks learn from your next meeting," the speaker told them. "I certainly don't think you need to push it at your end. But just know that we're increasing the apparent acceptance of the kelp battery within the science community. I'd suggest only mentioning it if he brings it up."

"How do you plan on using Jewell?" Gene asked.

"She's going to be there if we need an additional meeting between Jim and Harry," the speaker answered.

"In what capacity?" Amber asked.

"Our current plan is to have her arrive after you and Harry are at the club," he told her. "We'll also have our own dealer as we did the first time you went there."

"Is she just a distraction?" Jim asked. "Or is she playing some other role?"

"Right now, she'll be responsible for the final solution," the speaker informed them. "You and Amber have become too obvious, and if something happens while you're involved or around, it could raise suspicions."

"Are we supposed to know her?" Amber asked.

"Definitely not," the speaker told her. "She'll arrive later, as I said, and wait until there's an open seat at your table. Once seated, she'll do whatever is necessary to get Harry's attention."

"Both times we've met, we've gone to dinner," Amber said, looking at Jewell. "Is she supposed to go with us, or are you planning on Harry wanting to take her?"

"Our plan, unless we get any other information, is that she'll join you at dinner," the speaker answered. "But everybody needs to be in their own cars. We can't afford to have Harry alone with Jewell. Nor do we want all of you at the restaurant when we administer the spice. Shortly after arriving, you and Jim will get a phone call regarding your real estate investment program, and you'll need to leave."

"But that leaves Jewell alone with Harry," Jim said, shaking his head. "I thought that was to be avoided."

"She won't be alone at Lumbini," the speaker answered. "We'll have a waiter that will ensure everything goes as planned. Since he'll be serving your table, it won't appear unnatural. And, he'll testify that you and Amber left well before dinner arrived. That keeps the suspicions from you two."

"And if our names are brought up?" Jim asked.

"The only people that might provide any information on Billy and Maria Pratka are Larry, the two dealers, the maître d', the limo driver, and our waiter," Gene informed them. "Larry won't remember your names; the house dealer won't recognize any pictures of the real you, the maître d' might remember a couple that dined with Harry on a couple of occasions, but again, no names. If the dealer is questioned, which we severely doubt, he'll only know that a couple named Pratka came a few times. Maybe he'll remember some basic information about where you're from, the battery stuff, possibly the real estate thing, but basically, nothing that could tie you to the unfortunate demise of Mr. Harry Wellington. And the limo driver can only tie the Pratkas to the Four Seasons."

"Are you still planning on using the suicide tree seeds?" Jim asked.

"More than likely," Gene answered. "Especially since he'll be eating Indian cuisine as you did on your first visit."

"How much time will I have after I spice his food?" Jewell asked.

"Our physicians say that he'll get an upset stomach about thirty minutes or so after ingestion," the speaker told them. "Then, within three or four hours, his heart rate will plummet, and he'll be discovered dead."

"What about the autopsy?" Jewell asked. "Won't they find the poison?"

"Very slight chance," the speaker told her. "It isn't one of the normal toxins that are tested for. As a matter of fact, it takes a very special and expensive test to confirm its presence in the body. And if discovered, which is extremely slight, it's a native of India and could have been ingested when one of the Indian spices used in that night's meal preparation was accidentally polluted during manufacture."

"Let's not get hung up on these details just yet," Gene advised. "Trust us on ensuring this will be another unfortunate heart attack. Cerbera Odollam has been used for more murders in India than you'd believe. And it's never been proven. That's what makes it such a perfect drug for our plan."

"I guess it's up to Amber and me to convince Harry that he needs to sell his contracts," Jim said as the sobering thought of another civilian death entered his head.

"We really don't think you can convince Harry of anything," Gene told him, knowing that Jim still had some issues with the methods that were sometimes necessary. "Unfortunately, sometimes a man's narcissistic nature prevents him from seeing what he needs to do for the good of others. Even if what he's seeing is a fabrication."

"And there's no other way of getting the Lithium except through Wellington Minerals?" Jim asked.

"No," Gene said, shaking his head. "We've explored every other option. Wellington controls too much of the known resources. Every legitimate offer, every attempt at appealing to his sense of duty to the country, every veiled threat, all have been rejected because of either his greed or his failure to comprehend what will happen to our space program if he doesn't support us."

"Okay, everybody," the speaker announced. "I think we've covered everything we needed to talk about. Please, if you have any other ideas or suggestions, remember to call our offices. In case you need the number, it's 410-546-9378 for this mission."

"All right folks, we need to head back to the airport and get everybody home," Gene said as they all stood. "I'll fly back to Texas with Jim and Amber. Jewell, I guess we'll drop you at your gate before we go over to the general aviation area."

"When do I get personal service like these two?" Jewell asked as they walked out of the building. "Seems like I've been around long enough to rate a private jet."

"They don't rate a private jet," Gene said, laughing. "I do. They just get to tag along."

Chapter 26

The next few days passed uneventfully as Jim kept busy around the house doing the normal chores and making small revisions to his plan regarding Charlie. He had approached him once a week ago as he was leaving work for lunch and explained that he didn't appreciate his continual harassment of his wife. Of course, Charlie denied any wrong doing and said Jennifer had misinterpreted his remarks.

He knew that Jennifer was still having to put up with his obnoxious banter and suggestive remarks, but she continued to tell him that she was handling it. He also knew from the way she acted that Charlie was becoming more than just a nuisance, and the fact that Charlie was a family member of her boss made it difficult to complain.

Watching the commodities markets to see if there were any major changes in the Lithium prices, he hoped that Harry would take note and have the financial acumen to accept the government's offer. If unaware of the manipulation of the market, it only made sense to accept even the reduced offer if it was presented.

If the government had reduced their initial offer, as had been discussed, Harry should at least try to regain that amount or use it as a basis for further negotiations. Jim knew that most, if not all, of his missions with Dark Water had been necessary, and even his first assignment in Atlanta had been clearly in the national interest. He trusted the company, at least he trusted Gene, and knew that drastic measures were sometimes necessary in war.

And war isn't always fought on the battlefield. It spills over into everyday life, and if won in the shadow land of covert operations, it could prevent the losses on the actual battlefield. There had been at least three attempts to assassinate Adolph Hitler before World War Two.

The first attempt in 1921 was politically motivated, and if the gunshots in Munich's Hofbrauhaus beer hall had hit Hitler, maybe the Nazi party would have never survived the opposition of the communists and the social democrats. Twenty years before the start of WW II, just one lucky bullet could have possibly prevented a political ideology that endures today.

In another attempt in 1938 at an annual celebration of surviving the first attempt, Maurice Bavaud tried to shoot him because, as a Catholic, he opposed Hitler, who he thought was a threat to the Catholic church and the incarnation of Satan. He never got a clear shot because of the crowd raising their arms in the Nazi salute.

In 1939, Georg Elser built a bomb with a 144-hour timer and positioned it where Hitler was again celebrating the Beer Hall putsch. Unfortunately, Hitler moved his speech up an hour and left the building eight minutes before the bomb exploded killing eight people and injuring dozens of others, but not Hitler.

If any of these attempts had succeeded, maybe the six million Jews and sixty million others wouldn't have died because of Hitler and his policies. In addition to those directly killed in the war, the thousands more who lost limbs, those who starved during and immediately after the war, and the political ramifications that followed for decades might have been averted.

Of course, sometimes an assassination could be the start of a war, such as when Gavrilo Princip shot and killed Archduke Franz Ferdinand of Austria and his wife Sophia, the Duchess of Hohenberg. Gavrio, from a Serbian family living in Bosnia, and his accomplices, started a chain of events that would result in the death of over forty million and the other millions that died of starvation and disease.

The decision to take a life when you're facing the enemy and he's trying to take yours, or one of your comrades, is much easier. As he had learned in Vietnam, life on the battlefield was cheap. Even his covert operations in the Middle East were easily reconciled. Although he didn't know exactly why each mission was executed, he at least knew there were actual combatants facing each other.

And he personally knew of hunter/killer teams in Vietnam whose missions were to enter the village of an unfriendly tribal chief and eliminate him. Again, Jim knew the rationale behind these missions. More soldiers might die if the targets hadn't been assassinated.

But this seemed to be a financial decision. Justifying a killing over money didn't sit right with him. But, as so many that had disagreed with any of the wars that had been fought, someone somewhere had made a decision that was based on knowledge that he didn't possess. That's where the trust factor came into play. If you trusted your Commanders, you went into battle with a clear conscious. If not, the war would probably be lost.

So, after due consideration, Jim finally came to the conclusion that he knew he would reach. He was being given orders. And a good soldier follows those lawful orders. Besides, he concluded, he wasn't the one who would perform the final solution. His mission was just to convince Mr. Harry Wellington to renegotiate a reasonable offer.

Funny, Jim thought. Here I'm making plans that may involve the removal of a man for being an asshole to my wife, yet I'm debating the issue of removing a man for financial reasons involving the country's security. Funny.

Chapter 27

The following morning, Jim kissed Jennifer goodbye and headed for the airport. The flight to Mexico went smoothly, as did the return to DFW. The final flight to Tucson was delayed slightly due to a minor maintenance issue, but Captain Bandy pushed the speed up enough to make an on-time arrival.

After checking into his room, Jim was watching Law and Order when he heard someone knocking on his door. "Just a second," he said as he slid off the bed.

Opening the door, he saw Amber standing there with a few mini–Jack Daniel's bottles and a Coke in her hand. "Night cap?" she asked as she smiled at Jim.

"Sure," Jim said stepping aside to let her into the room. Glancing both ways down the hall to make sure they were unobserved, he shut the door and turned to see Amber mixing their drinks.

"Cheers," she said handing Jim one of the glasses.

"Cheers," Jim said, tapping her glass with his. "To what do I owe the pleasure?"

"I just thought we might go over what we plan to do tomorrow night," she answered, taking a small sip.

"I don't know," Jim admitted, shaking his head and motioning to a chair. "I guess we just keep playing our role and hope Harry decides to do the right thing."

"I've thought about that," Amber said solemnly as she sat. "I just don't get the feeling that he's going to fall for the battery thing. I know I'd want a lot more provable information before I made a multi-million dollar decision."

"You're right about that," Jim agreed, sitting on the bed. "Harry's a narcissistic pig, but certainly not a stupid one." Pausing, he continued, "I don't think the company can put out enough verifiable information to sway him."

"Nope," Amber said, taking another drink. "And the new deposit in Australia, that may have a chance because it's still unproven and can't be verified either way yet."

"Agreed," Jim said, leaning back on the pillows and putting his feet up on the bed. "I think we should abandon the battery idea and concentrate on the Australian discovery."

"How do we do that?" Amber asked as she slipped her shoes off.

"We need to make a call," Jim said, sitting his drink on the table beside the bed.

Dialing '9' for an outside line, Jim called 410-546-9378 and waited for it to be answered. "Good evening," he said, smiling at Amber. "Would it be possible to speak with General Barker?"

Hearing the answer, Jim nodded to Amber and told her Gene would be contacted.

A few minutes later, Jim said, "Good evening, General. Hope I'm not disturbing you."

After being told that it was all right, Jim told him, "Amber and I are discussing the battery issue, and we both think it's not going to work."

Waiting for the response, Jim then said, "Yes, sir. We'd appreciate it if you could talk to us about it tomorrow night."

"Yes, sir," Jim finally said. "We'll see you tomorrow. Good night."

Hanging up the phone, Jim looked at Amber and said, "He agrees and said they'll issue a statement sometime tomorrow that says the research proved to be economically unfeasible to produce the amps and watts necessary."

"Good," Amber said, leaning forward in her chair. "I just hope Harry believes that the Lithium prices will continue to fall. I'd rather not have to eliminate him over the price of some dirt."

"I agree," Jim said looking at Amber and noticing that there was nothing on beneath the T-shirt she was wearing. "I'm just hoping that we don't need to use Jewell."

"What's between you and her?" Amber asked, noticing Jim's glance down the front of her shirt.

"Nothing," Jim said, picking his glass up from the table. "We've just known each other for a long time."

"I think there's more to it than just knowing each other," Amber said, standing and walking to where she had sat the other minis. "I get the feeling that there was probably something in your mutual pasts."

"We sort of tried to get together several years ago," Jim admitted, looking at the extremely short shorts she was wearing. "Nothing ever came of it."

"Just two ships that passed in the night, unseen but somehow noticed?" Amber said, smiling over the top of her glass. "That's a shame."

"What could have been, what should have been, but wasn't," Jim said, getting up to mix another drink. "It's past. But we've remained friends. And that's important to me."

"I think she'd like to be more than friends," Amber told him as she stood by the bed and waited for Jim to come to her.

"And I think you're reading more into this than there is," Jim said, looking down into Amber's eyes. "I'm happily married, and Jewell knows that."

"Doesn't stop someone from wanting more," Amber said as she moved up against Jim. "I know it wouldn't stop me."

"Doesn't stop me from wanting either," Jim said as he took a step back. "But, wanting and doing are two entirely separate issues."

"What do you want?" Amber said, closing the distance between them again. "If you could have something, something you wanted, would you take it?"

"I don't think we're still talking about Jewell, are we?" Jim asked as Amber reached behind him to set her glass down.

"Not a chance," she said as she pulled his head down to hers.

Chapter 28

Jim waited until she realized that he wasn't kissing her back and then quietly said, "We can't do this, Amber."

Gently putting his hands on her shoulders and pushing her back, he continued, "I told you, just because I want something doesn't mean that I'll do it. That's not the way I am."

Amber looked down and said, "That's one of the reasons I'm attracted to you. You aren't that way."

"But if I did whatever I wanted, then I would be that way," Jim told her as he stepped around her. "I'd be just like all of the others that give in to their desires."

"Not even once?" Amber asked as she turned to face him.

"Once?" Jim asked. "Once with you? Or, once with just any woman? Or just with one other woman? Once never ends with once.

Besides," he continued, "if once was all right for me, would it be all right for Jennifer to do it just once?"

"You're a strange man," Amber said, picking up her drink and walking over to the chair. "I guess I already knew that. And I know how lucky your wife is to have a strange man like you."

Jim smiled and said, "I guess I'm just a little old-fashioned. Maybe goes back to my mother and dad. I don't think they'd like it if I abandoned everything they taught me about being an honorable man."

"Is that part of the reason you have such a hard time justifying this particular mission?" she asked as Jim sat on the bed.

"Part of it, I guess," he answered as he leaned back. "I've seen too much death to not wonder if I'm doing the right thing. Maybe I'm getting soft."

"I just think it's that you have a strong sense of morality," she told him. "Some people get so hardened doing this kind of work that it has little to no effect on them. I think you're one of those few who will always try to justify it in your mind. If you can't justify it, I bet you'd try to convince the company to find another way. Or, you'd refuse to do it."

"I honestly don't know," Jim told her. "I've always done what I thought was the right thing. But I know that sometimes I don't know everything and have to trust the people that make the decisions."

"I think that's one of the reasons the company recruited you," Amber said as she stood. "I bet that there have been lots of others that were released because they didn't worry about the ethics of each mission or were too anxious to use the most extreme measures. There's got to be a balance of following orders blindly and questioning the orders."

"It basically comes down to trust," Jim replied. "Sort of like most things in life. Trust is what keeps things from going to hell. If you don't have trust, you don't really have anything."

"Are we still talking about this mission or something else in your life?" Amber asked, heading for the door.

"Everything in my life," Jim told her as he followed her. "And most importantly, my personal life."

"She's a very, very lucky woman," Amber said as she opened the door and turned to face Jim. "I hope someday I get that lucky, too. Good night, Jim. You are such a strange and wonderful man. Never change."

"The man for you is out there somewhere," Jim said as he held the door open, "and he'll be lucky to find you."

"I'm sure he is," Amber said as she turned away. "I'm just getting tired of waiting for the stupid bastard to realize it and come get me. Anyway, good night, and I'll see you in the morning."

"Good night, Miss Amber," Jim answered as she walked away. "Tomorrows always shed a new light on things."

Shutting the door as she walked down the hall, Jim shook his head and wondered what had caused her to think they could develop some relationship outside of work. "Maybe," he thought, "I've given her the wrong signal. I don't see how, but maybe it's my fault."

Gathering the empty bottles, he was heading for the door to toss them in one of the trashcans by the vending machines down the hall when the phone rang. "Hello," he said as he looked at the four empty bottles.

"Hey, honey," Jennifer said. "How's the trip going?"

"Fine," Jim answered. "Same old routine. Just another night in another hotel. One more night, and I'll be home."

"I know," she told him. "I'm ready for you to get back."

"I've only been gone one day," Jim reminded her.

"And I'm still ready for you to be home," Jennifer replied. "I don't care if it's one day or one hundred. I'll always be ready for you to come home. I just wanted you to know that. For now, just get some sleep and hurry back here."

"I will, baby," Jim said. "You have a good night, too."

Hearing the click as Jennifer hung up, he thought about what might have happened if he'd let Amber stay.

Chapter 29

The next morning, Jim was up early, replaying in his mind for the umpteenth time how to resolve Jennifer's problem. He was certain after last night's call that she was worried. Although not completely unusual for her to call when he was on a trip, this one was different. She didn't have any news or issues to talk about. Just the tone and the few words about how she missed him told him what he needed to know. Charlie was now moved up to the resolution stage.

Meeting the crew in the hotel lobby, Jim was anxious to get to DFW and do a dry run on his still-evolving plan. The most critical aspect would be the timing. Since he was officially away on a trip, the short three-hour wait at DFW could prove to be the Achilles heel or the cover story he might need. There was just enough time unless traffic was an issue.

The other timing issue was if the flight got in as scheduled or was delayed even a few minutes. There was little he could do to prevent that, but since it was his leg to fly, he'd try for every shortcut he could get and push the speed up slightly as long as Captain Bandy didn't try to assert his opinion. Even five minutes less time could mean the difference between success and failure.

Once airborne and away from the local controller's area, Jim asked Robert to request direct to DFW. Hearing his request approved, Jim made the slight heading change and adjusted the speed slightly higher. Noticing that the computer now showed them arriving fifteen minutes ahead of schedule, Jim relaxed and thought about how best to get out of the airport and drive to where he was almost sure Charlie would be having lunch.

Less than one hundred miles west of DFW, they were given clearance to descend. Pressing his luck, Jim let the airspeed drift up to try to gain another couple of minutes. Now, if only they could get changed to the east side of the airport for landing, he would have an extra twenty-five to thirty minutes.

Unfortunately, there appeared to be too much traffic on the east side, and clearance for runway 18 right was the only option. Still, Jim had managed to cut twenty minutes off the flight time. Now, if Robert would just taxi at his normal snail's pace, he should be able to get to Mesquite and back with plenty of time to spare.

As soon as everybody was off the plane, Robert asked, "What are you going to do for the next three and one-half hours? Care to have lunch, and I can debrief you on why it's unnecessary to try to get in early?"

"I wish I could," Jim lied. "But I'm meeting my wife for lunch today. That's why I was trying to get here as early as I thought reasonable."

"I don't think you've thought this through," Robert told him in a condescending tone. "What if you'd burned the extra fuel to fly faster and had been told to wait because your gate was still occupied? You'd have wasted gas and not gained any time."

"I understand," Jim replied with the appropriate amount of chastisement in his voice. "I know you're right about the gate thing; I guess I was just interested in going to lunch with my wife."

"Just so you remember," Robert continued to lecture, "this airline has been running on schedule a lot longer than you've been here. And, the only reason to waste fuel is to try to get back on schedule, not to get in early."

"Yes, sir," Jim said, almost unable to keep the disdain from his voice. "I'll remember that. Now, I've got to go find my wife and grab a quick lunch. I'll see you at the gate for Baltimore."

Leaving his bags in operations, Jim took the employee train to the parking lot and hurried to his truck. Changing to a sweatshirt, he headed out of the north entrance to the airport. Less than twenty minutes later, he was parked a half block from the little restaurant where he had seen Charlie go numerous times. He just hoped he'd come today.

Thirty minutes later, Charlie drove by and parked his new BMW convertible in the small gravel lot beside the building. The few cars already there made it more difficult for Jim to hide in plain sight, but it also meant that it would probably be easy to find a spot, especially if he parked as far as possible from the building.

Jim waited fifteen more minutes, which he figured would be sufficient time to take care of the problem, and headed back to DFW. Traffic was still light, and he was back in the parking lot with over an hour to spare. Once back at the airport employee parking lot, he changed back into his uniform shirt and put on his jacket and hat. The employee train was just leaving when he got to the small waiting area.

Knowing that another one would be along in ten or fifteen minutes, Jim was satisfied that there would be plenty of time to execute his plan.

Chapter 30

The flight to BWI was uneventful, and once at the hotel, Jim quickly changed into his jeans and T-shirt. Waiting for the phone to ring, he thought about what he could do to avoid having to take any drastic measures with Charlie. Right now, he didn't think it would help, but he would try meeting him one more time to try to impress on him that continued harassment of Jennifer would not be tolerated.

Grabbing the phone after the first ring, he heard again that rooms 302 and 304 would be the staging area for their transformations into Billy and Maria. Turning on the TV to provide room noise, he put the Do Not Disturb sign on his door and headed for the stairs.

Gene opened the door when he arrived and knocked. "Good afternoon, Jim," Gene said, shutting the door. "Ready for your last try to convince Harry that he needs to sell his Lithium contracts before the market drops even further?"

"I'll do my best," Jim answered. "What's the verdict on the battery issue?"

"We're releasing a news article later this week in the Scientific American that removes the process from serious consideration due to excessive costs and low power output," Gene told him. "You might even want to break the news to Harry to show that you're completely forthright with your dealings since you've already discussed the program with him."

"On another issue," Gene said as Jim stripped down to his shorts and socks, "Jewell won't be coming tonight."

"Oh? Why not?" Jim asked as the prostatic belly was fastened around his waist.

"We decided that if we were going to try one more time with Harry, having her here wouldn't serve any purpose at this point," Gene explained. "She'll be available next week if needed."

"I suppose that's smart," Jim said, shaking his head. "Less exposure for any recognition issues later."

"Exactly," Gene agreed. "And she might distract from you and Amber trying to convince him that he needs to sell his contracts."

Trying to remain as still as possible while the fake wrinkles were being attached, Jim looked at Gene and asked, "Has he been made the reduced offer we discussed?"

"Yes, the offer was dropped to approximately three and a half million," Gene replied. "The offer was rejected without any discussion."

"He seems pretty sure of himself," Jim said as the wig was adjusted. "Is there a chance that he knows for sure that the latest discovery of Lithium in Australia isn't real?" "I don't think so," Gene answered. "His team of geologists were digging all over the internet and making phone calls all week. I think we've convinced them that it's a viable find."

"It surprises me that Harry wouldn't at least come to the table to see if he could get a better price, maybe even the original offer," Jim said, putting the trousers on. "What could he be thinking?"

"We think he's just wanting to get additional proof that there is an actual discovery," Gene told him. "Nothing else makes sense. He can't be aware of our program to deceive him. He'd be raising holy hell if that were the case."

"I suppose so, knowing his ego," Jim acknowledged. "Has he made any attempts to gain access to the property? Booked flights for his geologists to go there?"

"Not yet," Gene answered. "Everything we've supplied through every channel he's looked at should have convinced him that it's a high probability discovery. We're not sure why he hasn't sent his team."

"And the uncles?" Jim asked, buttoning up his shirt.

"They've been making some pretty loud noises," Gene told him. "They seem to believe that the company is missing a once-in-a-lifetime opportunity to take advantage of the current offer before the price drops even further."

Gene got up to open the connecting door when they heard the knocking. "You look wonderful," he told Amber as she came in wearing a new evening gown and jewelry. "I suppose you'd like to take your entire Maria wardrobe home when this is over."

"That would be great," Amber said as she watched Jim tie his shoes. "But I don't think there's any place around where I live that these clothes would be appropriate."

"You ladies would dress like that to go to Walmart if you could," Jim joked as he finished putting on the cufflinks and jacket.

"Okay, if you two are ready, let's get you to Larry's and see what we can accomplish tonight," Gene announced as

Amber straightened Jim's tie. "Just remember that this is probably the last chance we have to get Harry to see the folly in holding onto his stock."

Immediately upon entering Larry's, they headed to the same table where they recognized the dealer from their first visit. It appeared that the company had given Harry's dealer another night off, as Gene had told them a week ago. Taking their seats, they played cautiously, waiting for Harry to arrive.

Less than thirty minutes later, Harry arrived with the same lady who had accompanied him when they first met. "Evening, folks," Harry said as he took one of the open seats. "How are the cards tonight?"

"Reasonable," Jim said as another hand was dealt. "Of course, the dealer seems to have the advantage no matter how reasonable my hand is."

"That's the truth," Harry agreed as he pushed a stack of hundred-dollar bills to the center of the table. "I just feel luck tonight. Don't you, Val?"

"I certainly do," she said, smiling at Harry. "I'm sure I'll be very lucky tonight if I get a seat."

"You can have mine," a man in a gray suit said, standing. "I've lost enough for one night. Maybe you'll be luckier in this seat than me."

Valerie took the open seat beside Jim, and Harry passed another stack of bills to the dealer for her chips.

"How's the Baltimore renovation project coming?" Harry asked as he placed a bet for the next round of cards.

"It's moving about as fast as a snail crossing a four-lane road in the middle of August," Jim said, looking at his cards.

"And that means?" Harry said, motioning for another card.

"Well, the snail is getting his tushie toasted as his tail is frying on the hot asphalt, but he can't seem to get any speed up," Jim answered. "He knows he's got to get across the road before he's burnt to a crisp, but he's pretty sure either the cars or the heat will do him in before he gets there."

"Now that's descriptive," Harry told him, laughing at the thought of a snail frying on a hot road. "But I fail to make the connection with the housing project."

"We're pushing as hard as we can," Jim explained, "but the city and the developers seem to be immune to our time schedule."

"Is that so important?" Harry asked as another round of cards were placed in front of the players.

"Yes and no," Jim told him. "A lot of what we're trying to do is tied to investing this year to avoid some looming tax issues. But I'm worried that if this drags on much longer, my sisters will find another pet project in their Save the World mission."

"Would that be so bad?" Harry asked as he lost another hand.

"Only in that we've invested a lot of time and money in this one," Amber answered. "And I sort of like this one. Some of my sisters' other ideas are so farfetched that only a lunatic would consider them as feasible."

"Not to change the subject," Harry said, finally winning a hand. "How's the battery project coming?"

"I'm afraid that snail is now escargot," Jim said, placing another bet.

"That's too bad," Harry told him. "I suppose you're dropping the whole kelp issue now."

"Not at all," Jim responded. "As a matter of fact, the kelp feed slurry is proving to be better than expected."

"And the financial data shows we are ahead of our original projections," Amber said, smiling at Harry. "We now estimate a breakeven point second quarter of next year."

"That's if Mr. Jackson stays on track and the production facilities maintain their cost estimates," Jim added. "Then, if everything our marketing department tells us comes to fruition, we'll clear almost two million by the end of the third year and forecast at least that return annually for the near term."

"That's encouraging," Harry admitted. "I suppose you have contracts for all of the ingredients in place, don't you?"

"Oh, yes," Jim answered. "We've contracted for a ten-year run and an option for another ten with a two percent rise in price locked in."

"How's your investigation into the Australian discovery going?" Amber asked as she watched Jim win another large hand. "I think you said you were sending a bunch of geologists over there to see if it was worth investing in."

"Actually, I said I would send a team to see if it was an actual Lithium deposit of the size and scope reported," Harry said, correcting her. "And only after verifying the probability by other methods."

"Oh, sorry," Amber said, amazed at how touchy he seemed to be on this issue.

"No problem," Harry said, winning another hand. "I'm just being extra cautious about the veracity of this sudden discovery."

"I'm certainly not a stockbroker or investment manager," Jim said, "but I've noticed quite a drop in the price of Lithium over the last week or so. Doesn't that mean that the market thinks there's about to be a supply or demand shift?"

"It could mean anything," Harry said, losing his bet. "Mainly, the markets tend to overreact to bad news and have to make large corrections when they discover the news was false."

"Now, that seems like something I could bet on," Amber said. "Buy future Lithium so that when the Australian thing falls through, I will make a fortune when the price goes back up."

"You already have a fortune, my dear," Jim said, increasing his bet. "Besides, didn't your daddy teach you not to bet on oil futures? Well, this is the same thing. Bet on what is there today, not what you think will be there tomorrow."

"And, what about what happens when the market predictions are correct?" Harry asked as he started removing his chips. "Then you've bought a bunch of minerals that are worth less than the original drop in price."

"What do you suggest?" Jim said, cashing in his chips. "You've made a good living determining what the future in minerals holds."

"I recommend we go to dinner," Harry said, cashing in his and Val's chips. Turning to her, he continued, "Will you be joining us, my dear?"

"Afraid not," she said, kissing him on the cheek. "I've made plans for this evening that don't include talking about the price of seaweed or dirt."

"Shall I drive?" Jim asked as they prepared to leave.

"That will be fine. I'll just escort Val to her car and meet you outside," Harry said, putting his hand on Val's waist. "You guys decide what you'd like for dinner tonight, and I'll select the place."

Chapter 31

"So, what's it to be?" Harry asked as he walked up to where Jim and Amber were standing beside the limo.

"Seafood," Amber answered as their driver opened the rear door for them.

"But, of course," Harry said, smiling and turning to the driver. "Do you know how to get us to McCormick and Schmick's?"

"Of course, sir. Down on the inner harbor," the driver responded as he shut their door.

"I think you'll like this place," Harry told them as they left Larry's. "Some of the freshest seafood in Baltimore. Not to mention, they keep a very special wine for me."

"Sounds good," Amber said as she watched the checkerboard of blighted areas slide along their route.

"The harbor area is one of the best places to find excellent restaurants, but you don't want to wander even a block away," Harry remarked as he noticed Amber frowning at the burned-out buildings and groups of people standing on the street corners.

"Really?" Jim asked. "I would have thought that the local police and city officials would keep that area secure. If for no other reason than to attract the tourist trade."

"They try," Harry told him. "At least they make a show of trying. But it still comes back to the underlying problem of poverty and neglect."

"That seems to be the problem we're having," Amber remarked. "The city appears to be making a show of trying, but almost three weeks of calls and pleas for information have provided us with zip."

"I understand," Harry said. "The city is great about decrying the problems but is worthless about providing a solution. Their answer is always increased taxes and another handout program to fund."

"Seems like there are enough so-called welfare programs," Jim said, shaking his head. "Maybe they need a public works program where the people have to work at something to collect their checks."

"And drug tests," Amber added. "No test, no money."

"But the city says that's unfair," Harry said as they approached the harbor. "Their concept is that drug use is a disease and needs to be treated. Denying them the basics of life would be cruel and unusual punishment."

"What about the denying of my ability to control the rewards of my work?" Jim asked as they stopped in front of the restaurant.

"Ah, therein lies the problem," Harry said as they got out of the car. "You think you deserve to keep what you earn. But they, the city, know that you made your money off the backs of the downtrodden. Therefore, they are entitled to part of your outrageous earnings."

"Haven't they figured out that if you let people keep the majority of their earnings, they'll open more businesses and employ more people," Amber said as they went through the door into the restaurant. "I've never seen a poor man hire anyone. It takes a man with money to invest. That's the solution, I think."

"Mr. Wellington," the maitre d' said as they entered. "I have your usual table ready. Will there be any more guests joining you this evening?"

"Afraid not," Harry said as they followed him to a table with an excellent view of the harbor. "I hope you have a bottle of my wine chilled."

"That we do, sir," he said as he held a chair out for Amber. "I'll have it sent right out."

"Excellent. Better bring two bottles," Harry said as he took a seat beside Amber. "Let me know if I need to make another order. I want to be sure there's always enough for me and my guests."

"I'll check, sir," he said as he signaled for one of the waiters. "I'll be right back with the bottles while you place your orders."

"No need for the menus," Harry told the waiter as he arrived. "I think we'll start off with the coconut shrimp and Maine lobster bisque for each of us. Then, Chesapeake Rockfish, Lobster mashed potatoes, and pan-roasted wild mushrooms."

"Excellent choice," the waiter said, bowing slightly. "And to drink?"

"Domaine Ramonet Montrachet Grand Cru," Harry answered, smiling slightly.

"I'm not sure we have that on our wine list," the waiter said with a puzzled look on his face. "I'll have to check."

"Don't bother," Harry said smugly. "I believe the wine will be here before you can turn in our order."

"Yes, sir," the waiter replied, backing away from the table. "I'll be right back with the shrimp and bisque as soon as possible."

"Now," Jim asked as they were left alone waiting for the wine and their meals, "what are your plans regarding the Lithium field they discovered?"

"I'm sending a couple of my people over there tomorrow," Harry answered. "They seem to think it bears looking into."

"What sort of information do you think you'll get, and how will that affect your contracts?" Amber asked as the maitre d' arrived with their wine and glasses.

"Just getting a better handle on the scope of the discovery, if there is one," Harry said as the wine was poured. "I refuse to accept these unsubstantiated rumors. Especially when I have millions at stake."

"I understand," Jim said, tasting his wine. "Now, this is an excellent white. Where did you find this?"

"Little area in France," Harry answered. "They're really known for their red wines, but this one caught my attention while I was over there on vacation. And at about one thousand eight hundred dollars a bottle, I think it's worth every cent."

"Holy cow," Amber whispered. "I better not spill a drop. What's that, about a dollar a teaspoon?"

"The good things in life are expensive," Harry said, smiling. "Haven't you folks figured that out down in Texas?"

"I guess we're still getting used to having money," Jim said, nodding. "Maybe some of it is that we were raised to be a little less flamboyant. Regardless of how much money the family has, displays of wealth are considered in poor taste."

"Oh, come on now," Harry chastised him. "People know you're wealthy. Enjoy what you've got. It's not your fault that you've got more than them. I think part of being wealthy is to show others what they are missing. Maybe it will make them work harder to get the same as you have."

"That may work up here," Amber remarked. "But, down in Texas, especially in the small towns, you're sure to alienate your neighbors."

"So?" Harry asked in disbelief, "Who really cares what they think?"

"I guess that's the difference in what we call the 'New England' attitude and our more friendly outlook," Jim told him. "Out where we live, you never know when you'll need someone's help. In some ways, a lot of areas in Texas are still relatively unsettled, and your neighbor may be the only thing between you and disaster."

"How'd we get off on this subject?" Amber asked, trying to get the conversation back to finding out what Harry was planning.

Just as Jim was getting ready to answer, the waiter arrived with their appetizers. "Enjoy," the waiter said as he set the dishes around the table. "Let me know if there's anything else I can get you. And your main course will be ready as soon as you've finished here."

"Maria's right," Jim said, taking a piece of shrimp from his plate. "Good food requires a lighter conversation. What do you plan on doing if the Australian discovery is as large as the market seems to think?"

"Now, there's an interesting question," Harry answered. "If possible, maybe I can get a contract on the majority of it. Then I can restrict the production to maintain the price I want."

"And if you can't get the contract?" Amber asked.

"I'll cross that bridge when I get to it," Harry told her. "Bottom line.....I really doubt that the discovery is as large as reported. I fully expect the price to return to the same level as before this new Lithium field came into the news."

"I guess your best advice would be to sell futures," Jim said, nodding. "I could buy Lithium at today's price and sell it in a month or so at the recovered price. Based on your expertise, I think that would be an astute investment."

"Haven't we already discussed that regarding oil futures?" Amber asked.

"That was oil," Jim told her, shaking his head. "Here, we have an expert on mineral acquisitions that has given us some inside information."

"But it's still an unknown," Amber argued as they finished their dishes. "Oil, gold, silver, or any of the iums we've discussed. I prefer a little more certainty in my investing."

"But there's something else," Harry said as the empty plates were removed and the main course arrived. "Something that is based more on gut feel than available information."

"What's that?" Jim asked as his plate was placed in front of him.

"Something doesn't feel right about this," Harry said as they started eating. "It's just that I've been negotiating with a major user of Lithium, and all of a sudden, there's this new discovery. I've been in the business of knowing the market for minerals for a long time. And, the timing on this seems to be suspicious."

"So, what do you plan to do?" Amber asked as she took a sip of the wine. "How can you determine what the truth is?"

"Part of it will come from the team I'm sending over," Harry said as he forked a piece of fish into his mouth. "But, regardless of what they report, I'll probably wait for the market to stabilize before I make any drastic changes in my negotiations."

"Sounds like you've made up your mind," Jim remarked as they were finishing the first bottle of wine and waiting for the maitre d' to open the other bottle.

"Not necessarily so," Harry said as the wine was poured. "But I've developed a pretty good feel for the market over the years. This drop in price just seems premature compared to other market moves. I just think someone is trying to manipulate the price."

"Why would they do that?" Jim asked as they were finishing their meals. "And I can't imagine any person, or company, being able to manipulate the price like that."

"You're just a little naive," Harry said as the waiter arrived with their bill on a silver tray. "I'm talking about one of the largest companies in the world."

"And who would that be?" Amber asked as Harry put several hundred dollar bills on the tray.

"Your very own government," Harry answered. "More specifically, the Department of Defense, or one of their more clandestine organizations."

Chapter 32

Once Jim and Amber were back at the hotel and removing the clothes and prosthetics, Gene asked Jim, "What do you think?"

"I think we have a real problem," Jim said as he removed the belly paunch. "Especially if you think Harry will change his mind about selling his contracts before the end of the month."

"I was wondering about that," Gene admitted as he watched the makeup artist remove the wig and wrinkles from Jim's face. "We noticed he made reservations for two of his geologists to fly to Sydney. It doesn't take much of a stretch of imagination to know that he's concerned that the Australian discovery may have some merit. I'm not entirely sure our efforts over there will withstand the additional scrutiny."

"That's not why I think we have a problem," Jim said as he put on his jeans and T-shirt. "I'm concerned that he suspects the manipulation of the market price of the Lithium."

"Did he say that?" Gene asked.

"Not directly," Jim answered. "But he voiced his suspicions that the government, more specifically the DOD, has some involvement."

"I guess that doesn't surprise me," Gene said, shaking his head. "Harry's been in the mineral business for a very long time and has a keen sense about market fluctuations. I'm sort of surprised that it's taken him this long to voice his suspicions."

"What now?" Jim asked as Amber knocked and entered the room.

"I'm afraid we'll have to proceed on the assumption that we'll only get the contract problem resolved through Harry's uncles," Gene told them.

"Do you think we'll have to take care of the problem next week?" Amber asked.

"Probably," Gene answered. "Especially since there's a chance that our Australian discovery ruse will be revealed if his geologists dig deep enough. And, unless we get some latitude regarding the time line from our government agency, we'll have to plan on removing Harry from the equation."

"Assuming we need to enact the final solution, do you still plan on using Jewell?" Amber asked.

"Probably," Gene said. "I just don't think we should use either of you since you've gotten a lot of exposure being around him."

"I disagree," Jim told him. "I think the introduction of another person will place increased emphasis on that individual."

"What do you mean?" Gene asked.

"Let's assume Amber and I take care of the problem," Jim explained. "We can't be recognized as who we really are. And, our false identities are pretty well established with the few people who have had contact with us. We have a history with Harry that shows an amicable relationship that should exclude us from suspicion. Jewell, if brought in, would probably become the prime suspect because she shows up and Harry dies."

"First, let's not forget that the reason we're using the specific poison is because it's practically untraceable," Gene explained. "And, as you know from the past, a single encounter is much less likely to be remembered as to specific details about the person than repeated encounters."

"I understand that," Jim reiterated. "But, since you're going to introduce Jewell as an eye-catching lady, much as you did with Amber, she'll be remembered. Especially with the male population, we'll be encountering."

"But the same thing can be said of me," Amber interjected.

"To a certain extent," Jim agreed, "but you've become a fixture, just another of the familiar faces. Jewell, on the other hand, will catch the eye of every male she encounters. Even the females will see her as a new threat, and they've already dismissed you as a potential competitor for their male counterparts."

"Jim has a point," Gene said, nodding. "Our studies show that a person who has had repeated exposure, especially women, seems to become unremarkable. When a new face, especially an attractive lady, enters the scene, everybody notices."

"That's what I'm trying to point out," Jim said. "I think Amber and I will be the best solution, if it's absolutely necessary, to remove the obstacle from the negotiations."

"How do you plan on administering the poison?" Gene asked. "You'll need some distraction, and I don't think we can count on Amber keeping him from seeing any unusual movement."

"What about having Jewell come into the restaurant?" Amber asked. "Maybe she can come by our table and distract him long enough for Jim or me to put the powder on his food."

"Possible," Gene admitted. "But, the most crucial thing is to be absolutely sure he doesn't notice. Even the slightest suspicion will become a catastrophic failure, and we'll never get the chance again."

"Not to forget that the evidence will be right in front of us, and deniability will be almost zero," Jim said, nodding. "This has to be an absolutely fool proof plan. Up close and personal is always the best way to ensure a positive result, but it's also the most dangerous for the person taking the action. Even the slightest misstep could expose both the person and the organization."

"You're right about that," Gene agreed. "We need this to be airtight. I think we need to find a way to use Jewell as a distraction. And, without a foolproof distraction, we don't stand a chance."

"Agreed," Jim said. "I still remember her performance in Atlanta when she gave me the opportunity to approach our target while his attention was on her."

"Exactly," Gene told them. "I think we can probably have her enter the restaurant and be escorted to a neighboring table. Probably brush against Harry or just a hint of a smile."

"I think it would be necessary to have her slightly behind and to the side of our table," Amber suggested. "That way, he has to turn his head enough that his peripheral vision would not pick up the movement necessary to administer the powder to his food."

"I think that's probably the right approach," Gene told them as he checked his watch. "I'll need to get back to Quantico and game this for the next few days. We may need to enact a slight rearrangement of the tables or at least have the chairs at your table moved slightly to get the right angles. In the meantime, you guys get back to your rooms, and I'll contact you sometime next week with a fully developed plan."

Jim waited to follow Gene from the room, asking, "Can I have a minute of your time, General?"

"Of course," Gene answered. "What's on your mind?"

"There's a favor I'd like to ask of you," Jim told him. "Just a little background investigation on a certain individual."

"Is it connected with the current assignment?" Gene asked.

"Not at all," Jim replied. "This is sort of a personal issue."

"What's the issue?" Gene asked.

"There's this certain individual that's been causing a little problem back home," Jim told him. "He's being a real pain in the ass for Jennifer."

"How so?" Gene asked, wondering what the problem was.

"He's been trying to get her to go out for drinks or go to dinner when I'm on a trip," Jim admitted. "She told me she's tried several times to get him to quit, but so far, it doesn't seem to have any effect on his behavior."

"Just what sort of information would you need?" Gene asked, thinking about what he'd do to any man that bothered his own family.

"Just the basics," Jim told him. "Background on schools, any run-in with the law. Court cases. Anything that she may be able to use to persuade him to leave her alone."

"I'll see what I can dig up," Gene said, nodding. "I'll try to have what you need when you get home tomorrow or the next day. Just don't do anything you'd regret."

"I won't," Jim agreed, handing Gene a slip of paper with Charlie's name and the name of the company. "I'm just going to let Jennifer handle this for now. If I need to have a more formal discussion with Mr. Charlie Weitzel, I'd like some ammunition to fire in his direction."

"Got it," Gene replied, turning to leave. "I'll send you a copy of the report when I get it from research. Now, you head back to your room and get some sleep. We still have problems with the current assignment that require my attention, too."

"Good night, sir," Jim said, turning away. "And, thank you."

Chapter 33

The morning after Jim got home, he was watching the news and drinking his third cup of coffee when the phone rang. "Hello," he answered, wondering if Jennifer was calling from work.

"Mr. Lashley, if you will kindly walk to the end of your driveway, there's a package for you," the voice said before disconnecting.

Probably Rob again, Jim thought as he set his cup down and headed for the door.

As soon as he opened the front door, a nondescript white sedan pulled away from his driveway after dropping a manila envelope out of the driver's window. Not even seeing a profile of the driver, Jim walked across the yard and picked the envelope up.

After looking both ways at the road to see if anyone had noticed the drop-off, Jim went back inside his chair and opened the package. Noticing that it was an in-depth biography of Charlie Weitzel, he sat it on the table beside his chair and went to the kitchen to refresh his coffee.

Returning to his chair and turning down the volume on the TV, he sipped his coffee while he read the history of Charles J. Weitzel.

Charlie had applied to the Naval Academy upon graduation from Mesquite High School over twenty years ago. However, his low grades and scores on the aptitude test kept him from that prestigious institute. Even his rather wealthy benefactor, his uncle, couldn't pull enough strings to get him accepted.

After graduating with a bachelor's degree in accounting from the University of North Texas in Denton, his uncle was able to secure him a slot for Air Force pilot training after completing Officer Training School in San Antonio, Texas.

Less than six months after leaving college, Charlie was removed from his pilot training class for failure to meet the standards required for solo flight. After a formal hearing removing him from pilot training, where he was reassigned to missile training, he called his uncle to request a family hardship discharge.

Having successfully avoided serving in a missile silo for his remaining four years, Charlie joined his uncle's company as an accountant. Now, after almost twenty years in that position, Charlie was still one of the junior accountants vying for the position of head of the accounting department.

Additionally, there were several pages of information showing that Charlie had numerous complaints against him from other women who had previously held Jennifer's position. Several had resulted in the ladies' departure without any fanfare, but some had resulted in payments thinly disguised as severance pay.

Not proven, but highly speculated, a couple of the complaints had resulted in marriage problems and separations. All told, Mr. Charlie Weitzel had probably been instrumental in almost every woman who had held Jennifer's job leaving the company under suspicious circumstances from the first day he had joined his uncle's firm.

I think it's time to put a stop to Mr. Charlie's shenanigans, Jim thought as he quickly reread the data. Checking the time, he knew that he could be standing beside Charlie's car when he would most likely be leaving for lunch.

Slipping on one of his old flight jackets, squadron patches in full view, Jim pulled the 'Vette out of the garage and headed for Jennifer's office. Pulling in and spotting Charlie's car, he parked in the row behind it and waited.

Almost twenty minutes later, he spotted Charlie leaving the building and heading for his car. Jim waited until he was almost there before stepping from his car and approaching him.

"Excuse me, Charlie," Jim said as he stopped beside the driver's door of Charlie's car. "I'm wondering if we could have a word."

Charlie looked at Jim's well-decorated flight jacket and asked, "What do you want?"

"The same thing I thought we had resolved a couple of weeks ago," Jim answered, staring into Charlie's eyes.

"And that would be?" Charlie replied, trying to maintain what he assumed was a defiant posture.

"Leaving my wife alone," Jim told him, leaning forward into Charlie's personal space.

"You just listen to me," Charlie replied, taking a step back. "This is private property, and you have no right to discuss my company or its operation."

Crossing his arms, he continued, "And you think you can intimidate me with your fancy little fighter pilot's jacket with all the cartoon patches? I've heard that you think you're some sort of war hero. Lots of medals and crap. All I think about that is that you were too stupid to stay out of the military and got your ass shot.

And now you think you're a hotshot airline pilot," Charlie said, sneering at Jim. "Well, I think you took advantage of all the money we taxpayers spent on your education and training and then used it to get a job that I bet civilian pilots would be better qualified to hold. If you ask me, you're no better than those people who live off the welfare programs people like me have to pay for. We paid for the training. We paid for the fuel you wasted flying around the country getting drunk at Officer's Clubs. We paid for the bombs and bullets you wasted trying to prove how macho you were. And now, we keep paying so you can sit your ass in the front of an airplane that we spend good money on getting around on our business trips.

Now, if your little wife doesn't like working here in my company, she can quit," Charlie finished. "And, you can get in your little crappy car that my taxes probably bought and get your ass off my property.

Jim stared at him for a moment and finally said, "I came here to ask you politely, one more time, to quit bothering my wife. I've asked before, and now I'm telling you.....leave her alone."

"You don't get to tell me anything, war hero," Charlie said, thinking that he had the last word. "Now, as I asked before, get off my property."

Jim stood with his head cocked slightly to one side and quietly said, "Little man, you don't know what or who you're dealing with. You're what we used to call a polecat. If you don't know what that is, I'll tell you. It's a skunk. A sneaky little creature that sprays piss all over the place when it's scared. You're probably pissing your pants right now, aren't you, scooter. Now, before I get in my car and let you get on with your pathetic little nebbish life as a shoe clerk for your uncle, who is the real owner of this company, I'm telling you for the final time.....leave my wife alone. This ends right here, right now. Or you'll come to understand that real men don't put up with sniveling little skunks like you."

Charlie wisely kept his mouth shut as he saw the menace in Jim's eyes. Seconds later, Jim turned and walked back to his car. Pulling out of the parking lot, Jim saw Charlie slam his door shut and speed away.

Jim had hardly gotten into the house when the phone rang. "Hello," he answered, wondering if Charlie had gone back and said anything to Jennifer.

"I hope the information was useful," Gene said. "Now, maybe we can get back to the business the company is paying us to do."

Smiling, Jim replied, "Very informative. I was wondering what made the short little shit have such an attitude. But, that aside, what can I do for you, General?"

"I've got Jewell and Amber with me," Gene told him. "Can you meet us at that little pizza place for a late lunch?"

"I guess you mean Tomato Joe's," Jim answered. "I'll be there in ten minutes."

Chapter 34

Jim was seated at one of the tables in the empty dining room when Gene walked in with Jewell and Amber. Rising, he said, "Hello, General and ladies. Please, have a seat."

"I ordered tea for everybody if that's all right," he continued. "It should be delivered shortly.

"Tea is fine," Gene acknowledged. "This may take an hour or more, so I think we need to order an appetizer or something. What do you recommend?"

"The calamari is excellent," Jim answered as William, the owner of the restaurant, came to their table with four glasses of tea.

"We also have hot wings," William told them. "Mild or spicy."

"How about an order of each?" Jewell said, glancing around the small restaurant.

"Sounds good to me," Amber echoed. "Do you have any garlic bread?"

"Of course," William answered. "We bake our own bread. Would it be ok to bring a basket of our garlic parmesan cheese bread?"

"That sounds great," Jim said, taking one of the glasses of tea.

As soon as William left, Gene started by telling Jim what the company had determined would be the best approach to distracting Harry. The reason for the meeting would be to work on the timing that would ensure that Harry's head would be turned sufficiently to ensure he did not observe Jim put the spice on his meal.

"As you probably already know, the field of view for the majority of people is approximately ninety degrees to either side," Gene told them. "It is slightly wider, up to one hundred and six degrees in some rare cases."

"You're talking about from where the person is looking, right?" Jewell asked.

"Yes," Gene replied. "If a person, in this case, Harry is sitting where you are and looking directly across the table at Amber, you can plainly see both Jim and me."

"Yes, I can," Jewell acknowledged.

"Now, the vision isn't real clear at the outer edges, but it will detect the slightest motion," Gene explained. "That's nature's way of letting us see threats, something coming for us, to either side of where we're concentrating. Since we humans are predators, like lions or eagles, our eyes are focused on the front. This is primarily to allow us to gauge distance as well as clarity of the focused object."

"Is that why cows have their eyes more to the side?" Amber asked.

"All prey animals have that," Gene told her. "That allows them to see almost completely behind them just by turning their eyes slightly while their heads are down. And you'll also notice that if any two prey animals are together, they tend to stand head to tail. That gives them a maximum view of their complete surroundings."

"I've noticed that with horses," Jim confirmed. "They will stand like that unless they are in a herd of several horses."

"Ok, now that we understand the basics of why we see the way we do," Gene said, bringing the conversation back on track, "we need to explore how to best take advantage of nature to ensure our prey doesn't see our slight motion when Jim reaches for his plate."

"How am I going to deliver the spice?" Jim asked after William left the basket of warm bread and several small packages of butter.

"It's going to be a liquid," Gene answered. "We tried several methods, shaking it from a container like salt or pepper or pouring it from a packet. Every one of them took noticeable movement. Even if Harry turned his head to look to either side, a normal movement of about thirty to forty-five degrees, it was easily observed."

"What if he turns ninety degrees or more?" Jewell asked, buttering a slice of the bread.

"Probably not noticeable," Gene informed them. "But that much of a turn of his head isn't probable given the situation. Even when we placed our distraction at an adjacent table, the normal person would only turn sixty degrees or so. That still meant that any movement within the one-hundred-degree cone is possibly noticeable."

"What's that got to do with the delivery system?" Jim asked.

"We'll use a small three cc syringe," Gene told them, pulling one from his shirt pocket and handing it to Jim. "We tried several sizes to determine which would be the least noticeable, ease of carry, and still provide sufficient spice to do the job."

As Jim was looking at the syringe, William walked back to their table with a tray carrying the calamari and hot wings. "Will there be anything else?" he asked.

"Not for now," Gene told him. "We'll come around to the front if we need anything."

"That'll be fine, sir," William said, leaving them alone.

Taking the syringe from Jim, Gene put the tip in his glass of tea and pulled the plunger back to fill it. "Now," he told them, "it's only about six inches long and can fit in the palm of Jim's hand."

Demonstrating the best technique to hold the syringe, he reached for the pepper shaker on the table in front of him and depressed the plunger as he passed Amber's plate, where a slice of bread was lying.

After picking up the pepper shaker with the same hand that held the syringe, Gene asked, "Did you see what I just did?"

"What?" Jewell asked. "You held the syringe and also the pepper. I don't get it."

Setting the pepper shaker down, Gene opened his hand and showed them the empty syringe. "If you look at Amber's bread, you'll see a wet spot spreading across it."

As Amber picked the bread up, Gene continued, "And that was in full view of each of you. Did any of you notice that I squirted the tea onto her bread?"

As each of them shook their heads, he told them, "The key is in the expected movement and any slight distraction. Even without the distraction, we probably would be able to administer the required dosage."

Letting them think about what they had just seen, or more aptly, not seen, Gene announced, "Now, let's try that again. This time, I want you to try to catch me."

Gene refilled the syringe and hid it in his hand before looking at Amber and nodding. As he reached for the pepper shaker, Amber scooted her chair back slightly, causing a slight scraping sound. As soon as he pulled the pepper shaker back, he asked, "Did either of you notice when I dispensed the liquid?"

Looking at Jewell and then Gene, Jim answered, "No, I didn't."

"Me neither," Jewell admitted. "I thought you were going to do it when you reached for the pepper."

"Me, too," Jim said. "You must have done it when Amber moved her chair."

"That's exactly right," Gene told them. "Even the slightest distraction will cause your eyes to momentarily shift to the movement in your peripheral vision. That's what has kept man alive when he was being stalked. Or what makes the prey animal immediately turn to see what any slight movement is."

"How do you plan on providing the distraction?" Amber asked.

"Much the same as what I asked you to do before we picked up Jewell," Gene answered. "But we'll be a little less subtle. In this case, Jewell will be escorted to the table directly behind you."

"How do we assure she will be seated at that table?" Jim asked.

"That's already arranged," Gene answered. "You remember the waiter we said would be there? He's been notified that Jewell will be dining there, and an anonymous caller will make the reservation for both of them. He will ensure that the table beside yours will be vacant until her arrival."

Chapter 35

Gene handed Jim the syringe and said, "Now, you try it."

"Will she be there when we arrive?" Jim asked as he filled the syringe with tea.

"No, she'll arrive after your meal is delivered," Gene answered. "That way, we get the maximum distraction, and Jewell is only there for a couple of minutes."

Watching Jim toy with the syringe, Gene suggested, "Grip it like a dagger. Have the body in your palm and hide the extended plunger along your thumb. That gives you the maximum concealment and minimizes the movement required to dispense the liquid."

"How thick is the liquid?" Jim asked as he repositioned the syringe in his hand.

"Slightly thicker than the tea you're using," Gene answered. "We tried several concentrations to see which one would deliver a lethal dose and still keep the viscosity low enough to make the fluid easy to dispense with minimal effort. Another factor was color. We decided that a slight tan tint would match most curry dishes. The most important factor was what would be a lethal dose for someone Harry's size. After several experiments, we determined that a little under one cc would be sufficient. So, If you can manage to empty the syringe into one of the dishes he orders, and he eats at least half of it, he'll never see the sun rise again. "

Jim squirted the tea back into his glass and refilled the syringe as he asked, "Do I need to completely fill the syringe?"

"No," Gene answered. "That is a three-cc syringe identical to the one you'll be using. It will be preloaded, of course, with slightly less than two cc's. That makes the plunger only half extended, therefore easier to conceal."

Squirting half of the tea back into the glass, Jim said, "OK. Let's see how well I manage to do this."

"Before you do, let's stage the area," Gene said, sliding his chair back. "At the restaurant, you will be to Harry's left and Amber to his right, just as we're sitting now. Jewell, please move to the table behind Amber and sit facing the same direction as I am."

Once Jewell had taken her seat, Gene directed, "Now, when I turn and look in her direction, I'm not quite facing her. But my eyes are turned further to the right even though my face is pointed to Amber. Now, here's a critical point. Amber, you have to give Jim the signal when my eyes are focused on Jewell. All Jim can see is that my head is turned. Turning the head doesn't necessarily mean the eyes are directed away."

Placing a small piece of bread on the plate in front of him, Gene directed Jim, "Your concentration must be on where you're dispensing the liquid. It has to be on any portion of the dish where it won't be noticed. And, it must be something that will absorb the liquid instead of it being noticeable on the plate."

Gene turned his head to Amber and reiterated, "Slightly nod at Jim when I look at Jewell."

As Gene shifted his eyes further to his right to look directly at Jewell, Amber gave an almost imperceptible nod. Jim moved his right hand from his lap, and Gene turned to him, saying, "Another thing, Jim. You have to move the syringe from your lap when you see Jewell approach her table from behind Harry. Just reach for your napkin, which should be in your lap, where I'd recommend you position the syringe after you take your seat and palm it. When Harry's head starts to turn, place your hand beside your plate and be ready for Amber to give the signal. Now, with your hand by your plate, let's do this again."

Jim put his hands in his lap and waited for Gene to turn back toward Amber. As his head began to swivel, he put his hand on the table beside the plate in front of him and waited. As soon as Amber saw Gene's eyes shift, she repeated the subtle nod. Jim looked directly at the small piece of bread and slid his arm so that the tip of the syringe was directly over it. Depressing the plunger, the tea hit the plate beside the bread and splattered.

"That's what we're here to work on," Gene said, turning back. "Not only do you have to hit the target, in this case, the piece of bread, you have to keep from using too much force. Otherwise, you will splash either the liquid you're squirting out of the syringe or the liquid you're aiming at."

"Let's start over," Jim said, refilling the syringe to the two cc mark. "I'm going to do a couple of practice squirts. I know I was overly aggressive on that one."

Jim repeatedly filled and dispensed the tea several times as they watched. "Now, how much different will the pressure be when I use the mixture?" he asked as he managed to squirt the liquid back into the glass with little noticeable effect on the tea.

"Only slightly more," Gene answered as he observed Jim's technique. "Combined with the stress of the moment, I don't think you'll notice it. Just remember, you probably have a couple of seconds, so don't rush. Amber will be watching Harry's eyes, and if he starts to shift back to you guys, she'll let you know."

"If I see Jim hasn't completely emptied the syringe, I'll do something to keep his attention in my direction," Amber suggested.

"Good idea. All right, let's try it again," Gene said as Jim partially filled the syringe and put it in his lap.

Just as Gene started turning his head, William walked in and asked, "Anything else, folks?"

Jim took the opportunity to lift his hand and deliver a perfect shot onto the bread as Gene said, "I don't think so. Could you please bring the check?"

Turning back to Jim, he said, "OK. Ready?"

Jim smiled and replied, "I'm done. Unnoticed?"

Gene looked at the empty syringe beside Jim's plate, smiled, and said, "Excellent. We can plan and practice, but the key is the ability to react to any opportunity."

Amber winked at Jim and said, "I think we'll make a good team, don't you?"

As William brought the check to the table, Gene took it and said, "If you ladies will give Jim and me a few moments, I'll get everybody headed home."

As soon as Jewell and Amber had left, Gene asked, "What's going on with this Charlie character?"

"I tried to talk to him this morning," Jim started. "But he went into some tirade about me. That man has a real problem with people that achieved the very things he attempted but failed at so miserably."

"I figured that," Gene agreed. "I've seen it numerous times before. People who don't have the ability or the fortitude to rise above mediocrity carry a huge grudge against anyone who accomplishes what they couldn't. Either it's a college degree they failed to obtain, a position they don't get within their field of expertise, or any facet of their lives where they see others that they consider less worthy surpass their achievement."

"That seems to be the case here," Jim agreed. "But he seems to be hell-bent on proving that he's some sort of ladies' man. I'm not sure exactly how many women he's harassed, but I know from what Jennifer has told me about how he tries to pressure her; she's not the first."

"I gathered that from the report," Gene said, nodding. "I'm going to do a little more research on the women that previously held Jennifer's position, as well as any other sudden departures involving a female. I'll be willing to bet that little Charlie has tried to stretch his tentacles further than an adjoining desk, so to speak."

"I appreciate that," Jim said as they turned to leave the dining room.

Gene stopped quickly and asked, "Just what do you plan on doing? I sincerely hope you're not considering confronting him or threatening him in any way."

"I'm not sure yet," Jim confessed. "I was so pissed this morning that I may have said something. But I still hope that he realizes that I'm not going to sit by and let him make Jennifer's life hell there at the company."

"Give me a couple of days," Gene said as they started again for the door. "I'll also look into the company and see if we can't use some leverage to convince Charlie's uncle that he has a real problem on his hands. I sure don't want you involved in anything that would possibly disrupt our plans."

"I'll give you a couple of days," Jim said, looking directly into Gene's eyes. "But, if it's not resolved by the time I get back from the next trip, I'll make sure Jennifer or any other woman Charlie sets his sights on won't be bothered."

Chapter 36

Jim was sitting in the living room watching the news when Jennifer came in from the garage and called, "Hey, you. I need a drink. Would you come make us a Jack and Coke while I slip into something a little less formal?"

"Not a problem," Jim said, getting up. "I was just thinking about that myself."

He had just finished pouring the small splash of Coke that they both deemed sufficient when she came in wearing a pair of cutoff jeans and a T-shirt. Handing her one of the glasses, he asked, "What's the occasion?"

"It's just been one of those days," she answered, tapping her glass against his.

"Anything special?" Jim asked, looking into her eyes.

"Pretty much the same thing," she replied, taking a prolonged sip. "Just that I'm getting so fed up with the crap."

"Quit," Jim said, knowing that she wouldn't. He knew how much she wanted to work and fill the hours he was away.

"It's getting to that," she told him, putting her hand on his arm. "I love my job, but..."

"What happened today?" Jim asked, taking her hand and leading her into the living room.

"Charlie came in from lunch so upset," Jennifer said, sitting beside Jim on the couch.

"How so?" Jim asked, knowing it had something to do with their little discussion.

"He's just an ass," she replied. "And he's starting to make snide little remarks about military people, their wives or husbands, especially anything having to do with pilots."

"We've heard all of that before," Jim consoled her. "Especially back in the late sixties and early seventies. That's nothing new."

"I thought we'd gotten over that," she said, shaking her head. "All of the looks we got, wondering if the cook or waitress was spitting in our food just because we were in the service. Most people don't think that way anymore. There's even a token of respect from just about everybody now."

"Some people just have to belittle everybody that they think has accomplished something they couldn't," Jim said, wondering if he should tell her what he had discovered about Charlie.

"This seems too vindictive," Jennifer told him. "Almost personal. Have you said anything to him?"

"Of course not," Jim lied. "I told you, you're a big girl. I want you to take care of it. But I will step in if you want me to."

"And I've heard some rumors," Jennifer said, taking another big drink.

"About?" Jim asked.

"Apparently, he has had some issues with other women at the company," she told him. "Several people before me have quit."

"Why don't you go to his boss?" Jim asked.

"I'm not sure that would do any good," she told him. "His boss is his uncle, and from what I've heard, Charlie is the only child of his late brother."

"Still, maybe you should say something," Jim suggested. "Maybe his uncle doesn't know what Charlie has been doing."

"I don't see how he can't," Jennifer argued. "How can he not know when so many people have left the job?"

"I'm sure Charlie has an answer for every complaint," Jim replied. "Guys like him always have an excuse for why people quit instead of standing up for themselves. It's up to you, but I think you should confront Charlie directly when someone else hears. Maybe then his uncle can't deny it."

"He never says anything out of line when there's anyone else around," Jennifer explained. "He'll always smile and say things like That's a nice dress, or You look happy today. Nothing that would seem out of place except that I know how he thinks."

"I've known pilots like that here in the airlines," Jim agreed. "It's not so much the exact words but the insinuation. That and the leering smirk. Some guys just think they can say or do anything. And it's not just the pilots, most of whom just want to do their jobs. Some of the male passengers even seem to think they have carte blanche to say anything to our female Flight Attendants."

"I'm sure of that," Jennifer said, getting up and heading into the kitchen. "Refill?"

"Right behind you," Jim answered, rising and following her. "Speaking of behinds....."

Jennifer turned and smiled at him, saying, "Are you insinuating anything, Colonel Lashley?"

"No insinuation intended," Jim said, smiling as he set his glass on the counter and put his arms around her waist. "Just plain outright admiration."

Jennifer put her glass on the counter and put her arms around his neck, saying, "You always were a butt man, Jim Lashley."

"Ever since I learned what the word callipygian meant," Jim told her as he pulled her close.

"I think you invented that word to describe what you liked," she said as she kissed him. "And I think you're trying to distract me."

"Me?" Jim asked mockingly. "Why would I want to distract you?"

"I don't know," Jennifer said, looking into his eyes. "Something I've heard you and General Barker say a few times."

"What's that?" Jim asked, smiling at her.

"Misinformation, misdirection, fabrication, distraction," Jennifer told him with a glint of humor in her eyes. "Does that sound familiar?"

"I may have heard those terms once or twice," Jim answered, seeing the familiar seductive look. "Maybe it had to do with false advertising on television?"

"Oh, I think you boys were discussing something besides advertising," she said, running one of her hands down the back of his neck. "You guys think you're sooooo secretive. I've been around you two for too long. I don't know everything you boys do when you get together but don't think you're fooling me completely. And before you say classified or need to know, here's something you do need to know."

"What's that?" Jim asked, slightly stunned that she suspected there was more to his life than being an airline pilot.

Pushing him slightly away and walking out of the kitchen, she turned her head, smiled at him, and said, "I'm taking a shower, and I just may need a hand with something."

Chapter 37

The next morning, after Jennifer left for work, Jim headed north to Sunnyvale and the Kearney Feed Store. There, he picked up a thirty-five cc syringe and a two-inch long ten gauge needle. Along with them, he added a box of sterile vinyl gloves, a pair of cotton work gloves, a handful of sterile masks, and a box of square gauze bandages. After paying cash for his purchases, he tossed his purchases into the seat of his truck and drove further north to Allen.

Arriving at Cabela's, he wandered about the store for a few minutes until he found the bow and arrow hunting department. There, he found a small bottle of Moccasin Joe Skunk Scent. Noticing the label said it was triple strength, Jim smiled and headed to the checkout area.

Back at his truck, he put everything in the bag from the feed store and stashed it beneath the seat. Back in Mesquite, he stopped at the Goodwill store and walked in. Finding a pair of used jeans that he knew would fit and a heavy denim shirt, he carried them around the store until he found a baseball cap and a pair of oversized sunglasses. The final item was a pair of rubber boots that would fit over the black boots that he wore when flying.

The next stop was at the nearby Walmart, where he bought a pair of heavy-duty rubber gloves that reached halfway up his forearms and a plastic container that would hold all of his clothes after making sure it was polyethylene, stamped LDPE on the bottom, and the number four within the triangle. Finally, he stopped by the Renal Art Glass Studio, where he had previously made arrangements to buy a gallon of hydrofluoric acid under the pretense of etching some glassware for an anniversary gift.

Using extreme caution, he put all of his supplies and clothes into the plastic container and slid it beneath the seat on the passenger side. The rubber boots were too large to fit into the container, so he slid them beneath the seat on the driver's side.

After everything was completed; he drove home and called Jennifer at work to see if she wanted to go out for lunch. Hearing that, she did; Jim took a quick shower and was just walking out of the house when the phone rang.

"Hello," Jim answered, wondering if Jennifer had changed her mind or something had come up.

"Got a minute?" the familiar voice of Gene said.

"For you, always," Jim answered. "But I'm supposed to take Jennifer to lunch in a few minutes, so one minute is about all I can spare right now."

"This won't take long," Gene told him. "I just wanted to tell you that we're doing a little more research into the women that have left work where Jennifer is. There are several that have agreed to talk to us, and a couple that told us they had signed nondisclosure agreements."

"How long do you expect it to take to find out exactly what happened?" Jim asked.

"Probably no more than three days," Gene answered. "We've already made initial contact, and everybody except the nondisclosures are meeting with some of our people today and tomorrow. I think we can convince the remaining ladies, including the ones that signed the agreements with Charlie's lawyers, to give us a statement."

"That sounds good," Jim told him. "How many are there?"

"We've located and confirmed that at least fifteen women were either fired or quit due to Charlie's reluctant pursuit. Now, exactly what do you want us to do with the information?"

"First, I'd like a copy," Jim answered. "After that, I'll leave it to you and the company to do whatever you deem necessary to impress upon Charlie's uncle that his nephew has no place within the company."

"Any suggestions about that?" Gene asked.

"I don't know," Jim confessed. "Maybe have as many as possible sign intention to file suit for wrongful termination? Maybe a sexual harassment complaint with the appropriate state authorities? I'm sure there's someone at Black Water that has experience in this sort of issue."

"Probably so," Gene agreed. "I'll look into it. In the meantime, again, don't do anything rash. Just remember, we need you taking care of our company business, not some petty grievance by a nobody like Charles."

"I understand," Jim told him. "But, there's a line in my personal life that I won't allow to be crossed. And, you know damned well you wouldn't allow the same behavior if it was one of your family involved."

"You're right," Gene said. "And, for your information, you and Jennifer are as much my family as anyone. I understand your frustration and feelings about what's going on. But let's put this into perspective. Charlie is a pimple on an elephant's ass, a minor irritant that will be squashed as soon as the elephant can find a tree to rub his butt on. I'm just asking you to give us, me in particular, the time to find the tree."

"I've agreed to leave it alone until I get back from my next trip," Jim replied. "That is unless Charlie forces my hand. I know my loyalty lies with the company, but that's a distant second behind my loyalty to my wife. And even a pimple can become infected and cause problems if not treated. Now, I'll go one step further and tell you that I will notify you if I decide to do anything. I'm not saying that I won't do something, but at least you'll be informed."

"I guess that's fair enough," Gene admitted. "I can't really blame you for the way you feel, and I'm sure you'll be discreet and make sure the trail leads away from either you or Jennifer. Just be sure that if you do decide to do something, it's proportional in measure."

"Not to worry," Jim replied. "I was really pissed after Jennifer told me about what was going on, but I agree with the pimple metaphor. He's nothing more than a skunk that needs to be shooed away."

"Good," Gene told him. "Now that we're on the same page, you go get Jennifer, avoid Pepe Le Pew, and have a nice lunch. I expect the information we have on the additional ladies will be available when you get back home."

"Thanks," Jim said before hanging up. "I appreciate your help and your understanding."

Jim walked out and pulled the 'Vette out of the garage. Thinking back to the conversation with Gene, he wondered about the Pepe Le Pew comment. Coincidence? There certainly seemed to be an abundance of them with this company. But I did bring up the skunk thing. Maybe he's just a fan of old cartoon characters.

Chapter 38

Jim parked next to Charlie's BMW and looked closely at the door handles and the convertible top. Satisfied that his revised plan would be easy to execute, he walked into the building and directly to Jennifer's office.

"Hey," he said at the doorway. "How about lunch with a lonely man who has too much time on his hands?"

"Your treat or mine?" Jennifer asked, smiling.

"Definitely mine," Jim answered as she came from behind her desk. "Anywhere in particular you want to go?"

"I'm in the mood for lasagna," she told him as she took his hand. "How about Tomato Joe's?"

"Sounds good," Jim replied as they headed for the door. "How's work going?"

"We'll talk about that when we get to the restaurant," she answered. "I'd rather not talk around here."

"Now, that sounds intriguing," Jim said, holding the door open. "Clandestine, maybe?"

"You'll find out soon," Jennifer said as Jim opened the door of the 'Vette for her.

The quick drive to the restaurant was silent as they listened to the oldies station on the digital radio/CD player Jim had installed shortly after moving to Mesquite.

Waving at the owner as they headed for the rear, Jim held the chair at the table so that he would sit across from her and have a view of the opening to the room.

"What'll it be, folks?" the waitress asked, arriving with menus and two glasses of water.

"Lasagna," Jennifer replied.

"Same if William's daughter made it," Jim told her, handing back the menus.

"She did," the waitress said, smiling at how quickly people learned who made the best dishes at the little family restaurant. "I'll be right back with some bread. Does either of you care for a salad?"

"No thanks," Jennifer said, taking a sip of the water. "I can't eat all of the lasagna, let alone having a salad and bread."

As soon as the waitress left, Jim asked, "Okay, what's going on at the office?"

"Charlie came into my office this morning," she answered. "He's really upset about something you did."

Realizing that Charlie must have told her that they'd had a conversation, Jim said, "I suppose it has something to do with me telling him to leave you alone."

"Definitely," Jennifer replied. "I thought you said you'd let me handle this."

"I was," Jim said, nodding as the waitress brought a basket of bread and butter. "But there are some things that you don't know about him."

"Such as?" Jennifer said after she left.

"There are several women, as you already know, and some have been paid off," Jim explained.

"How do you know that?" she asked, taking a slice of bread.

"I asked a friend to do some checking for me," Jim answered honestly.

"Which friend?" Jennifer asked, looking directly at him.

"I'd rather not get into that," Jim told her. "That's not important. What is important is that there are several women whose lives have been impacted, and I'm not going to sit by and let him ruin your life or mine."

"Does this have anything to do with whatever you and General Barker do?" Jennifer asked.

"No," Jim answered truthfully. "I'll admit that I asked him to use someone in his organization to check on Charlie because I was concerned."

"What did he find out?" she asked.

"I don't have everything yet," Jim told her. "I'm waiting for him to check into a couple of women who signed agreements to never talk about it."

"What are you going to do then?" she asked, hoping that Jim would let her handle it.

"I'll wait and talk to you," Jim told her. "All I want is for him to leave you alone, but he doesn't seem to understand that I'm not like the other people. I won't put up with his crap."

"Just what did you say that made him so mad?" Jennifer asked as the waitress arrived with their orders.

"I just told him to leave you alone," Jim answered. "But he got rather personal about things. He told me you could quit; he didn't need me telling him how to run his company and how I'm nothing but a stupid freeloader. He really hates military people."

"I think you did more than just tell him to leave me alone," Jennifer accused Jim. "The way he was talking, you made some not-so-veiled threats."

"I never actually threatened him," Jim denied. "I may have intimidated him a little. Maybe called him a few choice names."

"Oh, yes," Jennifer told him. "Something about him being a shoe clerk? Does that ring a bell?"

"Yeah, I called him a shoe clerk," Jim admitted. "Like I said, he pissed me off when he started talking about me and my service as if everybody that wore the uniform were nothing but welfare recipients."

"Anyway, I don't want you to do anything unless you talk to me first," Jennifer demanded.

"I don't plan on it," Jim said, knowing that unless things changed soon, he would be doing something. "But this needs to be resolved this week. That aging Lothario needs to be reminded that the women who work there aren't his property, especially since he's just another employee himself."

As the lasagna arrived, Jennifer told him, "If I can't convince him to leave me alone by the time you get back from your trip, we'll discuss whether or not I should just quit or both of us approach his uncle."

"That sounds fair enough for me," Jim replied taking a fork full of the steaming lasagna. "But all bets are off if he tries to start anything with either you or me."

"I don't think he'll start anything with you," Jennifer said, dipping a slice of bread into the juice around the lasagna. "I get the impression that he'd just as soon never see you again."

"That's fine with me," Jim replied. "But it's his choice as to whether or not I need to show up."

"Not to change the subject," she said, looking at Jim, "just what do you and General Barker do?"

"Not much," Jim answered. "He calls on me to give technical advice sometimes. Mostly, I think he just wants to hang around and discuss the old days.

"Who does he work for?" she asked, deciding not to press any further.

"Some company called Black Water," Jim told her as he blew across the fork full of lasagna.

"What do they do?" she asked, taking a drink of water.

"They provide security for various countries and companies," Jim told her. "Some of the things Gene and I discuss do involve situations when he needs to advise them about certain aspects of an operation."

"Sounds rather boring," Jennifer said as she finished her meal. "We need to get me back to work, or Charlie will have an excuse to fire me."

"That would be fine with me," Jim said, picking up the ticket. "But then he'd hire another woman, and this little situation would never be fully resolved."

"You really want to nail him, don't you?" she asked as they headed for the door.

"Even if he wasn't bothering you, I'd want to stop him from harassing other women," Jim admitted. "Just guess I'm old-fashioned. Men don't get to touch or make crude suggestions to ladies."

"Not even if the lady is your wife?" Jennifer said as she smiled deviously at him. "Maybe you can suggest something later tonight."

"Now that's certainly possible," Jim said as he started the car. "Just don't tell anybody about it."

"Just the ladies at work," she replied as she leaned over and kissed his cheek. "Makes them jealous."

Chapter 39

As Jim turned the corner to his house, a white sedan pulled away from the curb beside his mailbox. As it continued down the street, Jim pulled into his driveway and parked. Walking back to the street, he opened the mailbox and pulled out an envelope with no address or other markings on the exterior.

After opening the garage and pulling the 'Vette inside, Jim carried the letter in and opened it while he watched the news. Seeing the list of women's names, he knew that Charlie had been at this for several years. Looking back at his brief stint in the military, it became obvious that he had been trying to get women to meet with him ever since he had joined his uncle's company.

There appeared to be at least eight women who had demanded something in return for not reporting his unwanted advances or for quitting their jobs. The final page described the plan for lawyers to meet with Charlie's uncle. Once shown the evidence of Charlie's misdeeds, the hope was that the uncle would at least put a leash on him.

Noticing that the lawyers planned on visiting the uncle on the same day that he was leaving on his next trip, Jim assumed that this was an effort to resolve the issue before he got back. Hoping that everything would be taken care of before he left for Baltimore and thereby avoiding the necessity of his plan, Jim called the number now etched into his memory, wanting to talk to Gene.

"Light Industrial Waste," came the familiar name.

"General Barker, please. Jim Lashley calling," Jim replied.

"One moment, please," came the response.

A couple of minutes later, Gene answered the phone, saying, "Good afternoon, Jim. What can I do for you?"

"Just calling to tell you that I got the information," Jim told him. "I told Jennifer that I'd show it to her, too."

"That's perfectly fine," Gene said. "I think it would be beneficial for her to know exactly what our plans are."

"I sort of promised that I'd let her take care of it for now," Jim said. "This may appear to be contrary to what I had told her."

"Not necessarily so," Gene explained. "If you'll notice, there are no mentions of you, me, or our mutual company. And, if you look again, you'll see the letterhead on the last page is from the office of a local law firm."

Jim looked again at the last page and saw that it was indeed from the firm of Carrillo/ Tibbels, P.L.L.C. "I recognize the name," Jim told him as he put the page down. "Aren't they the ones that run that obnoxious TV advertisement, The Texas Shaft?"

"Yes, they are," Gene said, chuckling about the ad. "But they have a connection with our parent company, so they're the logical firm, regardless of their taste in advertisements."

"' The Texas Shaft---I'll put it to them,' or The Wrecking Ball---I'll destroy their day.' Makes you wonder who their primary target audience is," Jim ventured. "Late-night accident victims? Or, maybe spousal abuse clients?"

"Actually, they're primarily criminal defense," Gene told him. "They do handle some accident victims and family law, but that falls mainly to the junior staff. The heavy hitters take on some pretty high-profile clients."

"I'll leave that to you," Jim said. "I just want this over. And, if this is the solution to the problem, I'll take either one, the Texas Shaft or the Wrecking Ball."

"Of course," Gene agreed. "Right now, one of the lawyers, not sure if it's the Texas Shaft or the Wrecking Ball, or both, will meet with the uncle day after tomorrow and present him with a proposal. The uncle's choice will be to expect a joint civil lawsuit filed by all of the women on the list for sexual harassment and wrongful termination or to ensure that there will be no further incidents with Charlie. How he handles his personnel problems will be left to his discretion."

"That sounds good," Jim agreed. "I'll tell Jennifer what the plan is when she gets home tonight. I think she'll agree that this is the best approach."

"I hope so," Gene told him. "Again, I want to avoid any confrontation between you and Charlie. I just don't see any benefit to you in that scenario."

"Oh, I think I'd benefit," Jim argued. "I'd love to punch that little weasel in the face. Seeing him prostrate on the ground beside his beloved little Beemer would be a great benefit to my feeling of justice."

"I understand the feeling," Gene agreed. "But, think of the possible ramifications. Both to you, Jennifer, and our mission. We have higher aspirations for you than knocking some minor irritant on his ass.”

“I promised to give you until we get done with Baltimore,” Jim replied, nodding. “But, if Charlie’s reaction isn’t to go softly into that good night, I may need to reevaluate my response.”

“I’m sure you have a plan in place for that event,” Gene told him. “I’m just asking that you make sure nothing interferes with our current operation. We’ve invested too much time, money, and effort in this. Not to mention, it must be resolved this week.”

“You have my word on that,” Jim told him. “If I even think there’s the slightest thing that would derail our negotiations, I’ll give Mr. Charles a very wide berth.”

“That’s good enough for me,” Gene agreed. “Do you have any questions about Baltimore?”

“Not really, not unless something’s changed,” Jim answered.

“Some minor adjustments,” Gene told him. “But we do need to ensure that you guys go to Lumbini for dinner that night. We’ve got our waiter on staff that night and have a backup plan should any of you fail to make it to the restaurant.”

“That shouldn’t be a problem,” Jim said, nodding. “I’m pretty sure if Maria suggests that she’d like to go back there, Harry will trip over his tongue, calling ahead for a table.”

Laughing, Gene replied, “No doubt. I just wish I could be there to see what he thinks of Jewell when she walks in and sits at the table next to you.”

“It’ll probably stop his heart,” Jim said with a slight smile. “Yes, I think it’ll be absolutely heart-stopping.”

That evening, when Jennifer got home, Jim mixed them both a drink while she changed into a pair of shorts and a tank top. When she came into the living room, Jim handed her the papers he had gotten from Gene along with her drink. "Read these," Jim said as she sat beside him.

As soon as she had finished the last page, he asked, "What do you think?"

Jennifer took the page that listed all of the women and said, "I didn't know that there were this many. It's almost unbelievable."

"It appears that he's been an ass ever since he was hired," Jim agreed. "And I have a little more information on Mr. Charlie that explains his attitude toward me and any other pilot."

"What's that?" Jennifer asked, looking at the page from the law firm.

"He tried to be an Air Force pilot but washed out of the program," he answered. "Then his uncle stepped in and got him out of his obligation due to family issues."

"So, he wanted to be a pilot but couldn't make it?" Jennifer asked incredulously. "I guess he resents anybody he feels is more successful or capable than he is."

"I believe you're correct there," Jim said, taking a drink. "Now, he's turned his failure into a bitter disdain for those that succeeded. I ran into several of those before I retired. Always resentful of people who accomplished what they couldn't. The worst thing is, they let it influence the rest of their lives."

"And they make it miserable for everybody else," Jennifer agreed as she held the letter from Carrillo/Tibbels. "Now, what do you think these lawyers are going to do? Did they really get all of these women to agree to sue Charlie and the company? And how did they find them so quickly?"

"To be honest," Jim answered, "I don't think they all agreed to sue. I'd be willing to bet that the lawyers just researched everybody that was ever employed there, separated the females that no longer were there, and compiled the list."

"So, you don't think they really intend to sue?" she asked, looking again at the list of names.

"I'd be willing to bet that it's more bluff than anything," Jim said. "I'm sure the lawyers could get several of the women to join a suit, but I sincerely doubt that they've gotten all of them to sign on to a lawsuit. Especially those that signed nondisclosure agreements, or whatever it was when they were paid to leave."

"What do you think I should do with this information?" she asked, laying all of the papers on the couch between them.

"I believe the plan is for the lawyers to contact Charlie's uncle in a couple of days," Jim answered. "I think you should wait until they've had a chance to talk to him and let him decide what to do with his nephew."

"What if I told his uncle that I was going to join the lawsuit?" she asked, pointing to the list of women.

"Then, you'd have to explain how you got this information," Jim told her. "I still think it would be best to just let the lawyers handle it for now. I'm pretty sure Charlie's uncle doesn't want the expense or negative publicity of the lawsuit. But, if the problem isn't resolved before I get back, then I think we should both go to the uncle and explain the situation. But I'll still let you decide."

"You're probably right," she agreed. "Plus, if I took these papers to the uncle, Charlie would know that I was trying to cause problems. That would certainly make things worse."

"No doubt," Jim said, smiling. "Then, I don't know who he'd hate the most, you or me."

"Oh, I think he'll hate you more than anybody," she told him, laughing. "You have the tendency to piss people off just by being around."

"Really?" he asked, smiling. "I always thought most people loved and admired me."

"Some do," she agreed. "But you and every fighter pilot I've ever met have an ego problem that is impossible to overlook."

"Ego? Me?" Jim said, gathering their glasses to make another drink. "I'm just a shy, bashful, unassuming country boy."

"Maybe thirty years ago," she said, following him into the kitchen. "Now, not so much. I think that little country boy died on that hill in Vietnam with all of his friends. What survived is much different. The only thing shy about you now is you're still a little bashful when you're around ladies you don't know."

"Is that such a bad thing?" Jim asked, handing her a drink.

"Not at all," she said, smiling. "I'm pretty impressed with the man that came home. I'm sure the boy that went up that hill was a nice kid, but he's barely a shadow of what came down."

"I'm glad you feel that way," Jim said, putting his arm around her as they headed back to the living room. "Now, how'd you like the rare chance to mattress wrestle a poor veteran who has a slight ego problem?"

"Rare?" Jennifer replied, changing directions toward the bedroom. "Rare would be the day that you don't want to mattress wrestle... or whatever you decide to call it that day."

Chapter 40

The next morning, Jim took a roll of black electrical tape and a roll of white waterproof first aid tape out to his truck. After cleaning both the front and rear license plates with an alcohol solution, he used the two rolls to alter the letters and numbers. Satisfied that the revised plates would pass unless closely inspected, he sprayed a little water on each and blew ashes from his barbeque grill on them. Now, they looked like the dusty plates and bumpers that were on most of the local pickups driving around the dirt and gravel roads in the area.

After rechecking all of the things he hoped he wouldn't need when he returned from Tucson in two days, he went inside to pack his suitcase for the upcoming trip. Everything ready, he took a book he had been reading and tried to concentrate on the story. Failing that, he tossed the book on the end table and headed out to the garage. Hoping to catch Charlie at the office, he started the 'Vette and headed there. Not wanting to have a repeat of the last encounter, he planned on trying to talk to him calmly and rationally.

Pulling into the parking lot, he shut off the engine and was climbing out of the car when Charlie came out of the building. Seeing Jim's car, he headed directly toward him.

"Just the man I need to talk to," Charlie said as he got closer.

"Good," Jim answered. "I was hoping we could clear up a little misunderstanding."

"What misunderstanding?" Charlie asked when he stopped just inches from Jim. "I don't think there was any misunderstanding unless you don't understand English."

Jim backed up a foot and replied, "Look, I didn't come here to rehash our last conversation. I just wanted to apologize for letting things get out of hand."

"You certainly need to apologize," Charlie said, taking another step toward Jim. "And I suspect that you're behind what's going on with my uncle."

"I don't know anything about your uncle," Jim said, taking another step back. "I just don't want any animosity between us. My wife loves working here, but you need to leave her alone. That's all I'm asking."

"And I suppose you don't know anything about some fancy lawyers coming to see us tomorrow?" Charlie sneered. "Just a coincidence?"

"I don't know anything about that," Jim lied. "I'm not interested in anything except the situation involving my wife. As I've tried to explain, she loves her job here, and I want her to be happy. She's concerned that your attitude toward her will eventually cause her to leave. I don't want that. And I don't think you really want that either."

"You have no idea about what I want," Charlie argued. "And I think I made it perfectly clear the last time that you're not welcome here. About you not knowing anything about the lawyers, I don't believe you. It's just too convenient; we have an argument, and lawyers show up."

"Why would I know anything about that?" Jim asked, wondering if the real purpose of their visit had been leaked to Charlie.

"A potential lawsuit about wrongful terminations?" Charlie tried to explain. "Just days after I tell you that your little wife can quit if she doesn't like it here, these sleazy lawyers send us a notice that there's some problem with recent personnel changes. Don't try to deny that you had nothing to do with that."

"How the hell would I know anything about personnel changes?" Jim argued, shaking his head. "The only personnel that I'm concerned with is my wife. I don't care about who quit, got fired, or resigned for whatever reason. If you have an issue with whomever these lawyers are representing, I suggest that you talk to them."

"I plan to do just that," Charlie said. "And, I plan on finding out if you had a hand in any of this. And, if you did, you can expect that our lawyers will be coming to see you."

Jim held his hands up and replied, "Look, Charlie, I didn't come here to argue. I'm sorry if there's a problem with some former employees. But, once again, I'm just concerned with my wife. And, as I just said, she wants to keep working here. And that's impossible if you continue to harass her. All I'm asking is that you leave her alone."

"Who said I was harassing your wife?" Charlie demanded. "Maybe she needs to reconsider what working here entails. I've never said anything that could be construed as harassment. I stop by and try to be friendly, but I guess she's so sensitive that she can't take a mere compliment without worrying if there's some hidden meaning."

"She told me that you've tried to get her to go out for a drink or have dinner with her when you know damn well that I'm out of town," Jim accused. "And she's repeatedly told you no. All she's asking is that you stop asking her. Can't you take 'no' for an answer? Maybe that's why you have legal issues regarding personnel problems."

"I don't think you have any right to tell me how to treat my employees," Charlie countered. "I believe we've covered this before. This is my company, and I'll decide how to treat them. And, as far as I'm concerned, asking anyone for a friendly drink or taking them to dinner isn't harassment. It's just common courtesy to treat my employees to a drink or dinner occasionally."

"I'm not arguing about how you treat other employees," Jim replied, getting angry. "I'm only talking about my wife, who has repeatedly told you she's not interested in having a drink and certainly doesn't want to go to dinner with you. And if she considers your repeated attempts to get her to go out with you harassment, then it is harassment. For the final time, I'm asking you to stop asking her for anything that's not directly work-related. Please."

"And, I'm telling you for the final time, stay out of my business," Charlie demanded, thinking this conversation would end with Jim backing down. "You just tend to your little pilot job and leave the running of my company to me."

"Your company?" Jim demanded, taking a step toward Charlie. "You mean your uncle's company. And regarding my little pilot job…at least I made it through pilot training. Something you failed to do. And I didn't need somebody to bail me out of my commitment to the service, as you did when you were being sent to be a missile puke. Yes, I know all about how you tried to be an Air Force pilot and washed out during the first stage of training. And now, who do you work for? Your uncle! Probably because nobody else would hire a little piece of shit like you. So, don't run your pathetic little mouth about anything that you can't do or about men and women who can accomplish something besides counting beans in the back room of your uncle's company. And even the other bean counters seem to be doing more to get ahead than you. How many times have you been passed over for promotion? And with your own uncle making the choice as to who gets promoted? You can't seem to even manage that. What a pathetic little loser. I've had it with you, shit for brains. One more complaint from my wife, and you'll regret the day you ever looked at her or tried to lecture me. Now, that's something that even a smelly little skunk like you can understand."

Jim turned and walked back to his car, now knowing that Charlie didn't possess the intelligence to appreciate anything other than direct action. His attitude toward him and Jennifer wouldn't change. As he started the car and headed home, he had very little confidence that Gene's plan to send in the lawyers would do anything except further antagonize him. Shaking his head as he drove home, he knew with almost certainty that he would be forced to carry out his plan in two days.

Some people just can't seem to understand how to treat a lady. Especially another man's wife, Jim thought as he pulled into his driveway. Time for a lesson in basic respect.

Chapter 41

Once back in the house, Jim called Jennifer at work and told her that he'd had another run-in with Charlie. Promising to tell her more about it when she got home, he then called 410-546-9378. When the familiar voice announced Light Industrial Waste, Jim asked for General Barker.

"Good afternoon, Jim," Gene said. "What's on your mind today?"

"General, I'm afraid I probably have something to tell you that you don't really want to hear," Jim told him.

"Why don't you just tell me and let me decide if I want to hear it or not," Gene told him.

Pausing for a second, Jim said, "I had another little discussion today with Charlie. It didn't go so well."

"I thought you were going to leave that to us," Gene said, chastising him. "Right now, you have more important issues to worry about. And we can't afford to start over with our program. You know that. Why did you want to open a can of worms that isn't that important?"

"I just wanted to apologize to him for my behavior the other day," Jim tried to explain. "I went there with the intention of showing him that I don't have any ill feelings about him. But, it sort of got out of hand."

"What do you mean 'out of hand'?" Gene asked.

"After he started accusing me of bringing in the lawyers, I sort of told him that I knew about his background in the Air Force," Jim answered. "Then, I made some rather personal disparaging remarks about him and his lack of achievement in anything he's tried to accomplish."

"You just can't seem to leave this alone," Gene scolded him. Pausing for a couple of seconds, he then asked, "What do you plan to do now? I don't believe that you'll ever convince him that what he's been doing will come back to haunt him, so what else can you do? That's why we decided to approach the uncle and tackle the problem from the top down."

"You're right about me convincing him of anything," Jim agreed. "I honestly just wanted to defuse the situation when I went there. I almost begged him to leave Jennifer alone. He's such a narcissistic ass that nothing I say will ever convince him that she has no interest in ever seeing him outside of the office."

"All right," Gene finally said. "I sort of knew it would come to this, knowing you and suspecting that Charlie was too dumb to take the easy way out. I wish the lawyers hadn't shown their hand until you were gone on your next trip just to avoid this exact situation. We've crossed that bridge and need to keep our eyes on what's next."

"I understand," Jim agreed. "At this point, I think the only acceptable resolution is for Charlie to leave the company. Anything else will continue to be a problem for Jennifer. Either he goes, or she'll quit. And as I've already said, he'll just keep on, and another man, or woman, will have to deal with him."

"I know you're right," Gene replied. "And I know you'll never kick the can down the road for someone else to deal with. You've always been sort of stubborn in that respect; it's also one of the reasons I've always depended on you to take care of every assignment we've given you. I guess I shouldn't have expected anything else. So, as I initially asked, what do you plan to do now?"

"Nothing unless things escalate," Jim answered. "I still plan on letting your lawyers deal with his uncle and see if they can't convince him that Charlie needs to go."

"And if things escalate?" Gene asked.

"Probably just a subtle little slap in the face," Jim answered.

"I suppose you've already made plans for the little slap, haven't you?" Gene asked.

"More or less," Jim admitted.

"I'm assuming that I can't convince you to just accept whatever happens with our legal plan?" Gene asked.

"As I said, unless things escalate," Jim told him, shaking his head. "If he does anything to Jennifer after today, the rules change."

"All right," Gene finally acquiesced. "What do you need for us to do? Is there anything that you may need to make sure this can't come back to haunt you?"

"No," Jim answered. "I've got everything covered. I honestly hope I don't have to do anything. I'm going to talk to Jennifer tonight when she gets home and let her know that I'd rather her quit than keep enduring the harassment or worse. But, even if she does, the root of the problem is still there, as we've already discussed."

"If she quits, at least we've gotten the problem out of the personal realm, and maybe you'll let us resolve it," Gene suggested.

"I don't have a problem with that," Jim admitted. "But, as long as that little piece of crap is left to bother anyone, I'll never be happy. Especially with his attitude toward me and other service people. He needs a reality check."

"I suppose you're referring to the little slap?" Gene asked. "Just make sure whatever you do can't come back to you or interfere with our main goal in Baltimore."

"I'll make sure," Jim told him. "I have no intentions of anyone ever knowing what I do if it comes to that."

"Good," Gene said. "Now, is there anything we need to discuss about the Baltimore problem?"

"No, sir," Jim answered. "Not unless things have changed. Between the ladies and me, I think everything has been covered. And, as before, I hope you guys can convince him to take your advice, and none of the plans will need to be taken to the next level."

"I understand," Gene said before hanging up. "But the clock is ticking, and time is quickly running out. I'll see you in a couple of days. In the meantime, use caution with your personal issues."

"Yes, sir," Jim said before hearing the click that meant Gene was gone.

When Jennifer got home later that evening, she tossed her purse on the couch and said, "You've really screwed things up this time."

"What do you mean?" Jim asked, turning the TV off.

"Charlie is ranting about how you've sent lawyers to look into personnel issues and that you've been digging into his personal life," she explained. "And, now he's threatening to fire me."

"At least he isn't asking you out to dinner," Jim said, knowing immediately that it was the wrong thing to say.

"No, I don't think he'll ever do that again," Jennifer said as she shook her head. "Now, I may lose my job. And that's because you can't let me take care of him. You just don't get it. I'm a big girl. I can take care of worms like him. I don't need your heavy-handed method of dealing with a cockroach. Why didn't you just leave this to me?"

"I honestly tried," Jim told her. "I fully intended on letting the lawyers do their thing and leave the rest of it to you. But he took my attempt to apologize as a sign of weakness. When he started telling me how it was none of my business how he ran his company and brought up the pilot issue again, I sort of lost my temper. I know now that I shouldn't have gone there, but all I wanted to do was to try to defuse the situation and let it go."

"Well, that didn't work," Jennifer said, crossing her arms. "Now, I suppose I'll have to quit my job. I certainly can't keep working when he's there to make my life miserable."

Jim stood and put his hand on her shoulder, saying, "Look, I'm sorry I got involved. I just want you to wait for a few days before you make any final decision. I think his uncle may finally open his eyes and see what harm Charlie is doing to the company and how it will impact them if the lawsuit continues. I know you don't really want to quit, and I don't want you to. Please, let's wait until I get back from my next trip. Three more days, then you make your decision. That's all I'm asking."

"Three more days," Jennifer replied, looking into Jim's eyes. "I suppose I can do that. But I won't be threatened by that little jerk. It's gotten to this point because of your involvement. But I'll admit that the real issue is his problem with respecting me or any other woman that works there."

"Thanks," Jim told her, putting his arms around her. "I think you'll be happy with the final solution to this little issue."

"I'm not sure I'll ever be happy there unless he's gone," Jennifer said, putting her arms around Jim's neck. "And I sure don't want to hear about what you and your friend Gene are planning. You've got your three days. I'll just leave it at that."

Chapter 42

The following day, Jennifer had left for work when Jim carried a spray bottle full of water, a roll of paper towels, and his suitcase out to the truck. Checking to make sure that all the material he had bought was still stored out of sight under the passenger side of the seat, he tossed his suitcase on the seat and returned to the house.

A few minutes later, he came back out wearing his uniform and locked the front door. Taking a quick look at the license plates to ensure they still looked authentic, he headed for the airport.

Finding a spot close to where the employee train stopped, Jim took a quick look again at the license plates to make sure the tape hadn't come loose and headed into the small loading platform to wait for the train. As it arrived, he noticed Robert's car pulling into the parking lot. Crap, he thought, I really wished he'd call in sick. But it's only three more days.

Quickly getting into one of the two cars, he hoped the doors would close, and the train would leave before Robert could park and get there. Luck was with him and the train was pulling out when Robert was leaving his car. Smiling to himself, Jim gave silent thanks to whatever power kept him from spending even another fifteen minutes with one of the few Captains that he hated flying with.

Once at the terminal, Jim headed down to Operations to gather his kitbag and check for any changes. Seeing an envelope that contained several new pages for his flight publications, he signed into the computer and printed a copy of the crew list for the flight. Noting that Amber had already signed in also, he left operations before Robert arrived and went to the gate for the flight to MEX.

As he walked down the aisle of the terminal, he watched the passengers and other crew members. Seeing no one that he knew, he continued past one of the many kiosks until he finally arrived at his gate. Seeing Amber sitting in one of the chairs, he walked over and took a seat beside her. "Anything new?" he asked as he leaned back in the plastic chair.

"Nope," she answered. "I saw that we're still flying with the little prick."

"I noticed that, too," Jim said, laughing. "It's the last trip of the month, and I doubt that I'll ever see him again."

"Small blessings," Amber replied. "I'd rather have a bladder infection than spend another month listening to his inane blather about how we should do our jobs."

"That's not a nice thing to say about our illustrious Captain," Jim told her, smiling. "I was actually referring to anything new regarding Baltimore."

"Oh," Amber answered. "I haven't heard anything since we met a couple of days ago. How about you? Anything new?"

"Not regarding that," Jim answered. "I'm just hoping that Jewell makes it. The little syringe thing really needs some distraction to make it work. I'd hate to be caught squirting something into his food."

"No, that wouldn't be very good," Amber agreed. "Have you thought about what you'd say if you were caught?"

"Nope," Jim told her, shaking his head. "What could I say? Here, Harry, I've decided you need some extra spice in your shrimp?"

"I guess there's no answer," Amber agreed. "And, I bet he'd call for the maitre d' and have us held pending someone analyzing his food. No, there'd be no way to deny what had happened."

"The only thing that could save us would be if the waiter the company put there could grab the plate and destroy the evidence," Jim suggested. "I just hope he's paying attention and can assist us if something goes wrong."

"Have you ever had a close call?" Amber asked.

"Not really," Jim answered. "The company seems to plan things pretty well. How about you?"

"Only once," Amber admitted. "It was sort of like this, except I was the distraction."

"What happened?" Jim asked.

"Well, the setup was similar. Except, my partner was supposed to put something in her drink," she told him. "I was supposed to drop my napkin and let the target pick it up. While she was bending down, my partner accidentally knocked her glass over and spilled it."

"That's not so bad unless the target saw something other than a simple spilled drink," Jim replied.

"Well, the target saw the eye dropper my partner had in her hand," Amber explained.

"Your partner was a lady?" Jim asked. "What was the supposed relationship?"

"Our target was lesbian," Amber explained. "She was trying to seduce my partner. I was supposed to be an old short lived affair, but now just friends."

"Wow, that's a little different," Jim said, shaking his head. "But I guess that's not so abnormal these days."

"No, you'd be surprised at how many women running businesses are open to that sort of relationship," Amber said, noticing that Jim was truly astonished.

"I suppose so," Jim said, nodding. "I guess it's like you Flight Attendants. I know there are lots of guys back there that prefer their own kind. I guess I never thought much about the female side of things, especially in a business atmosphere."

"Oh, there are several female Flight Attendants that only want another female, too," Amber said, nodding. "Lots of intrigue happening behind those closed cockpit doors."

"I've heard about two ladies finding out that their 'boyfriend' was the same guy," Jim told her, smiling. "I'd hate to be caught in the middle of a female versus female over another female dispute."

"Why would that be any different than two guys over another guy?" she asked. "Isn't that the same thing?"

"Of course," Jim said, defending his position. "I was more referring to two women fighting over a man. Or two straight male Flight Attendants fighting over a woman."

"I don't think it matters," Amber argued. "Two of any people that find out that they're being cheated on will have the same issues."

"You're probably right," Jim admitted. "I just never thought about the same emotional aspects being there."

"That's because you don't have to deal with the drama in the back of the airplane," Amber explained. "I'll bet that there are more than the occasional drama issues up there in the cockpit.”

“Not really,” Jim told her. “There are a few comments about ex-wives or girlfriends, but I haven’t heard much about personal issues. I know there are a couple of alternate lifestyle guys I’ve flown with. But they pretty much keep their private lives to themselves.”

“That’s because most of you pilots are such macho, egotistical prima donnas,” Amber remarked as Robert walked up.

“You must be talking about our former military members,” he said as he looked from her to Jim. “Most of us that came up through the civilian system don’t have that stick on our shoulders. But, be that as it may, we need to get on board, and I’ll brief you guys on the trip down to Mexico.”

As Robert walked away, Jim whispered, “That’s because guys like him have no reason to have a big ego. I want to hear about what happened when your partner spilled the drink that we were talking about.”

“Not much,” Amber said, following Jim down the jet bridge. “She just said she was using some artificial sweetener in her tea. Then she asked if the target would like to try it when the waiter brought her another glass.”

“Did she?” Jim asked as they got to the airplane.

“Yes, she did,” Amber answered. “I think she’d have said yes to anything my partner suggested. She was really interested in her.”

“Sounds like attractions work either way,” Jim said as he tossed his suitcase in the forward closet.

“Sure does,” Amber replied. “And, I’ll bet we all act according to some hormonal program. Regardless of our attraction, we all act like rabbits in heat. I’ll bet that even you have your moments.”

"More than moments," Jim admitted as he put his flight bag in the cockpit. "But I'm more like a bunny in need of constant petting. And I know my wife would turn me into a little eunuch bunny if I ever let another woman pet me."

Chapter 43

The trip to Mexico City and back was uneventful, arriving at DFW exactly on time. Once clear of Customs, the entire crew headed to the gate for the final leg of the day to TUS. The airplane they were supposed to take to Tucson was going to be at least fifteen minutes late arriving, which meant that they needed to accelerate the preflight and boarding if they were going to get the passengers to TUS on time.

"What do you think, Captain?" Jim asked as the plane finally pulled up to the gate. "Should we call the dispatcher and get authorization for a faster speed and try to get the airline back on schedule?"

"I don't need any authorization," Robert answered. "As the Captain, I can make these decisions on my own. It's your leg to fly, and I'm directing you to fly twenty knots faster to make it there on time. This is what I was trying to explain to you last week. There are times when it's acceptable to push the speed up, and there are times to just follow the flight plan. I'll brief the Flight Attendants to make sure they have sufficient time to complete their service, but we'll plan on cutting at least ten minutes off of the flying time."

"Even if you cut fifteen minutes off the flying time, that still leaves them over two hours," Jim countered. "And, since it's only a beverage service, that's plenty of time."

"Again, this is where my background in civilian aviation comes into play," Robert chastised him. "I'm responsible not just for the crew but the entire passenger load as well. I believe it's important to make sure the passengers, as well as the crew, know that I'm doing everything humanly possible to get back on schedule. Some of these people are making connections with another flight and need to be reassured that we'll get them there on time."

"What if we request to take off from the east side, like runway 17R," Jim asked. "That would save us at least ten minutes."

"That's a waste of time," Robert countered. "The FAA isn't interested in our scheduling problems. I doubt very seriously if they'd approve of that, so we won't even ask."

"Okay," Jim said, nodding. "I was just thinking of ways to cut a little time off. Just so we can get the passengers to Tucson on time for their connections."

"That's all right," Robert told him, not hearing the sarcasm in Jim's tone. "A few more years with the right Captains, and you'll turn out to be a fine Captain yourself someday."

"I surely hope so," Jim said, trying to hide his disdain. "I know I've got a lot to learn. For now, I better run down and start the exterior inspection as soon as I can."

A few minutes later, after coming to the cockpit, Jim told Robert that he needed to go back to the computer for a minute to check on something. Back at the gate agent's podium, he called the DFW tower to ask for an old friend from his Marine unit. Hearing him answer the phone, Jim asked, "Are you still trying to tell us poor pilots where to go? That's all you ever did back when you were a real Marine."

"Is that you, Lashley?" came the response. "Still pushing iron around the skies, I see."

"Yeah, it's me," Jim said. "Do you suppose you could do an old Marine buddy a favor?"

"Depends," the tower controller said. "What do you need?"

"I'm heading to Tucson, and we're about fifteen minutes behind," Jim told him. "It would really help if you'd give us the east side for takeoff."

"When are you leaving?" he asked.

"As soon as we can get everybody on board and shut the doors," Jim answered. "Should be within fifteen minutes or so."

"I think I can work that for you; what's your call sign?" the controller asked.

"American 944," Jim answered.

"I'll pass it to the ground controllers and get you out of here as quick as I can," he replied. "Semper fi."

"Semper fi," Jim responded. "I owe you a beer."

"At least," the controller said. "See you at the club next week for the reunion."

"Your drinks are on me," Jim said before hanging up.

Jim rushed back down the jet bridge and climbed into his seat just as Robert was finished telling the Flight Attendants that he was going to try and get them back on schedule.

Jim had finished setting up his instruments for the takeoff from the east runways when Robert took his seat and called for the checklist to start the first engine.

The engine had just finished starting when the gate agent stuck her head in the cockpit and announced, "Everybody is on board, Captain. Thanks for hurrying to get us out of here."

"Not a problem," Robert said as she turned to leave. "That's my job: keep the airline on schedule."

Once the engines were started and they had pulled away from the gate, Jim switched the radio to the ground controller and announced that they were approaching the taxiway.

"American 944, cleared to taxi to 17 right," the ground controller replied. "Switch to tower, 126.55."

"26 55," Jim said, switching the radio. "Tower, American 944 for 17 right."

"American 944, you're cleared for takeoff from 17 right, contact departure 118.55 when airborne," the controller said. "And have a good flight, Jim."

Robert steered the plane onto the runway and said, "Your aircraft, I've got the radios."

Jim made a normal takeoff and executed a right turn when the controller directed as they passed five thousand feet. Now, almost fifteen minutes earlier than predicted, Jim smiled to himself, thinking it's better to have good friends who will help you when you need it than all of your weak-ass civilian flying. Semper fi, douchebag.

Once headed west and climbing through ten thousand feet, Robert turned to Jim and said, "I suppose you had something to do with that. And, after I told you we wouldn't ask for the east runways."

"You heard me on the radio," Jim answered. "I never asked for anything. We were given that runway when we came off the ramp."

"Then what was that last remark from the tower?" Robert asked. "How did they know you were flying this trip?"

"Oh, that was probably one of the controllers that I knew back in Vietnam," Jim answered. "I had talked to him earlier about a reunion and told him what I was flying this week. I guess he remembered it."

Robert sat quietly, staring at Jim, and finally said, "All right, I guess that's probably what happened. But, in the future, make sure you don't try to go around any of my orders."

"Wouldn't dream of it, sir. You know us military types, always following orders," Jim said. "Do you still want to push the speed up as you directed or use a normal cruise since we'd probably get there early if we went any faster?"

"Just fly at normal speed," Robert told him, turning away. "I'll tell the passengers that we're going to be on time. You've got the radios until I get back."

"Yes, sir," Jim answered.

Chapter 44

Once in his room at the hotel in Tucson, Jim called home to check on Jennifer and see how things were going at work. As soon as she answered, he knew something was wrong. "Hey honey, what's going on?" he asked, hoping it was nothing serious.

"I've been fired," she said, almost sobbing. "That little prick Charlie came in this morning and told me I had until the end of the week to clear out my desk."

"Did he give you a reason?" Jim asked.

"Not really," Jennifer confessed. "He just said that it wasn't going to work out and that I needed to find another job. He even said he'd write me a good recommendation. But I know it's got something to do with what's happening with those lawyers."

"I don't see how some legal issues could cause him to want you gone," Jim told her. "I'd bet it's more to do with you not wanting to have a drink or dinner with him than anything you've done. And, I hate to say it, but I'm pretty sure some of the blame is because I told him to leave you alone."

"Maybe so, but I'm going to talk to his uncle tomorrow," Jennifer told him. "I want to make sure that he knows what Charlie is doing."

"How about waiting until I get back?" Jim asked. "I'll be glad to go with you to see the uncle, and at least I'll have a chance to explain my actions."

"I don't know," Jennifer complained. "I want this resolved as soon as possible. I just can't believe that they'd fire me. Everybody has told me that I'm doing a great job. What the hell does Charlie think he's doing?"

"I know you're upset right now," Jim explained. "But if you'll think about it overnight, you'll see it differently in the morning. Please wait until I get home. I think his uncle will pay more attention to both of us if we tell him what really happened. Will you do that for me?"

Jim listened to her breathing on the phone for several seconds before she finally said, "All right. I'll wait until you get back. But if he says one more word to me, I'll go straight to his uncle and tell him how I feel."

"Good," Jim said, relaxing slightly. "We'll take care of this when I get there. But if you decide you want to quit, that will be fine with me. There's always another job."

"Not a chance," she told him. "Even if I wanted to quit, I'd never take this sort of treatment lying down. You know me better than that, Jim Lashley."

"I sure do," Jim said, laughing softly. "That's one of the many qualities about you that I love ... and fear."

After saying goodnight, Jim dialed 410-546-9378 and waited to be connected with General Barker. Hearing him answer, Jim told him, "Jennifer was fired today. I've asked her to wait until I get home to do anything, but she's pretty pissed."

"I suppose you're calling me to advise me that you plan on doing something," Gene said.

"Pretty much," Jim answered. "Have you heard anything from the lawyers?"

"Not yet," Gene admitted. "They've just started advising Charlie's uncle of the situation. I think they plan on giving him what they are presenting as options tomorrow."

"I'll wait until I get back to DFW before I make up my mind," Jim told him. "But that little shit needs a lesson. Even if we get some action out of his uncle, I want him to know that I'm not going to sit by and let him treat my wife like he's been doing."

"Please don't tell me you're going to confront him again," Gene asked.

"Nope," Jim answered. "You know I wouldn't jeopardize our mission or myself. He'll never know I was around, but he will get the message."

"All right," Gene finally agreed. "If you need any assistance, let me know. Especially if anything happens that will impact our Baltimore operation."

"I will," Jim told him. "As you've always told me, I've got a plan, a backup plan, and a way out. Don't worry. I'll be on the airplane to BWI as scheduled."

"I'll worry until I see that you've taken off from DFW tomorrow at noon," Gene said. "You know that I'm going out on a limb with this, don't you?"

"I know," Jim said. "And I appreciate it. I also know you'd be doing the same thing if you were me. I'll see you tomorrow night."

The next morning, Jim was waiting in the lobby for the rest of the crew to come down for the ride to the airport. Amber walked up and sat beside him, asking, "Have a good night?"

"Pretty much like any other," Jim answered. "Same flat pillow, rough sheets, some odor that I can never really identify, and nobody to tuck me in."

Laughing, she responded, "I've offered on more than one occasion to tuck you in. So, don't list that as one of your problems."

"I never said there were any problems," Jim said, smiling. "And, you know why I can't let you tuck me in. But if you want to come smell my room, maybe you can solve that riddle."

"I'll let you sniff that out for yourself," she replied as the rest of the crew arrived. "Besides, I'm pretty sure it's the same as my room. And, no, I can't figure out what it is, either. Maybe some exotic potpourri?"

"Only if they buy it in bulk from some third-world country," Jim said as he stood and held out his hand to help Amber get up. "Sort of reminds me of a campfire made with dried buffalo chips."

The trip back to DFW got in ten minutes early due to stronger winds from the west than were forecast. As soon as everybody was off the plane, Jim told Robert, "I'm going down to operations for a few minutes. I'll see you at the gate in a couple of hours."

Leaving his suitcase and bag, Jim checked the computer to see which gate he needed to come back to and headed for the employee train back to the parking lot, hoping he wouldn't run into anyone he knew.

As soon as he got to his truck, he looked around to make sure he was unobserved and started changing clothes. Once he had his uniform folded neatly on the seat and wearing the clothes he had removed from the container, he pulled on the rubber boots and headed out of the airport.

Twenty-five minutes later, he turned the corner about a half of a block from the restaurant where he hoped Charlie would be for lunch. As he drove past, he saw his BMW sitting toward the rear of the parking lot. Making a quick U-turn, he parked beside Charlie's car so that if anyone came out of the restaurant, they couldn't see it.

Walking around the front of his truck, he opened the passenger door, pulled on the vinyl gloves, and donned one of the masks. Next, he filled the syringe with the skunk scent and placed it on the ground beside the empty plastic container. Then he took out a couple of gauze squares and pulled on the heavy rubber gloves. Picking up the syringe, he stepped over to Charlie's car and squirted a small amount of the scent onto the gauze. Wiping the door handle carefully, he then plunged the needle through the canvas top directly above the driver's seat. Depressing the syringe slowly to make sure nothing sprayed out, he squirted the remaining liquid onto the seat and dashboard.

Barely able to breathe from the noxious odor, he put the syringe, empty scent bottle, and gauze squares into the container, tossed his mask and both pairs of gloves in with them, and quickly snapped the lid shut. Putting the container in the bed of his truck to keep any fumes from getting on his clothes, he started the truck and headed away from the restaurant.

Pulling into a quiet residential area a few blocks later, he made sure there was no one outside and quickly changed back into his uniform. Checking to make sure the wind would blow any odor away, he put the clothes he had been wearing into the container with the syringe and other items. Then, he took the bottle of hydrofluoric acid and poured it over everything. Making sure he hadn't spilled any, he sealed the container and left it in the bed of the truck.

Back on the road to the airport, he pulled into a convenience store where he knew he could toss the container into the dumpster behind the store. Wearing the cotton gloves, he wiped the entire container to remove any fingerprints or oil from his hands and tossed it into the dumpster along with the rubber boots he'd also wiped down. Smelling the gloves to make sure they carried no odor, he removed them and threw them into the dumpster.

Back at the airport, he pulled the tape from both license plates and sprayed them to remove the ash that he had tossed on them. After wiping them dry with a paper towel, he put the tape and towel in the trash can before catching the train to the terminal. Once inside, he went to the kiosk where several types of food were offered and looked around to see who appeared to be ready to leave. Spotting one man who was heading back to get a refill for his drink, Jim walked over and spotted the receipt beside the empty tray. Picking it up, he turned quickly and headed for the nearest gate where he could use the computer.

After signing in to the computer, he looked at his watch and saw he had about ten minutes to get to his gate. Seeing that it was directly across the aisle from operations, he printed a copy of the updated trip and walked quickly to retrieve his suitcase and flight bag.

Jim had barely gotten to the gate when two uniformed airport security officers approached the gate agent. Seeing Jim sitting there, they came over and asked, "Jim Lashley?"

"Yes," Jim said, standing. "What can I do for you?"

"Would you please tell us where you've been this morning?" one of them asked.

"Flying," Jim answered. "What's this about?"

"Probably nothing," the officer said. "But could you please tell us exactly where you've been this morning?"

"Sure," Jim replied. "I left Tucson about five hours ago, came here, and now I'm waiting for my trip to Baltimore."

"How long have you been here?" the other officer asked.

Jim pulled the computer slip from his pocket and answered, "We got to the gate about two hours ago from Tucson. Then I went to operations and made some changes to my flight pubs. After I finished that, probably thirty minutes later, I came up to get something to eat."

"Can anybody vouch for your whereabouts?" the first officer asked.

"Not really," Jim acknowledged, handing him the computer slip. "Here's the exact time we got to the gate. Probably fifteen minutes later, when all of the passengers were off the plane, I walked to operations.

I didn't see anybody there that I remember. I made my changes as I said and then came upstairs to eat," he continued.

Taking the receipt from his pocket, he looked at it and handed it to the same officer, saying, "Here's the receipt for my meal. As you can see, it was stamped almost forty-five minutes ago. After that, I went back to operations, signed into the computer, got my bags, and came here."

Both officers looked at the computer slip and the receipt before handing them back to Jim, saying, "Looks like somebody made a mistake. Sorry for the confusion, sir."

"Not a problem," Jim told them. "Can you tell me what this is about?"

"We got a call about an hour ago," they explained. "Somebody thought you had been involved in some vandalism thing. But it's pretty obvious that you couldn't have been there."

"Really?" Jim asked. "Where was I supposed to have been a vandal?"

"Somewhere in Mesquite. That would have been impossible, given the time required. Don't worry about it, sir. We'll make sure the Mesquite police know that your time is all accounted for. Again, sorry for the confusion, and have a good flight," they finally said before leaving.

They had barely left when Amber walked up, asking, "Now, what did those guys want?"

"Nothing," Jim answered, smiling. "They just got some bad information, but I explained that they were wrong. Not a problem."

Chapter 45

After landing in Baltimore, Jim made a quick call to Jennifer after he got to the hotel. "What's happening back there?" he asked as soon as she answered.

"You wouldn't believe it," she said excitedly. "Not only did I get my job back, Charlie has been fired."

"You've got to be joking," Jim replied, smiling to himself. "How did that happen?"

"I got called to his uncle's office sometime around noon," she explained. "Charlie smelled like a run-over skunk. I mean, he stank. It was gross. Then he accused you of doing something, something to do with the skunk smell."

"He accused me?" Jim asked, knowing the answer.

"Oh, yes," Jennifer told him. "He demanded to know where you were, so I told him that you were flying and wasn't sure exactly where you were. Then, he told me he had called the police and that I better find out exactly where you were because he was going to have you arrested."

"Did you still have a copy of my schedule in your office?" Jim asked.

250

"Yes, and I told him I'd go get it, but he needed to do something because I couldn't stand the smell in that office any longer," Jennifer told him, laughing. "I thought the lawyers were about to puke."

"The lawyers were there? In the office?" Jim asked.

"Yeah, I guess they were all sitting around when Charlie came charging in, telling his uncle that you had done something to his car," she explained. "And once he started ranting and talking about the police, they sort of just sat back and watched."

"I'm surprised his uncle let them hear all of this," Jim remarked.

"It happened so fast," she said. "I guess everybody sort of forgot about them once Charlie started yelling about you and demanding that I tell them where you were. Anyway, they were still sitting there when the Mesquite Police officers came in. Then they asked me to get your schedule."

"I'm surprised the lawyers sat there if it smelled so bad," Jim said, laughing. "I wish I could have seen that."

"Anyway, when I came back with your schedule, the officers copied it and left, saying they would call the airport," Jennifer told him. "Charlie's uncle told him to go home and take a bath and then come back with some clean clothes on. That's when they told me to go back to work."

"When did Charlie get fired?" Jim asked.

"Well, it was maybe an hour later," she explained. "The uncle called me back to his office. Charlie was back, still smelled a little, and the two policemen were there. Anyway, Charlie's uncle handed him a report that showed that you'd been at the airport the entire time. Charlie said he didn't care about that; he insisted that if you hadn't done it, then you'd hired someone to spray skunk smell all over his car."

"What did the police say?" Jim asked.

"They said there was no proof that anything had been done to the car," she explained. "They said that maybe a skunk had sprayed the car while he was eating and that when he started the heater, it sucked in some of the odor."

"Sounds like it got rather heated," Jim remarked. "Were the lawyers still there?"

"I didn't see them," she answered. "But when the officers finally left, the uncle told Charlie to leave the office and asked me to stay."

"What did he want?" Jim asked.

"First, he apologized for Charlie accusing you. Then, he asked if Charlie had done anything inappropriate toward me," she told him. "After I told him about how Charlie kept asking me out for a drink or dinner, he just shook his head. And then I told him about being fired yesterday. That seemed to really bother him. Anyway, he told me that I wasn't fired and to please go back to my office. As I was walking through his secretary's office, I heard him telling her to get Charlie in his office immediately."

"That's some story," Jim said, shaking his head. "Is that when Charlie got fired?"

"I think so," she agreed. "I heard just before I got ready to go home that his uncle had given him until the weekend to clear out his desk. Oh, and the best part, he wasn't to talk to anybody about anything. I sort of overheard the uncle's secretary say something about lots of women suing the company because of Charlie. Can you believe it? Charlie fired, and I've still got my job."

"That's great, baby," Jim said, looking at the clock, knowing he had to get downstairs. "I guess you don't need me to go with you to see the uncle when I get back."

"No, I guess I don't," Jennifer said. "But I do want to know if you had anything to do with this."

"How could I have done anything?" Jim asked incredulously. "I was at the airport waiting for my trip to Baltimore. You heard the police confirm that."

"I'm not as gullible as most people, Jim Lashley," she said. "I also know you and your friends, like General Barker, know more about what happens than you let on. For now, I'm just happy that he's gone, and I've still got my job. But we will discuss this more when you get home."

"I'll be happy to discuss it," Jim told her. "I don't know how much I can add to what you already know. Maybe he did hit a skunk, or one just happened to spray his car, like the police said. I'm sure they looked at his car and didn't find any signs of vandalism."

"Maybe they didn't know where to look," she replied. "We'll talk tomorrow. But, in the meantime, thank you. For whatever you didn't do, thank you."

Chapter 46

Jim had just changed into his jeans when the phone rang. "Hello," he answered as he pulled on his boots.

"302," was all he heard before the line disconnected.

Hurrying downstairs, he thought about whether or not he should say anything to Gene about Jennifer's call. Finally deciding that he needed to be honest about what had transpired, he was prepared to tell him everything when he knocked on the door.

Gene opened the door, saying, "Looks like your little diversion didn't delay you getting here. How'd it go?"

"Fine," Jim said as he looked around the room and saw the same makeup artist and clothes from the previous times. "Would you like to hear about it?"

"Not really," Gene told him as he shut the door. "Right now, we need to concentrate on our target. Do you have any questions about tonight?"

"Not unless things have changed," Jim answered as he took off his jeans and T-shirt. "And since I'm here morphing into Billy Pratka, I assume nothing has."

"No, unfortunately, you're right," Gene said, sitting on one of the stuffed armchairs. "We've tried coaxing him in every conceivable way, but he's been steadfast in refusing every reasonable offer we've made."

"How about the uncles?" Jim asked as the stomach paunch was adjusted. "Are they convinced that a sale is their best option?"

"More than ever," Gene said as he watched the adhesives for the wrinkles and mustache being applied. "I'd bet that one of them will make a call tomorrow before noon trying to reopen the negotiations. Maybe they'd even be willing to accept a lower offer than what we initially made."

"And the Australian discovery?" Jim asked. "Still an option?"

"Even with his geologists there, Harry still hasn't disproven it. At least not that we know of," Gene answered. "That's why I think the uncles will accept a much lower bid for their contract."

"What about Jewell? Did she make it in?" Jim asked as the wig was fitted and secured to his head.

"Yes," Gene told him. "She's next door with Amber getting ready. Are you satisfied that you can manage the syringe? Or do you want a couple of trial runs before you leave for Dunnahoe's?"

"I wouldn't mind a couple of attempts," Jim admitted as he pulled on the new pants and shirt. "I'm not too worried about how much pressure to put on the plunger, but I have a little concern with what dish I'll be trying to 'spice.' That will make a difference in how much it may splatter."

Gene rose and took an empty syringe from his shirt pocket, saying, "I don't think it really matters since most of them have some amount of sauce. I'd highly recommend trying to put it on the entrée. That's the most likely to be fully eaten. Although we've calculated the ration so that even just over one-third of the spice is sufficient, I'd prefer he consumes at least half of it."

Jim took the syringe as the finishing touches were made to his makeup and asked, "Where is the actual one?"

"It will be in the limo," Gene answered. "It's taped to the lower portion of the rear seat. You'll see it when you're picked up at the hotel. I didn't want it in your pocket at Larry's. It would be too easy for someone to bump into you and maybe lose some of the liquid. I don't think you'll have a problem putting it in your pocket when you get out at Lumbini, especially since Amber will be getting out on Harry's side. When she leans over to get out, his eyes won't be looking at you."

"That's for sure," Jim acknowledged as he filled the syringe from a glass of water that Gene had brought from the bathroom. "The amazing thing is that he doesn't seem to care if people know what he's looking at."

"He probably thinks the ladies enjoy him looking," Gene agreed as he watched Jim squirt the water back into the glass several times. "Guys like him seem to believe that women dress especially so he can get a glimpse."

"Okay, to come in?" Amber asked as she knocked and cracked the connecting door open.

"Please do," Gene said, smiling at how different she looked. "As always, you are stunning."

"Sure," Amber said, laughing. "Five pounds of wig and makeup, ten pounds of latex across my chest, a corset that would constrict a boa and a wardrobe that would be the envy of any Hollywood starlet. Who wouldn't be stunning?"

Jewell walked in behind her, saying, "I don't suppose you have a photographer handy, do you? I think I'd like to have several shots made for my personal collection. I know I'll never look this good again."

"Both of you are naturally beautiful, with or without the makeup," Gene insisted. "We've just enhanced it."

"Enhanced isn't the word," Jewell quipped as she stuck out her chest. "Dolly Parton would be proud of this enhancement."

"Well, I imagine that you'll have no trouble distracting Mr. Harry Wellington," Jim remarked. "Not to be crude, but you'd distract every male within a hundred yards. Harry might snap his neck watching you walk by."

"Just wait until I lean over and look at him from the neighboring table," Jewell joked. "I don't think you'll have any trouble doctoring his food. Hell, he probably wouldn't notice if you swapped plates, poured a bottle of cyanide in his wine, or dipped his fork in fresh dog poo."

"You just concentrate on your job," Gene told Jim. "Regardless of his interest in Jewell, there's still a chance that something could go wrong, and we'll be caught with the proverbial egg on our faces. Not to mention, everything we've done to get to this point will be wasted."

"Speaking of that," Jim said, returning his attention to the syringe, "what's our backup plan?"

"Show him, Jewell," Gene instructed.

Jewell opened a small black purse she was holding and removed a derringer-like silenced pistol. "This is the emergency backup," she said as she showed Jim the single shot twenty-two weapon. In case anything happens to expose any of us, I'll put one very well-placed bullet in the side of his head."

Jim looked at Gene and asked, "Do you think this is the way to go? Especially if we're sitting in a public restaurant, and with the way she looks, how do you expect us to get out of there?”

“Like she said, this is the emergency backup,” Gene explained. “Should she have to exercise this option, I’m counting on nobody seeing or hearing the shot. Once she pulls the trigger, she’ll just walk past and out of the door. You two will just push your chairs back and leave the restaurant.”

“You don’t think this will be noticed?” Jim asked incredulously. “At the very least, Harry will fall over backward or face down onto the table.”

“Probably,” Gene assured him. “Any attention, and we don’t expect any initially, will be directed to Harry. Much like a drunk passing out, everyone’s eyes will be on him. Or, possibly, on Jewell as she walks out. Meanwhile, you two just get up and leave. By then, I doubt you’ll be noticed.”

“Are you comfortable with this?” Jim asked Jewell.

“Completely,” she answered. “I’ve watched the simulations at Black Water headquarters several times. Dark Water had collected numerous reenactments from some of their overseas assignments, and the subject usually displays no reaction for anywhere from fifteen to forty-five seconds after the shot. Especially when a small caliber gun is used at a very close range, that’s plenty of time for you to exit the table. Probably even the restaurant since attention will be diverted to Harry as he collapses.”

“And we still have a waiter there,” Gene reminded them. “If he sees Jewell get out of her chair, he’ll also provide some distraction. Either dropping a plate or knocking over a chair. Trust us; we’ve gamed similar scenarios at restaurants across the world. We didn’t actually kill anybody during these situations, but our actor recreated the exact movements we observed from Dark Water’s videos and experience. Questioning the patrons later revealed that less than one percent of them could accurately describe either what happened or the people involved."

"And remember," Jewell added, "this is truly an emergency backup. None of us, especially you two, can be discovered. I sincerely hope that I don't have to do anything more than let Harry look down my dress. But we absolutely can't afford to be caught."

"Okay," Jim finally said. "What about our plan up to the point of emergency backup? Do we want to take separate cars, I mean us and Harry?"

"Yes," Gene answered. "We're sure there won't be any reaction to the spice for thirty to forty minutes after ingestion, but we don't want you around when the initial effects start."

"Won't that seem odd since we've always ridden together in our car?" Jim asked.

"Not really," Gene explained. "Amber was briefed on how to provide the excuse for you guys to take separate cars. She's going to need to leave Dunnahoe's and return to the hotel before heading to the restaurant. You'll ride with Harry and meet her at Lumbini later. That way, you can leave at any point after you've administered the spice."

"Kind of you to let me know about this before now," Jim complained.

"Unfortunately, we didn't make the decision until this morning. And I believe you were rather busy before you left DFW," Gene told him pointedly. "One of our gaming situations showed that the lack of Harry having a car brought up the question of how he got there. Granted, that's only important if he collapses at the restaurant. If we need to exercise Jewell's option, we don't want an unnecessary investigation into the transportation aspect. We fully expect any investigation into the shooting, should it resort to that, be inconsequential to you guys."

"That's true," Jewell agreed. "Nobody at the restaurant knows any of our names. Our appearances are so radically altered that recognition will be virtually impossible. And should it be traced back to Dunnahoe's, your names aren't known."

"Even if someone anywhere remembers the Pratka name, or traces you back to the Four Seasons, or questions the limo driver, there's absolutely no way they can tie those fictitious Pratkas to any of you," Gene told them. "Even the cab that brings Jewell from the Four Seasons to Lumbini won't have a clue about her name or even if she was a guest of the hotel."

"Okay, let's say we follow the initial plan. I give Harry the entire syringe, and there's no reaction initially; what then?" Jim asked. "Do we just continue with our meals?"

"Yes," Gene answered. "If there are any symptoms, we fully expect Harry to excuse himself and want to go home. Our research shows severe abdominal discomfort doesn't occur until after thirty minutes or so. That leaves you plenty of time to finish your meal and make your excuses to leave. Having Jewell sitting alone close by is just another inducement for Harry to want you to leave."

"Not to bring that up, but why's she alone?" Jim asked. "A very attractive lady at an expensive restaurant sitting alone will draw lots of attention."

"She won't be there that long," Gene said. "She'll come in about thirty minutes after you get there. Your food will arrive before she enters and walks by your table. So, by the time she comes in, you'll already be eating. Timing-wise, she'll just be finishing her first glass of wine when you're almost finished. It will appear that she's waiting for her companion to arrive before she orders. Nothing abnormal about that."

"I really don't think Harry will be concerned about my lack of a companion," Jewell said, smiling. "When he gets a glimpse of my enhancements, I doubt if he notices anybody else at the restaurant. He'll even be hoping that nobody comes so he can be gallant and offer to be my escort until my date arrives."

Gene looked at the clock on the table and announced, "All right, people, we need to get going. We'll take everybody to the Four Seasons and discuss any other issues on the way over. One final thing: the waiter at Lumbini will notify us if Jewell has to execute the backup. Should that happen, we'll have a car standing by to get all of you away from the restaurant and straight back here. Any other questions before we leave?"

"What about any evidence we leave behind, such as fingerprints or DNA on the glasses or silverware?" Jewell asked.

"Not to worry," Gene answered. "I'm sure you were briefed when you first started working for Dark Water that all of your information in the Integrated Automated Fingerprint Identification System, or IAFIS, was changed to data that would lead any investigation away from you. Trust me, there's no way anyone can trace you through either fingerprints or DNA. Now… anything else?"

Hearing no objections, Gene opened the door and wished them good luck.

Chapter 47

Arriving at Dunnahoe's a few minutes later, they walked in and spotted Harry at his favorite table. Seeing who the dealer was, they knew that Harry would be winning tonight and probably in a better mood to celebrate.

"Any open seats here?" Jim asked as they got to the table.

"I was just leaving," a man told him as he raked his remaining chips from the table. "I think I'll try someone else; this dealer seems to have it in for me."

Amber took the now open seat, and Jim tossed ten thousand dollars on the table, saying, "Chips for the lady, please."

"How are you folks tonight?" Harry asked, smiling and looking at Amber's cleavage. "You certainly look good."

"Doing well," Amber answered. "How about you? Did your week go well?"

"Pretty good," Harry told her, unable to stop staring. "Anything new on buying a ghetto?"

"I'm afraid not," Amber told him as she slid five hundred dollars worth of chips onto the table. "My sisters are becoming quite a problem."

"Why's that?" Harry asked as he placed a thousand-dollar bet.

"They don't seem to understand how difficult it is to deal with the local city government," Jim said as another man at the table took his chips and left. Taking his seat, he continued, "Maria has tried to explain it, but they still act as if we're dealing with our people back home where we have considerable influence with the local agencies."

"I certainly understand that," Harry said, noticing that the dealer was signaling him not to take another card. "I've had a hell of a time trying to find out what's happening down in Australia with the supposedly world-shaking deposit of Lithium."

"I can't imagine dealing with another country," Jim said as he put ten thousand dollars on the table to exchange for chips. "I hate having to deal with even another state."

"But you're involved in California as well as Texas, aren't you?" Harry asked, pulling his winnings and stacking them.

"Yes, that's why I hire lawyers," Jim said, placing a bet. "I'm more of a hands-off type of manager. As long as things are going smoothly and the profits are within an acceptable range, I let the people I've hired take care of everything. I'm much more comfortable just dealing with the folks around Midland and Odessa."

"We've known most of those people all of our lives," Amber added. "They've always accommodated us with just about everything."

"You can get by with that if you never venture out of your hometown comfort zone," Harry told them. "If you want to run with the big dogs, you've got to get involved with at least national interests. I'm pretty much at the top of the food chain as far as global mineral acquisition is concerned. And I aim to stay there."

"Speaking of global, what seems to be the problem with the Australia thing?" Amber asked, leaning over toward Harry.

"Just some stumbling blocks trying to gain access for my geologists," Harry said again, looking down at the top of her dress. "I'm starting to really doubt if there's anything of that magnitude down there. I've never been stonewalled like this before when there was an actual find."

"Why would they stop you from trying to verify their operations?" Jim asked, noticing that the dealer was signaling Harry not to take a card. "I'd think they'd welcome you. Especially since you're in a position to bid on their product."

"That's what makes me think something is hinky," Harry said, signaling that he wouldn't take a hit. "Every other time I've ever tried to verify a new mining operation, I've been welcomed. There's just something amiss here."

"So, what are your plans?" Amber asked, following Harry's lead in standing pat with her cards. "Just give up?"

"I never give up," Harry said, leering at her. "Not when I want something so badly."

"But you seem to have lost some interest," Jim countered as all of them won the hand.

"Not really," Harry replied as he placed another bet. "I'm just going to wait a few weeks and let someone else do all of the leg work. I'll still be in a position to outbid anyone if there is actually enough there to make it worth my while. Which, as I said, I really doubt."

"You told me a few weeks ago that you were negotiating with a large company," Jim remarked. "And you insinuated that it was the Department of Defense. Are you still interested in making a deal with them?"

"I believe I also told you that I think they are the ones trying to manipulate the market," Harry said adamantly. "So, to answer your question bluntly, hell no! Why would I reduce my offer when I believe that they're behind this whole scheme to defraud me? I'll be damned if I let a bunch of government gofers take advantage of me."

"Again, what if the discovery is there?" Amber asked, seeing the rise in Harry's irritation at the mere mention of interference in his business. "How would you react?"

"I'd outbid everybody," Harry said, shaking his head. "I've got a stranglehold on the market without any new discovery. If it's there, and the government wants all of it, then I'll still have the rest of the known Lithium under my control. Hell, if the government buys that contract, my other contracts may even be worth much more. I think I'm in a win-win situation."

"Speaking of win-win," Jim said as he took another stack of chips of winnings. "I think we need to head for dinner. I've taken enough of Larry's money, and I'm starting to think that our kind dealer is in jeopardy of losing his job if all of us keep winning."

"Don't worry about my job," the dealer said, smiling. "My job is to let you win all you want. We seem to always get it back on your next visit."

"And that's the God's honest truth," Harry said as he asked to cash out. "As much as I win, I always seem to give it back sooner or later. Generally, sooner!"

"Yes, but then there's always next week," Jim said, smiling as he and Amber cashed their chips in. "I plan on coming back week after week until I own this place."

"Oh, no," Amber told him as she took the stack of hundred-dollar bills. "Then we'd have to live up here. No way!"

"But you'd get to see me every few days," Harry said, leering at her again. "Wouldn't that be worth it?"

"I can't think of anything I'd like better," Amber said, flirting. "But right now, I'm in the mood for Lumbini's wonderful Indian food! Before we eat, I need to run back to the hotel for a minute. Why don't you boys take Harry's car, and I'll meet you there?"

"That's fine with me," Harry said as they headed for the door. "Just don't keep me waiting. As much as I enjoy talking with Billy, he just can't hold my interest the way you do."

"Oh, stop it," Amber said as their limo pulled up. "I'm sure you say that to all of the women in your life."

"Maybe so," Harry answered as he held her door open. "But I truly mean it with you."

"Don't pay any attention to him," Jim said before closing the door. "Would you please check to see if I brought my medicine when you get to the hotel? I think I may have left it at home."

"Certainly, my dear," Amber said, knowing he was referring to the syringe taped to the seat. "I'll make sure. Now, unless you let me leave, we may have trouble getting a table."

"Never a problem," Harry told her. "As always, I have a standing reservation there. I'll call ahead and make sure they have a couple of bottles of Masseto Toscana IGT open

when we get there. You just hurry and get your cute little
butt over there."

Chapter 48

While Amber made the unnecessary trip to the Four Seasons and went inside for ten minutes, Harry and Jim drove to Lumbini in pretty much silence other than Jim's occasional remark about the checkerboard of burnt-out townhomes and blocks of abandoned buildings.

As promised, the maitre d' at Lumbini was ready and escorted them to a table near the rear of the restaurant. The two bottles of wine requested were on the table when they sat. As the waiter was pouring the wine, the maitre d' brought Amber and said, "I believe you gentlemen were waiting for this beautiful lady."

The waiter pulled the chair out so she would be sitting in the same position that they had determined would be the best for distraction when Jewell arrived. As she sat, Harry handed her one of the glasses and said, "Yes, I've been waiting for a beautiful lady like her for all of my life."

"You're such a schmooze," Amber said, taking the glass. "I really doubt that you've ever waited for anything. You're the type that would chase a rabbit down its hole if you were after it. Even knowing you couldn't possibly fit through the opening, you'd keep digging, trying to find a way."

"You're right about that, my dear," Harry said as they all raised their glasses. "I'm like a bloodhound that's caught the scent."

"The scent I've caught is mouth-watering," Jim said as he set his glass down. "Maria and I decided that we'd love one of the shrimp dishes again tonight. What would you recommend?"

"I'd recommend the Shrimp Korma," the waiter suggested.

"What's that?" Amber asked as she sipped her wine.

"It's jumbo shrimp stir-fried with garlic and ginger paste, then simmered in a tomato and coconut sauce," he explained.

"That sounds delicious," Amber exclaimed. "Anything else?"

"Of course, madam," he continued. "I'd also recommend side dishes of mushroom masala and Aloo Dum. The mushroom masala is thick slices sauteed with tomato, onion, green chilies, red chili powder, curry leaves, and cumin. Very delicious. The Aloo Dum is quarters of potato cooked with onion, tomato, and a mix of savory spices."

"That sounds perfect," Amber told him, smiling and looking at Jim. "I bet you never thought you'd be eating green chilies here in Baltimore."

"I bet they don't know about Hatch's green chilies," Jim said, smiling at the waiter.

"Oh, but we do," the waiter announced. "We order fresh green chilies from Hatch's daily. They're flown from Albuquerque to us every morning. We only serve the finest of ingredients."

"Amazing," Jim said, shaking his head as he reached across the table to take Amber's hand. "We serve Hatch's green chilies on just about everything we cook back home except for steak, of course. But I love it with scrambled eggs. I'll have the same as my lovely wife."

"Thank you, dear," Amber said as she passed the syringe. "I'm sure tonight's dinner will be much better than scrambled eggs with chili."

Harry sat his glass down and agreed, saying, "Might as well make it three. And we'd like mango kulfi for dessert, please."

"By the way," Amber said as the waiter walked away. "You did put your medicine in your luggage. I sat it on the bathroom counter for you."

"Thanks," Jim said as he put the syringe beneath his napkin on his lap. "I was worried that I'd need to get Dr. Alka to phone a prescription up here."

"What medicine do you need every day?" Harry asked as they waited for their food to arrive. "You seem to be in excellent health."

"Allopurinol," Jim answered. "I've developed a touch of gout. Probably from eating too much rich food."

"I understand," Harry agreed, nodding. "One of my vices is good food. Another is a fine wine, such as this Masseto to, and of course, beautiful women."

"I'll admit that you certainly know your wines," Amber told him as she leaned forward, smiling. "Every bottle you've recommended has been excellent. How did you learn so much about which wine goes best with which dish?"

"Mostly through listening to the waiters as I've traveled around the world," Harry explained. "I've found that the wines from Italy are among the best, especially from

Tuscany. Then it's just a matter of understanding that lightly flavored dishes, such as fish or chicken, go best with a white wine. Heavier flavors, such as steak or tonight's shrimp, need a dry red. I especially enjoy a good merlot."

"I thought you said that white wines go with fish or seafood," Jim said as the waiter approached with their plates. "I assumed that shrimp would be classified as seafood."

"You're correct, somewhat," Harry said as the plates were placed in front of them. "Because of the spices, especially curry, I find that the heartier taste of merlot is best."

"It doesn't matter to me," Amber announced as she took one of the shrimp from her plate. "As long as the wine is good, red or white doesn't matter."

Just as Harry was about to take a shrimp from his plate, the maitre d' walked toward them with Jewell following close behind. As they passed their table, Harry paused with his shrimp on his fork and watched as Jewell took a seat at the nearest table. Jim quickly removed the syringe and looked at Amber. She nodded as she watched Harry's eyes to ensure he was staring at Jewell.

Jim placed the tip of the syringe against the shrimp on Harry's fork and smoothly emptied it. Knowing that a lot of the liquid would fall into the sauce, he hoped that there was enough on the shrimp to have the desired effect. Returning the now empty syringe to beneath his napkin, he said, "This is excellent shrimp, and the sauce is unbelievable."

Amber smiled as she knew they had accomplished their role in tonight's mission. She, like Jim, just hoped that Harry would continue eating the sauce that came with the shrimp.

As he turned back from looking at Jewell, Harry raised his fork and took a bite of the shrimp, saying, "Now, that is a very beautiful lady. I don't think I've ever seen such an exotic creature around here before. I can't believe she's here alone. I know I wouldn't let her out of my sight if I was with her."

"Yes, she is beautiful," Amber said as she took a spoon full of the coconut sauce. "Have you tried this sauce by itself? I never thought garlic and coconut would taste so good together."

Jim mimicked her actions and agreed saying, "I think this would even go well with a rare ribeye steak."

"Now you're being ridiculous," Amber told him. "Maybe the mushroom masala, but coconut steak doesn't sound good to me. Harry, what do you think?"

Harry finally turned from leering at Jewell and asked, "What are you talking about? Steak and shrimp?"

Taking another spoon full of the sauce, Amber repeated, "No, I'm talking about how good this sauce is, how it would go with almost any dish, especially fish or chicken. Try a spoonful of it, Harry. Give me your honest opinion."

Harry took his spoon and filled it with the sauce, saying, "I think if you served this with every meal, Jim's gout would really be a problem."

Jim and Amber watched with interest as Harry sipped the sauce from his spoon. Now sure that he had eaten most of the liquid Jim had administered, they relaxed slightly and waited to see if he noticed any difference.

Taking another shrimp from his plate, Harry announced, "I agree with you. There are any number of dishes that this sauce would enhance. Contrary to what you Texans believe, good steak doesn't need any sauce. I personally like Kobe, but I imagine that you guys just toss a piece of Angus on the grill and pop the top off a bottle of beer."

"While I do enjoy a good steak," Jim said, watching Harry's face for any change of expression. "And while Kobe beef is among the best, a finely marbled ribeye from a black Angus is at the top of my list."

"I prefer a porterhouse," Amber said, smiling at Jim. "Grill it on a bed of Mesquite and cover it with sautéed mushrooms. Now, that's a meal."

"You guys need to try Morton's on your next visit," Harry said, taking another spoonful of the coconut sauce. "They have one of the best ribeye steaks around. And they're less than a mile from your hotel. I'd love to treat you there tomorrow night if you're still in town."

"I'd love to try one," Jim said, relaxing somewhat. "We do need to go view some of the property listings that our agent has arranged. But I'm sure we can be free any time after five."

"I'd be sure to be out of the areas you're looking at by five," Harry said as he refilled their glasses of wine. "What if I come by the Four Seasons and pick you up at around seven?"

"Sounds perfect," Amber said as she finished her meal. "If it's as good as tonight's dinner, I can hardly wait."

Noticing the waiter at Jewell's table, Jim said, "Not to rush anybody, but I do need to get home a little early tonight. I'm a little concerned that our California operation needs some minor adjustments."

"Problems?" Harry asked as he watched Jewell talking to the waiter.

"Not really," Jim answered as Jewell tipped the waiter and started to leave. "Just some changes in how we plan on marketing our product."

Jewell smiled seductively at Harry as she passed their table, and Amber announced, "While you guys are finishing, I need to visit the ladies' room and touch up my lipstick."

Harry watched Jewell head for the door and told Jim, "If I'd known she was going to be stood up, I'd have invited her to join us."

Jim smiled and said, "A lady like that would kill you, Harry."

"Maybe so," he agreed as he continued to stare. "But I've got an excellent cardiologist, and I'd have him waiting in the next room with a heart defibrillator."

Moments later, as Amber returned, Harry frowned and rubbed his stomach, saying, "I think I may have had just a little too much curry. My stomach is disagreeing with something. Maybe it's best if I leave you folks and head home myself."

"I'm so sorry," Amber said, showing the proper amount of concern on her face. "Is there anything we can do?"

"I'm sure it's nothing that a little bicarbonate of soda can't handle," Harry said as he grimaced. "I hope you'll excuse me. If you'll handle our waiter and bill, I'll take good care of you tomorrow."

"That's perfectly all right," Jim said as Harry pushed back from the table. "You go on home and take care of your problem. I hope you feel better, and we'll see you tomorrow night."

Chapter 49

As soon as they were back at their hotel, Jim and Amber went directly to room 302, where they knew Gene would be waiting. "How'd it go?" he asked as they walked in.

"I think it went fine," Jim told him as he sat and waited for the wig and wrinkles to be removed. "Amber got him to eat a couple of spoonfuls of the sauce that had the most spice. There may have been enough on the shrimp, but I think the first spoon of sauce would have done the trick."

"Good thinking," Gene told Amber. "Did you have any problems?"

"None," she answered as Jewell came through the connecting door. "Jewell's entry was perfectly timed, and Harry couldn't take his eyes off of her. That made the rest of it a piece of cake."

"That guy is creepy," Jewell said as she leaned against the nightstand. "I've never seen eyes like that except on a snake. I'd hate to be left alone with him."

"I don't think anybody has to worry about being alone with him now," Jim said as he removed the paunch from across his stomach. "Except maybe the mortician."

"How close did we cut it?" Gene asked as Amber started to head next door to remove her disguise.

"Harry was showing some signs of discomfort," Jim told him. "But we had finished most of the meal, and I don't think he'll connect his stomach ache with anything except the curry that he mentioned."

"Good," Gene told them as he stood. "You guys get changed, and I'll be in touch tomorrow. Congratulations, it sounds like everything worked out perfectly."

"By the way," Jim said as he stood to shake Gene's hand. "That little issue with the syringe being in the car could have caused a problem. Amber had to pass it to me in the restaurant, and there was an unnecessary chance that we could have been caught."

"I understand," Gene said as he looked from Jim to Amber. "That's just one of the problems with last-minute changes, such as having to take both cars. Once we determined that we needed Jewell as the emergency backup, the syringe had already been placed in the limo, and it got overlooked. That's one reason we hire only the best. Your ability to adapt and innovate is the key to our success. No matter how much we plan and game the scenarios, there's always a chance that something will fall through the cracks. Now, let's get this over, and I'll contact each of you tomorrow. We'll plan on a debrief later in the week to go over issues such as the syringe or anything else you may have seen. Until then, have a good night and fly safe."

The following morning, Jim was sitting in the lobby drinking a cup of coffee when Amber came down with her suitcase. Putting it beside Jim's, she headed for the courtesy coffee bar and asked, "Need a refill?"

"No thanks, I think I'll wait until we get to the airport," Jim said, smiling at her. "This isn't as bad as the stuff you brew on the airplane, but I plan on getting some Cinnabon coffee when I get rolls for everybody."

"Even our pudgy little Captain?" she said, laughing.

"Even him," Jim said, laughing with her. "It's our last flight together, and I thought I'd try to be nice."

"You're sure you didn't have just a little left in that syringe, are you?" she asked, walking back to where Jim was sitting.

"As much as I dislike him, and as much as I feel sorry for anybody that ever has to fly with him, I'd never do such a thing," Jim answered.

"Maybe just enough to make him a little sick? Just a drop or two on his Cinnabon?" she replied, smiling deviously.

"Oh, I've heard the stories about how you Flight Attendants put a few drops of Visine in the coffee you give people you don't like," Jim said as he saw Robert get off of the elevator. "That's why I drink Dr. Pepper and make sure the can isn't opened."

"We can always put it on the ice in the cup we bring you," she told him. "There are always ways. You just never know. That's why you need to be nice to all of us. We're always comparing notes on you guys."

"Good morning," Robert said as he walked up. "Everybody have a good night?"

"I can't speak for the rest of them, but last night was one of the best layovers I've ever had," Amber told him.

"Oh? Why's that?" Robert asked as the other Flight Attendants arrived.

"Nothing, really," she answered as she stood. "Just a hot bath, a good book, and knowing that this is the last trip of the month."

Jim looked at her, knowing she meant the last trip with Robert, and said, "I know what you mean. I'm looking forward to next month's flying. I've got training that takes me off of three of the trips, so I'm only flying six days."

"Where are you flying those trips?" Robert asked as they headed for the van to take them to the airport.

"Cabo and Chicago layovers," Jim told him as they loaded their suitcases. "Sort of extremes, hot in Cabo and cold in Chicago. But, the breakfast buffet in Cabo is unbelievable."

That afternoon, after Jim had arrived home and was washing the 'Vette, Gene drove up and pulled into the driveway. Getting out, he asked, "Do you think you might have a small bit of Jack Daniel's sitting around evaporating in your house?"

"I'm sure I have a shot or two," Jim said, walking over to shake Gene's hand. "But it never sits around long enough to evaporate because somebody swings by often enough to ensure it doesn't."

"What are friends for?" Gene asked as they entered the house.

"To drink your whiskey and steal your jokes?" Jim replied as he poured two drinks.

Handing one to Gene, he said, "Semper fi."

"Semper fi," Gene repeated as they tapped glasses.

"Now, I'm sure you didn't just come by for a drink," Jim said as he led Gene to the living room. "What's on your mind today?"

"First off, I'd like to apologize for the little syringe issue," Gene said, taking a seat. "That was unacceptable, and we've added another layer of people to look at every aspect of our operations. Especially when we make last-minute adjustments like deciding we needed two cars in the event we needed to use Jewell to solve any problems at the restaurant."

"That's all right," Jim argued. "You can't see every eventuality that can occur."

"No, but we can certainly try to do better," Gene said, frowning. "To think that such a small thing could cause such catastrophic results. There's too much at stake to take unnecessary chances like that."

"What's that old saying about the plans of mice and men?" Jim remarked.

"Ah, yes. Robert Burns," Gene answered, nodding. "But I hope we're smarter than a mouse."

Gene took another sip of his drink and looked at Jim seriously and asked, "Now, what the hell did you do to cause such an uproar with Charlie and the company?"

Jim smiled slightly and asked, "What makes you think I had anything to do with that?"

"Don't BS me, Jim," Gene said sternly. "I know your mind, and I know you've been planning something for weeks."

"Let's just say that I encouraged Charlie to react," Jim told him. "I know guys like him are quick to blame their most obvious adversary for anything that happens to them. It just so happens that I had the opportunity to orchestrate a reason."

"I hope we don't ever need to have this discussion again, Jim," Gene reprimanded him. "Now, do you want to know what happened?"

"Jennifer told me that Charlie was fired," Jim told him.

"That's most of it," Gene explained. "It wasn't part of the deal with the lawyers. As I said, how his uncle managed his personnel was his business. But the accusations against you were the final straw. And, as an added benefit, all of the ladies on the lawsuit decided to drop their charges."

"Now that sounds like a coincidence," Jim said, smiling. "I'm sure the lawyers called each and every one of them that very day, and they all agreed."

"About as much coincidence as a skunk in a restaurant parking lot the very same day, don't you think?" Gene told him.

"Coincidences abound," Jim answered, smiling.

"I know you think you had all of your bases covered, much the same as we did with the syringe," Gene finally said. "But, as you saw, even a minor glitch can pose unnecessary risks. In the future, if you ever feel the need to repeat something of this nature, please let me help you. We have people who can take care of things like this without jeopardizing our higher priorities."

"I understand, sir," Jim said contritely. "It's just that this incident involved my wife. If it was just me, I wouldn't have wasted my time on the little prick."

"I understand your feelings," Gene told him. "But remember that I'm always here. You and Jennifer have been a part of my life for many years, and I'm just as incensed as you are. Now, just promise me that you'll at least let me help you if you ever decide to do something like this again."

"I will," Jim said, knowing that Gene truly thought of him and Jennifer as family. "I just hope the situation never arises again."

"Good," Gene said, standing. "Now, if you have a few minutes, we need to go pick up Amber and meet Jewell at Love Field."

"As you wish," Jim said, gathering their glasses. "I'm sure you want to take your car, so I'll just put mine back in the garage."

"As you so keenly observed, three people and a two-seat car aren't compatible," Gene teased as they headed out. "Your superior powers of grasping the obvious are remarkable. Especially for a Marine."

After getting Amber at her house in Plano, they drove to Love Field and met Jewell at one of the small restaurants in the terminal. "I don't suppose you've already eaten," Gene asked as they took seats at the table where she was waiting.

"Nope," she said as she smiled at Jim and Amber. "I've been sitting here sipping tea, waiting for you to buy a poor damsel in distress a meal."

"As soon as the waiter takes our orders, and it is on the company, I'll tell you a little something I heard just a few hours ago," Gene told them as they took seats around the table.

A few minutes later, after they had placed their orders, Gene announced, "It seems that one Mr. Harry Wellington was discovered deceased in his bed early this morning. And within a few hours, as I predicted, his uncles sent a message to the Department of Defense asking to renegotiate the Lithium issue."

"How'd that work out?" Jim asked, nodding.

"It's ongoing," Gene said as he saw the waiter heading their way with a tray of plates. "Additionally, word has it that they appear to be willing to take the original offer, less ten percent."

"That's excellent," Jewell said as her burger and fries were set in front of her.

"And the cause of death?" Amber asked.

"The body is being autopsied," Gene answered. "Cardiac arrest will be the cause, and that will be the end of it."

"I just wish Harry would have been willing to negotiate fairly a month or so ago," Jim said as he picked up his burger. "Would have saved a lot of people a lot of grief."

"We all do," Gene told them somberly. "But sometimes people fail to do the right thing even if it's to their detriment. Pass the ketchup, please."

www.ingramcontent.com/pod-product-compliance
Lightning Source LLC
Chambersburg PA
CBHW071248300726
48975CB00002B/594